Replevy for a Flute

The Eddie Devlin Compendium

Replevy for a Flute

DISCARDED

T.R. St. George

Copyright © 2001 by T.R. St. George.

ISBN #:   Softcover   1-4010-4122-1

All rights reserved. No part of this book may be reproduced or transmitted in any form or by any means, electronic or mechanical, including photocopying, recording, or by any information storage and retrieval system, without permission in writing from the copyright owner.

This is a work of fiction. Names, characters, places and incidents either are the product of the author's imagination or are used fictitiously, and any resemblance to any actual persons, living or dead, events, or locales is entirely coincidental.

This book was printed in the United States of America.

To order additional copies of this book, contact:
Xlibris Corporation
1-888-7-XLIBRIS
www.Xlibris.com
Orders@Xlibris.com

FOR DENNIS

Replevy (in detinet). A legal action launched with a Writ of Replevin granted plaintiff by a court for the purpose of the immediate repossession of specific personal property of plaintiff rightfully taken but wrongfully detained by defendant: or, in lieu thereof, monetary damages to the value of the personal property when rightfully taken by defendant.

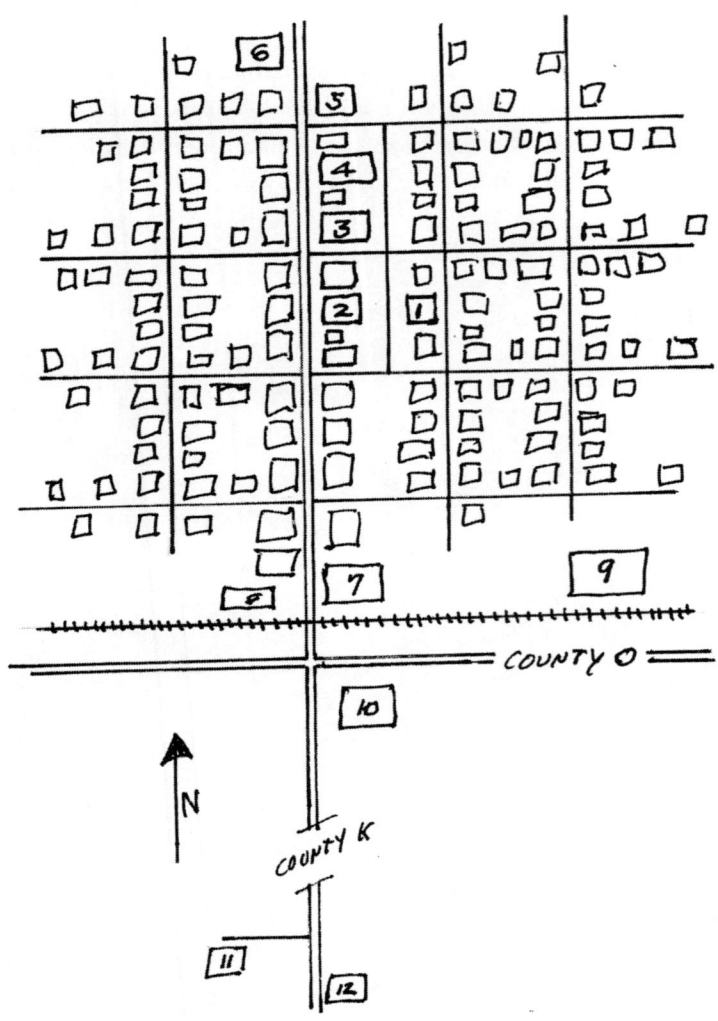

(1) Klamatty's Justice Court. (2) Hooter's Drugs. (3) Bonnie's Café. (4) Municipal Liquor. (5) Standard Station. (6) Fire Hall. (7) ADM elevator. (8) Old MSP&P Depot. (9) Stockyard. (10) Consolidated School. (11) Strudel's. (12) Hennessey's.

This is the fifth in a series of satiric, iconoclastic, little bit sexist (politically suicidal!) novels that track a gaggle of characters, Edward T. Devlin foremost among them, from the Stock Market CRASH of 1929 through The Great Depression, World War II, the Eisenhower years, the Kennedy assassination, Watergate etc. (the history is highly selective) to the Millennium and beyond. The previous titles, also published by Xlibris, are: Old Tim's Estate (1929-35), Wildcat Strike (1939), The Bloody Wet (1943-44) and Bringing Chesty Home (1948).

Author's Note. There really is a Hayfield, Minnesota, around 1,300 people live there, but it bears little resemblance to and is NOT the "Hayfield" depicted in these pages.

1.

For breakfast this bright May morning in the middle of the Middle West in the middle of the reign of Ike the Slicer (Thursday, May 17, 1956) Imogene (Apple) Strudel, twelve, big for her age, forty pounds overweight, a year behind in school, seated at the new Formica table in her mother's sunny farmhouse kitchen, plows steadily through a large glass of orange juice (from concentrate), a big bowl of cornflakes with milk and sliced banana and lots of sugar, two fried eggs, six slices of bacon, four slices of Wonder Bread toasted and buttered and slathered with strawberry jam, a large glass of 100% fat milk and two chocolate covered doughnuts.

"One thing about Apple," her mother, Mrs. Wolfe Strudel, the former Annie Seaver, often says. "She allas eats good." And all's right with the world, Annie Strudel reckons, if only a person eats good. Busy packing Apple's school lunch in a Mickey Mouse lunch bucket while Apple mines her nose with one forefinger and hunts down doughnut crumbs with the other, Annie also says now, "Hurry up, Apple! Or you'll miss the school bus again! Have you got all your books together and your homework? And your flute? For god's sake, remember. You forgot last week. You have to turn your flute in today. And the case. I didn't see the case. Did you leave it at school again?"

"Nuh," Apple, surveying the ore she found in her nose, says. "Sin my jacket. Can I have another doughnut?"

"No! You don't have time! The bus will be here. For god's

sake, hurry up! Get your stuff together. You miss the bus again and your dad has to drive you, you'll really get it! He's busy today. He's got to pick out the hogs he's shipping. You want a chocolate doughnut in your lunch?"

"Mmm. Two."

"All right, two. Now get yourself together! Get going!"

Apple gets herself together, collects the pink vinyl jacket she'll carry, her book-bag, the math homework she did not do and her flute. She stuffs the flute in one jacket pocket, along with its case.

This flute and its case are rentals, chattels owned by the Diptill Music Co. in St. Paul. They were placed in Apple's care when she signed up for Sixth Grade Band last September at the new Consolidated K-8 Elementary School in Hayfield, an educational great leap forward that replaced a dozen one-room country schools and the elementary school in Hayfield in which Apple spent six years struggling through five grades. Apple also struggled with the flute for awhile, though reluctant to practice, getting so she could produce occasional sour notes, but found music hard to read, soon abandoned plans for a musical career and wanted to drop out of Band. But her father, House District 33B State Representative Wolfe Strudel when the State Legislature is in session (and when it isn't too) nixed that idea. She'd signed up for Band, State Rep. Strudel said, and she by god was going to stay in Band! "Once you start something you by god finish it!" he said. Besides, the damn flute and its case was a nine-month non-refundable rental which, Apple by god better remember, cost a whopping $15 a month, and she, and he, by god, were going to get their money's worth! Like hell she was going to give the flute and its case back to the Diptill Music Co. up in St. Paul, which then no doubt would rent it again, double-dipping! Apple thereafter seldom fooled with the flute, failed Band the first semester and likely will fail it again, but the Strudels by god are getting their money's worth. So to speak.

"Damn it, Apple!" Annie Strudel says. "Hurry up!" She hands

Apple her lunch bucket and a doughnut to eat on the bus, case she gets hungry, helps Apple sling her book-bag over one shoulder, drapes the vinyl jacket over the book-bag and shoves Apple out the kitchen door.

It's a hundred-yard walk down the Strudel's long driveway, two gravel tracks between fields planted with corn, to blacktopped Winatchee County Road K, where the school bus will halt opposite the Strudel's big metal mailbox. Apple covers this distance slowly, squinting, the sun in her eyes, eating her doughnut. To her right, the big yellow school bus is halted at the top of Hennessey Hill, embarking Billy Hennessey and his little sister Mary.

* * *

Wolfe Strudel, Apple's heard this story a thousand times, by god walked to the abandoned country school in Simpson (a dot on the prairie fifteen miles away) in which he spent eight years on his way to high school, three miles each way in all kinds of weather. ("Uphill both ways, too," Annie Strudel sometimes mutters when Wolfe gets going on this.) Wolfe considers a school bus, never mind it's eight miles to Hayfield and the new Consolidated School, clear proof Apple's generation has gone soft. And what with the initial investment, repairs, part-time drivers and the goddamn insurance, the goddamn buses, there are four, cost and arm-and-a-leg to operate. The way his school tax jumped this year proves that. Though the Band and a Music teacher and a by god Art teacher, none of which Wolfe encountered or missed when he was an elementary student, also had something to do with the tax jump. Wolfe, like numerous other rural types sure (a) their school tax would go up and (b) their offspring would encounter and likely succumb to lurid temptations in a "big" school, bitterly opposed consolidation, but the goddamn State Department of Education pushed in through the Legislature. Wolfe has tried but so far failed to discover just how much the goddamn school bus service and those silly Art and Music teachers cost the Consolidated School District. The district superintendent, Hjalmar Peterson, Ed.D., forty years at the public trough, is a past master at obfuscating his budget and operating costs.

Rep. Strudel is known to be (as the saying goes) a close man with a dollar. Through four ninety-day Legislative sessions and four special sessions, picking up where his predecessor left off, he has earned a solid reputation for that. His predecessor, the late Alfred Olerude, the Hayfield Heating Oil & Propane Gas Co. in real life, twenty years in the Legislature, who though deceased these four years got sixteen write-in votes in the last election, never once voted "Aye" on any bill that included an appropriation (including those funding routine state government operations) or any kind of tax increase.

To little effect, unfortunately. "The goddamn Democrat-Farmer-Labors," which was what Republican Alf called the Legislature's usual majority, steadily dreamed up and adopted new ways to spend money (consolidating the schools, for instance) and raise taxes, but Alf stuck to his principles. The Capitol reporter for the Minneapolis Times-Register, a young fellow with a flair for words, first called Alf "The Watchdog of the Treasury" in the late Thirties and the rest of the state press, daily and weekly, soon so identified Alf in just about every story in which he was mentioned. Alf loved that phrase, put it on his letterhead and, stuck with it, cast the lone Nay on the '52 bill granting the state's World War II vets a $300 bonus. Some political observers thought that Nay might cost Alf his otherwise safe seat in the '52 election, but a coronary, he was eighty-two, carried him off first. On August 2. Just about the time he was launching, though he had no primary opposition, his tenth re-election campaign. Many who knew Alf guessed the coronary was triggered by the new tobacco tax the goddamn Democrat-Farmer-Labors installed to finance the bonus: three cents a pack on cigarettes effective August 1. Which, this theory is, proved too much for Alf when he encountered Chesterfields at 35 cents a pack in Win Hooter's drugstore in Hayfield, Win naturally rounding his prices off to the next nickel.

Whatever, it was then (specifically, while with other constituents he watched Alf's casket sink slowly into a grave in the cemetery shared by Hayfield's Protestant denominations) Wolfe Strudel, a registered Republican and former Winatchee County Young (under thirty-five)Republicans chairman, decided he by god would (a) become a politician and (b) run for Alf's old seat.

The next thing Wolfe did, that same afternoon, was phone old Heinrich (Dollar) Dobermann at the Dobermann Hotel in Winatchee Falls, the county seat, old Dollar the Falls' leading financier and a chairman emeritus so to speak of the Winatchee County Republican Committee.

The Dobermann Hotel switchboard put his call through to a secretary who inquired as to his name and business with Mister Dobermann and said "Mister Dobermann is busy," but when he said his business was "like politics" said she would connect him and did and a nasal irritable voice said, "Damn it! Who is this? What do you want?"

"Uh Mister Dobermann?" Wolfe said, "My name is Strudel. Wolfe Strudel. I'm from out south Hayfield. I don't know you remember me but I was the Young Republicans chair—"

"Strudel? Yes, I know that. What do you want?"

"Well I'd uh like to uh like talk to you, Mister Dobermann. Your convenience. It's sort of like a political business. Now old Alf's gone."

"May he rest in. I surmise you got your eye on his House seat. Think you're a candidate. All right, come and see me. Let me see." Papers rustled. "Four o'clock tomorrow afternoon. My office, the mezzanine, the hotel. I'm busy, you can wait."

Wolfe, wearing his blue serge suit and favorite green tie, parked his '46 Ford pickup outside the Winatchee Falls parking meter zone at 3:30 p.m. and walked to the Dobermann Hotel, a whopping four stories of tan brick, the best hotel in Winatchee Falls, built by old Dobermann late in the Roaring Twenties when the nation's future looked rosy and the Pretzell Chiropractic Clinic across West College Street, Winatchee Falls' chief claim to fame, was treating upwards of four-thousand patients a year. He took an elevator run by a man with one arm he knew but could not put a name to and found on the mezzanine a door with Dobermann Enterprises Inc. on its frosted glass.

"I'm Mister Strudel," he told the middle-aged woman typing at a desk in the tiny office beyond the door, who he took to be old Dobermann's secretary. "I have an appoint—"

"Have a seat," the woman said. "Mister Dobermann is busy." She went on with her typing. Wolfe took a seat, there was only one chair, and sat waiting for forty minutes. Then the woman, receiving some message by means he could not discern, said, "You can go in now."

"So I went in." This Wolfe telling Annie that evening at their kitchen table, Apple in bed, and subsequently a few relatives, How I Got Into Politics. "And old Dollar, he was sittin' there in a big leather chair behind a desk about the size a flatbed truck, papers all over it. He ain't much bigger'n a peanut, y'know. Well, you seen him places. Desk about up a that bowtie he allas wears. Looks like a peanut too. Little wrinkle face. Glasses on a string around his neck on his nose. But he's pretty damn sharp. Well, I guess everbody knows that."

"I know that," Annie said. "I knew Dobe I was just a little kid. My dad allas did his shirts, Dad was in the dry-cleaning business. Before Dobe, dad allas call him Dobe, got rich and built the hotel and bought the laundry. I talked Dobe a few times too, not much, when I work there. The newsstand the hotel. Before we got married."

"Yeah, well." This was Wolfe's story, not Annie's. "Anyway, he told me sit down and I did and he offer me a cigar, which I say no thanks I don't smoke, and light one up hisself. Cigar about a foot long look like a big dog turd."

Old Dobermann got his foot-long cigar going, the tip glowing, then for what seemed a long time puffed his cigar and silently studied Wolfe like (it seemed to Wolfe, squirming) he was some kind of insect or wheat mold old Dobermann had not seen before. What in fact old Dobermann saw was a muscular man (5-10, 190) with wide-flung ears, mean little pale blue eyes, a broad sunburned face and a lousy haircut, the haircut Annie's work, that saving the Strudels $1.25.

"So," old Dobermann, this inspection completed, said, finally. "Was I right, Strudel? You figure you'd like to run for Alf Olerude's seat in the Legislature, his House seat, now he's gone. You ever run for anything before? Ever been elected to anything? Besides chairman, the Young Republicans? How old are you?"

"Thirty-five," Wolfe said. "Hayfield Chapter, Committee Save Our Country Schools, elect me vice-chairman. And I'm a member the Hayfield Township Soil Conservation Committee. County Extension Agent appoint me that."

"You got other qualifications for public office?"

"Well uh I'm a veteran. I was a First Lieutenant, The War."

"You serve overseas? Wounded? Any medals?"

"I was in Europe. I ran a Motor Pool, colored truck outfit. I wasn't never wounded. War was sort of over when I ship out."

"You're a farmer, right?"

"Yessir. I got a hunnert-sixty eight miles south a Hayfield. The old Sheehan place. I raise around three-hunnert hogs. Spotted Poland Chinas."

"Where'd you get the money, buy the Sheehan place?"

"Well uh I uh won some money playin' poker, the Army. And I got a mortgage, my GI Bill."

Half that statement was a little white lie but nobody knows the true story, not even Annie. Well, former Lt. Strudel's former

First Sergeant knows it, but he was a colored man from South Carolina who planned to retire to the south of France when discharged with the money he made in the post-war blackmarket in Occupied Germany, and it was highly unlikely, Wolfe was pretty sure, old Dobermann and former First Sgt. Harold Higgins would ever share any confidences. And former Lt. Strudel, this salves Wolfe's conscience, was not actually in the blackmarket himself. He merely was on a retainer, $200 a week for eight wonderful months, paid by former First Sgt. Higgins in good American dollars, in return for which Lt. Strudel trip-ticketed company trucks to destinations, mainly Quartermaster supply dumps, when so requested by First Sgt. Higgins.

The rumor was First Sgt. Higgins was the Number Two or Three executive in a major blackmarket operation run by an Army Reserve colonel at Occupation Force Headquarters, but Lt. Strudel did not know and did not wish to know if that was true. He was content with his retainer, gave in fact some thought to remaining with the Occupation Force when his discharge came through, but all the blackmarket schemes were under investigation at the time.

Nothing came of that but Lt. Strudel was afraid something might. He took his discharge, came home with $6,000 in the lining of his GI overcoat, deposited the $6,000 in three segments in three Winatchee Falls banks, collected Annie and their infant daughter, Imogene, and went off to two years of Ag School at Land Grant U with his GI Bill, then withdrew his deposits, put a down payment on the old Sheehan place and went into the hog business.

"You married?" old Dobermann, still assessing Wolfe's qualifications for public office, said. "How long? You got a family?"

"Yessir. Nine years pretty soon. We got a girl name Imogene. But we call her Apple."

"Are you a good husband? Far as anybody knows. I mean, assuming, nobody is going to pop up the middle some campaign, claim you're the father her unborn child?"

"No. I mean yes. I mean no. Nuthin' like that!" Wolfe blushes. Blushes? Is he lying? No. The fact is, Wolfe is no ball of fire in this department and Annie, her libido is going strong, has taken to telling him that now and then. But Wolfe, up at 5 a.m to slop his hogs, spend a long day in his fields and slop them again before supper, is ready for bed by 9 p.m. He sometimes stays up, listens to the Ten O'clock News on WCCO, goes to sleep before it's over. But this is Wolfe's business (and Annie's). Not Dobermann's.

"Wife a local girl?"

"Yessir. Maiden name was Seaver. Before we got married. Annie Seaver. Fact, she work for you once, Mister Dobermann. Here the hotel in the newsstand."

"Don't remember her. High turn-over though in the hotel business."

That too in part is a little white lie. Old Dobermann remembers Annie then Seaver. Brash busty little number with her brains in her crotch his worthless son Clyde no doubt frequently screwed. One of many, but Clyde for a time also had the crazy idea he'd like to marry Annie Seaver. Talked him out of that foolishness, Clyde already married once and divorced, no children, but the goddamn lawyers' fees, highway robbery, and the one-time divorce settlement put a $7,000 dent in Dobermann Enterprises' 1940 bottom-line. Told worthless Clyde, then twenty-nine, a Dobermann Enterprises vice-president in charge of nothing, "Go ahead and screw the help, that's gonna be your principle occupation, but chrissake don't marry them!"

Old Dobermann paused in his inquisition at this point and silently puffed his cigar while waiting for his nerves to calm, worthless Clyde having set those nerves to jangling even in absentia.

This silence set Wolfe's nerves to thrumming. Sweat oozed down his ribs under his blue serge suit and he broke the silence. "What I was thinking."

"Never mind that," old Dobermann, recovered, said. "Tell me, Strudel, what's your philosophy in regards to government?"

"Well uh." That was a tough question, Wolfe never having given any thought to his philosophy in regards to government, but he found a straw to clutch. "I allas like the way old Alf vote. When he was alive. Not spend so gotdamn much money, I mean. Or raise taxes."

"What about that Veterans Bonus? Would you voted for that, Strudel, you were up there in the Legislature voting on it? Or against it, like Alf did?"

Another tough question. Wolfe chewed his lip, trying to guess the answer old Dobermann wanted to hear but reached no conclusion and finally said what he guessed was probably the truth. "Well I uh guess I prolly vote for it. I mean me being a vet and all. But there's lots vets in the state. Couple hunnert thousand, I read some place. I think old Alf, he vote Nay, that bonus, he piss off lots vets."

"Amen to that," old Dobermann said. "But Alf was a stubborn old fart. Tell me, Strudel, that three-hundred dollars mean much to you?"

"No. Not much. I got some hogs prolly worth that."

"What about, assuming, the two-thousand a session, too goddamn much, and all the goddamn per diem members the Legislature get? That mean much to you?"

"Well, yeah, some," Wolfe, embracing the truth again, said. "But not a whole lot." The goddamn per diem was a mystery to him and the $2,000 per annual session was not in fact his principal motivation. His principal motivation was to help run things the way they should be run and cut taxes (school, property, whatever) and otherwise slash what he took to be the exorbitant cost of state government. Beginning with the obscene $49,500 per annum pocketed by Gov. Knute Volvaag, a goddamn DFL. "What I think, Mister Dobermann, is there is too damn many people work for the state. Counties too. And what I seen them working, the Extension Office, Driver License place and other places, they is paid way too much. What I seen, they mostly just take coffee breaks."

"Amen to that, too," old Dobermann said. "So, assuming, you think you can stand up on your hind legs in public, Strudel, tell potential voters that? Tell them you're going to try and cut their taxes and fire all the incompetents employed by the State and so on? You got to think about speeches, you're a candidate. You had any experience in that line?"

"Yeah, some. I make plenty speeches, our School Board and some other School Boards and the goddamn State Board Education start talking they was gonna close a bunch country schools out there around Hayfield and consolidate them. Build a new Consolidated School, they called it, and bus the kids it!" This was a subject close to Wolfe's heart and pocketbook. "They talk about two years and I make about twenty speeches, tell them they was all crazy. But they went head and done it anyway! Our kid, she rides the bus the gotdamn new Consolidated School they build. Which they got a band there and a Music teacher and a Art teacher teaches something they call ceramtics. No wunner our school taxes went up like the price cars! I never had any that crap I was in school and I never miss it either! And the gotdamn buses! Run them gotdamn buses cost an arm-and-a-leg."

"Amen to all that too," old Dobermann said. "All I ever went was a country school. So, assuming again, Strudel. We're talking money now. You got any figure in your head for campaign expenses?"

"Uh well, no. Not exactly, I mean." Wolfe floundered. This was another tough question. His vague previous assumption was the State Republican Party or County Republican Committee, both of which frequently asked him for contributions with which to Save Our Nation, paid candidates' campaign expenses. "Tell you the truth, Mister Dobermann, I don't know how much a campaign costs."

"Well, not a hell of a lot," old Dobermann said. "Not for old

Alf anyway. He had a safe seat. That likely rub off some on somebody else is a good Republican. Maybe. Or you might grab on a Eisenhower's coattails, he gets elected. Polls got him way ahead of Stevenson. You'd have to spend a few hundred though, posters and so on. You in a position, Strudel, spend a few hundred, get yourself elected? That's assuming."

"Uh, well." Wolfe hesitated but took the plunge. "Oh sure. Few hunnert." He had his eye on a new (used) John Deere tractor priced at $1895 at Wobeling's Farm Implements outside Winatchee Falls but his old Massey-Ferguson still had a few miles in it.

"Let's see what we have here then," old Dobermann said. He laid his big cigar in an ashtray full of big cigar butts and ticked off what they had on his fingers. "You're no kid. You're old enough be respectable and responsible. A veteran. Married. Good husband, good father, blah-blah-blah. Honest farmer. You ever arrested for anything?"

"No. Well, I had some traffic tickets. When I was a kid. Before The War. Just speeding was all."

"Nothing since? No DWIs?"

"No. I ain't much a drinker."

"No criminal record then come back and bite you." Old Dobermann ticked that off on his little finger. "All right. Tell you what I'll do, Strudel. I'll give the County Chairman a call. Herb Holder. You know Herb. You understand, that's all I can do. There may be other candidates want Alf's seat. None I heard of though. Not yet. Any nomination of course be up to the County Committee. But I give you credit, Strudel, you come and see me before you jump in and get your feet wet. Throw your hat in the ring, the saying goes. I'll put in a word for you. And I'll give you some good advice. Don't go telling people you'll cut their taxes. You can't do that, the goddamn DFL controls the Legislature. All you say is you'll give that your best shot. I'll be in touch with you. Give my girl your phone number."

Old Dobermann (who, Wolfe remembered Annie saying, fear-ing germs, is reluctant to shake hands) turned to his papers.

"Oh gee, golly!" Wolfe said. "Thanks, Mister Dobermann! Thanks a lot. I really 'ppreciate you." But old Dobermann waved that off and Wolfe, dismissed, left, walking on air as another saying goes. Old Dobermann was much too modest. The County Republican Chairman himself for ten years, his personal contributions to the party coffers dwarf everybody else's in Winatchee County and are said to be not insignificant when compared to those made by the Dairy Interests, the Mining Interests, the Lumber Interests and various corporate executives in the Twin Cities. If old Dobermann told Herb Holder, once like Wolfe Strudel the Young Republicans chairman, "Herb, drop your pants at high noon in the middle of Broadway," Herb would drop his pants at high noon in the middle of Broadway. Wolfe's nomination for old Alf's seat was just about as certain as the sunrise.

Homeward bound in his '46 Ford pickup, Wolfe, though seldom given to fantasies, enjoyed one that afternoon. He'd soon be the House District 33B Representative, serve a couple terms, make a name for himself watch-dogging the State Treasury, then get elected to the State Senate, add mightily to his reputation, then, well, who's to say, the governor's wing in the State Capitol and the Governor's Mansion is not an impossible dream.

The Governor's Mansion. Wolfe, curious, went and had a look at the mansion, just the outside, it was at the time the subject of numerous rancorous editorials, during his annual (1950) trip to the Minnesota State Fair, where he was exhibiting a prize Spotted Poland China boar the crooked judges did not reward with a ribbon. What he saw was a massive three-story brownstone built by a lumber baron in 1882 on half an acre of land surrounded by a high iron fence on Summit Avenue, St. Paul's premier residential street. It looked (and looks) like a castle, a small castle with two towers, neither accessible, numerous cupolas and behind it a large former carriage house converted to a three-car garage. The lumber baron's last surviving heirs bequeathed it to the state in 1946, taking a juicy tax break. They were glad to get rid of it. The roof leaked. Likewise the ancient plumbing and there were bats in the attic and rats in the basement. But that's not the case now. The goddamn Democrat-Farmer-Labors who took control of the Legislature in 1948 when Gov. Knute Volvaag was elected to a four-year term promptly appropriated despite Rep. Alf Olerude's apoplectic opposition, this triggering the rancorous editorials, $200,000 with which to renovate the mansion: fix the roof, install new plumbing, new heating, a new kitchen and air-conditioning (!) in the main dining room and master bedroom. Those projects, however, were not completed until 1952 (the cost overruns ran another $100,000) and, ironically, it's Republican Governor Marcus Diptill, a widower and former state senator who rode into office on Eisenhower's coattails, handily defeating Volvaag's bid for a second term, lives in the mansion now, cared for by a staff of eight. Sleeps in the air-conditioned bedroom. Annie would like that, Wolfe surmised, sleep in an air-conditioned bedroom—

Then slammed on his brakes, his fantasy vanishing like a burst soap bubble, the pickup fishtailing. It was that or hit a large Holstein cow chewing its cud in the middle of County Road K. One of old Jerry Hennessey's cows, Hennessey too cheap (or too poor) to fix his fences. The Hennesseys are the Strudels' nearest neighbors but they're not very neighborly. They live at the top of Hennessey Hill, named for old old old Jerry Hennessey, the original homesteader, on a farm gone to rack and ruin. The barn and windmill lean at crazy angles. The old farm home has seen no paint in twenty years. The yard around it is full of broken and abandoned farm machinery. Several older Hennessey offspring, long gone, are serving with the nation's armed forces.

Wolfe drove around the Holstein and, home, his hogs slopped, supper over, Apple in bed, told Annie with no mention of the Governor's Mansion, that'll be a few years yet and he doesn't want to get her hopes up, How I Got Into Politics.

"Well, I hope it works out," Annie said. "We sure could use a couple thousand. Fix the house up. Get a new furnace. One them oil furnaces. But how you gonna run the farm, Wolfe, you're up in St. Paul up the Legislature?"

"I'll hire help," Wolfe said. "One the Hennessey kids. It's only the middle January middle April I be up the Legislature. Be home most weekends. Billy Hennessey prolly. Ain't he the oldest one?"

"No, that's young Jerry. Billy's more like twelve. Twelve going on forty, things Apple says. What his ma says too. But you got to hire somebody, you're up the Legislature there, that'll take a big chunk out a your two thousand."

"No. Not so big. It ain't like they gonna work full-time. Just two, three hours most days. Slop the hogs. Go get more slops couple times a week. Dollar-an-hour tops."

The slops Strudel's swine eat are the garbage he collects from the Community Hospital in Winatchee Falls, originally the food served patients, around 85 percent of which the patients do not eat because it is inedible. The swine won't eat all of it either but eat most of it.

"Whoeee!" Annie says. "Lissen him! Gonna pay somebody dollar-an-hour slop his hogs! You sound like you think you're old Dollar Dobermann, all the money he's got. But I suppose there be some left, that two-thousand."

"There's mileage too," Wolfe said. "Eights-cents-a mile I get, I think, I use my truck I'm on State business. Like drivin' back and forth, St. Paul. And per deem. I dont 'xactly know what that is but Dobermann mention it. Speakin' Dobermann. I know he's richer'n hell. Owns the hotel. Some farms he's works on shares. Some other buildings downtown. Hell, I don't know what all. But how'd he get to be so rich? I don't know that."

"I know that," Annie said. "Some it anyway. My dad told me. And Clyde. Dobe's boy. Only son. No sisters either. When I was working the newsstand, the hotel, me and Clyde talk some. Him and Dobe, they don't get along so good. Clyde's a pretty good guy 'cept he drinks like a fish." But enough about Clyde. He and a number of others are Annie's little secret or secrets. No virgin when she married Wolfe, she told him that. But neither was Wolfe. "My dad knew the Dobermann's. Who they were, I mean. They were just about the only Germans on Irish Ridge there, out east the Falls. Big family. Old Dobe was the last the litter. He was allas a little runt. All the Irish kids beat him up at school. His old man beat him too. Dobe finish school though, eighth grade, he allas pretty smart. Then took off. Run away from home and got a job the Western Union in Winatchee Falls. Deliver telegrams. With a bike he swiped. I don't know he ran away with everthing he own in a handkerchief tied a stick like that Horatio Alger. But pretty close, I guess. He slept in back the Western Union for quite awhile and got another job washing dishes the Tuttle Hotel for his supper. Before it burn down. Dobe hardly ever eat otherwise, my dad said, and he allas had two three jobs and save just about ever cent he made 'cept he bought some clothes."

"You tellin' me he save enough and build his hotel?"

"No. But he was nineteen, he got a teller job, the First National Bank. Twenty-six or so, he was one the vice-presidents. I told you he was pretty smart. He could do mortgages right in his head. I mean you give him a figure, a mortgage, and the interest and he'd tell you your payment ever month, twenty years, thirty, whatever. Just like that. Then he started sellin' real estate in his spare time and bought some himself. Old houses he rent or rent rooms in or cut up and made apartments."

"And save his money."

"Yeah. But where his real money come from, he married Valkyrie Gutknecht. Back before The War. Not the one you were in. The other one. Married her for her money, everbody allas figured. You ever see Valkyrie?"

"Yeah, I think. Couple times somethin' goin' on in town. Parade or like that. Big woman."

"Valkyrie about the size a silo 'cept shorter. She used to come down the hotel sometimes, I was workin' the newsstand. We talk some. She had a sit on one the couches, the lobby. Chairs wasn't big enough. But her old man owned the Gutknecht Brewery used to be by the river there. Where the Ford place is now. The old man died, Valkyrie got the brewery and just about everthing else was in the old man's estate. His big old house up West College Street there and all his money 'cept five-hundred dollars he left the First Lutheran Church. There wasn't no other hairs. Her ma died when she was a kid. Valkyrie was a kid, I mean. So Valkyrie inherit everthing and Dobe, my dad allas said, Dobe had his paws on it, old man Gutknecht was still in his casket."

"She died too, dint she? Valkyrie?"

"Yeah. End The War about. The one you were in. By then old Dobe had her on a allowance. Twenty-five bucks a week. She used to complain it wasn't enough. She told me about a hundred times she was sorry they ever sell the brewery. Dobe sold it some guy from up St. Paul year before Prohibition. It went belly-up pretty soon then. Dobe got a good price for it and put that money in the Stock Market. He was in the Stock Market all through the Twenties, my dad said. Pulled out a month before it Crash. That money, he bought up a bunch farm mortgages the banks was happy and sell once The Depression start and they foreclose on them. Dobe throw some the Irish kids used to beat him up off some those farms. He prolly owns fifteen, twenty farms he works on shares. And the hotel. And some buildings downtown there. And I don't know what all else. Clyde is gonna get it all, I guess, old Dobe ever dies."

Annie often thought about that, Clyde's eventual wealth, while working at the Dobermann Hotel newsstand in the early Forties and screwing Clyde (or going down on him) two or three times a week. Clyde in fact, he was Draft proof with of a football knee acquired somewhere in the course of a checkered college career, sometimes spoke vaguely of marriage. But old Dobe apparently scotched that idea. Clyde at any rate, right in the middle of one of her ministrations, said, "The old man says I better not get serious about you. But we can still have a lot of fun." Then Clyde, vaguely ashamed perhaps because he could not fight for his country though he'd never evinced any enthusiasm for that, went off to California to work in an aircraft factory and Second Lt. Wolfe Strudel, QMC, the Quartermaster Corps the next best thing to Draft proof, came home on leave, in uniform.

And here I am, Annie, suppressing a sigh, thought. But that was all water over the damn or under the bridge or whatever the saying is.

"I heard it said," Wolfe, feeling good now he was in politics and offering a little humor. "Guy down the Legion Club works one of Dobe's farms. He says old Dobe can't take it with him, he ain't gonna go." Annie laughs. "How old is he anyway?"

"Oh, gosh, I don't know. Eighty? Maybe more. I know Clyde said once he was like forty when he was born. Dobe was like forty, I mean. Clyde's more'n forty now. We allas used to wonder, me and the other girl work the newsstand, Fannie Leary, how Dobe and Valkyrie ever manage and produce Clyde. Conceive him, I mean. I mean him so little and her so big. We try imagine it. We think they might done it with that artificial insem'nation they doin' with bulls now. Except they wasn't anybody doin' that then. Not when Clyde was conceive."

"You got a dirty mind, Annie," Wolfe said. "I'm hungry. I think I like a fried egg san'wich and a glass milk."

"No you're not," Annie said. "It's ten o'clock. Let's go to bed."

Which they did and, being in politics a powerful aphrodisiac, enjoyed themselves and each other for nearly thirty minutes, just about Wolfe's limit in that department.

Herb Holder phoned the next day. He invited Wolfe to the County Committee meeting a week hence, 8 p.m. in the Hiawatha Room at the Dobermann Hotel. Wolfe went, wearing his blue serge suit and green tie, and treated the committee to his Philosophy of Government. Which in a nutshell was he'd never ever vote for any tax increase, any wage boost for state employees or (this drawing applause) any funds for the shiftless poor, shiftless handicapped or shiftless old-timers who failed to save for their Golden Years. "Pretty much the way Alf allas vote 'cept I might voted for the vets bonus and I'd like and get rid a the goddamn Department Education."

The County Committee, six members absent but the ten present a quorum, all of them solid citizens with comfortable incomes, promptly unanimously nominated and endorsed Wolfe Strudel for the late Alf's Olerude's House District 33B seat and pledged $500 toward his campaign expenses. Wolfe floated home in his pickup and, politics again an aphrodisiac, took Annie to bed, much to her surprise and delight, the second time in eight days.

Wolfe subsequently put around 800 miles on his pickup, spending $24.90 for gas and an oil change, driving all over House District 33B, half of Winatchee County and a thin slice of Dodge County, wearing either his blue serge suit and green tie or (this old Dobermann's suggestion) a plaid shirt and well-worn bib overalls. He addressed various farm groups (they saw the overalls), numerous 4H Clubs (the overalls and the kids were not voters but their parents were) and, wearing his suit, church groups and numerous service clubs: Lions, Elks, Kiwanis, Optimists, Rotarians, etc. The Optimists found him optimistic. The Rotarians applauded his views on government. He handily defeated three candidates running without party endorsement in the September primary (in which 20 percent of the registered District 33B voters voted) and set his sights on Wilbur Starbuck, a Winatchee Falls insurance man and the Democrat-Farmer-Labors' sacrificial lamb.

Wolfe's primary victory was celebrated at a "Strudel for State Representative" rally in the Winatchee Falls Armory, organized by the County Committee. The rally crowd was a little thin, no more than fifty potential voters counting the County Committee present.

"But it's allas hard," Herb Holder, surveying the great many cookies, chocolate chip and peanut butter, left over after the rally, said, "Get people's interest up in the Legislature contests. You want a take some cookies home, Wolfe?"

Wolfe took two dozen chocolate chip home. Annie puts a dozen away for Apple's school lunches and they ate the rest in bed then threshed around on the crumbs for thirty minutes, Annie's bare butt soon speckled with chocolate chips, a fine rousing time had by all.

Wolfe then spent $300 for election posters. They pictured Wolfe in his blue serge suit and exhorted voters to "Vote for Wolfe Strudel for State Representative," with a tag line, "He'll fight for lower taxes!" Wolfe wanted "He'll Cut Your Taxes!" but Dollar Dobermann nixed that, said again cutting taxes was not a realistic proposal while the goddamn Democrat-Farmers-Labors controlled the Legislature. Young Jerry Hennessey and his little brother Billy, using Jerry's beat-up '37 Ford, Wolfe buying Jerry's gas, put these posters up throughout the district on trees, fence posts, telephone and utility poles, Republicans' barns and silos if close to roads, etc. Which in mid-October, triggered just about the only excitement the District 33B House race produced, that reported thus in the Winatchee Falls Bugle Call:

GOP Candidate Accused
By Edward T. Devlin, Bugle Call Reporter

Wilbur Starbuck, the DFL candidate for the District 33B House seat in the upcoming election, today charged his Republican opponent, Wolfe Strudel of near Hayfield, with violating a city ordinance prohibiting the display of election material on public property.

Strudel, Starbuck told the Bugle Call, "has his election posters up on utility polls all over town and that's a violation." The Winatchee Falls Electric Co., Starbuck said, is a public utility owned and operated by the city and its poles are "public property" as defined by the ordinance.

A violation of the ordinance is a misdemeanor punishable by a fine of not more than $100 or 30 days in jail or both. Starbuck also said a violation might constitute an election fraud. He plans to file a formal charge in regard to that, he said. Strudel could not be reached for comment.

Starbuck, a Winatchee Falls insurance broker, and Strudel, who farms near Hayfield, are vying for the House seat held for many years by the late Alfred Olerude of Hayfield, who died in August while campaigning for another term. Olerude was long known as "The Watchdog of the State Treasury."

That gave Wolfe a couple of bad days. But Annie stalled off the goddamn reporter, Devlin, when he phoned. The Hennesseys were dispatched to remove the allegedly illegal posters or at least some of them. "There ain't no way," Jerry Hennessey whined. "Tell which them goddamn poles is utility poles or jist poles." And Starbuck filed his election fraud complaint, but County Attorney Sheldon Ravitz, a former Winatchee Falls city attorney come up in the world and a member of the Republican County Committee, was reluctant to pursue that matter on grounds the ordinance in question might be unconstitutional under the First Amendment, the one about free expression. Starbuck's complaint languished in Municipal Court then died, moot.

Wolfe Strudel by then, handily defeating Starbuck in the November general election (in which 49 percent of the registered voters voted and the late Alfred Olerude came in second with 162 write-in votes) was the District 33B Representative-elect, former Ramsey County State Senator Marcus Diptill, forty-four, was the governor-elect and Gen. Dwight (Ike) Eisenhower was the president-elect.

Old Dollar Dobermann phoned a few days later. He did not exchange any pleasantries with Annie, Wolfe was in Hayfield buying a high protein supplement for his swine, but told Annie, "Tell your husband I want to see him. Two o'clock tomorrow, my office."

Wolfe reported as directed. "Congratulations, your election," old Dobermann, aiming a foot-long cigar at Wolfe, said. "You be up in the Legislature now. So listen. Most the time, up there, you go ahead and vote what they call your conscience. No new taxes and that. What you told me. Vote Nay. But there might be times, some bills, once in a while, I might ask you vote Aye. I do that, you by god vote Aye! You understand that?"

"Yessir!" Wolfe said.

In January, Young Jerry Hennessey hired to slop the Spotted Poland Chinas, Wolfe went off to St. Paul by bus, leaving Annie the pickup, for his first legislative session. He was one of eight "freshmen" House members and both the Minneapolis Times-Register-Item, the Item just acquired by the Times-Register, and the St. Paul Monitor-Union ran muddy mug shots of the eight. The Times-Register-Item called him "Wolf" Strudel and the Monitor-Union called him "Rolf Studel" and transposed his mug with that of freshman Sven Olson from Benton County. A veteran legislator told Wolfe that was par for the course, let it pass.

Wolfe kept his head down throughout his first session, got a loose grip on the way things worked up in the Legislature, met some lobbyists, one of whom got him laid (and still occasionally gets him laid but that's Wolfe's little secret) and at lunches and dinners and cocktail parties paid for by lobbyists developed a near-addiction to large shrimp, the bigger the better, an expensive seafood he'd seldom previously encountered. He also got acquainted more or less with other House and a few Senate members and came to the conclusion (which he did not broadcast) that John McNally, an acerbic Times-Register-Item political reporter, was right when he said in one of his weekly Capitol Comments columns: "Despite much evidence to the contrary, the State Legislature is not entirely useless in that it provides part-time employment of a sort for many persons otherwise unemployable." McNally also opposed a move to extend the annual session beginning January 15 by thirty days to May 15 (this favored by many legislators) on grounds "the present 90-day session limits the damage our lawmakers are wont to inflict."

Wolfe voted his conscience throughout his first session, Nay to everything, no requests from old Dobermann for an Aye forthcoming. He was for a brief time as Alf Olerude's successor a minor though inarticulate celebrity, or curiosity, badgered by obnoxious reporters from the newspapers and, the worst kind, the television, the latter beginning to spring up like weeds or wheat mold. The television kind mostly looked to Wolfe to be about seventeen. They stuck microphones in his face, seeking snappy quotes he could not provide. Would he walk in old Alf's footsteps, the reporters asked? Wolfe soon grew tired of that question and reporters in general. Advised by old Dobermann, he settled on two answers, "No comment" and "I cannot confirm or deny," and the media soon lost interest in him. His charisma was dismal. It still is. He chaired no committees nor does he now. He was not a "reliable source" or a "source close to the House leadership" and there were other more colorful and articulate reliable sources "close to the House leadership." Several of those were said to harbor gubernatorial ambitions should Gov. Marcus Diptill step down or decide to run for the U.S. Senate. They were all years ahead of Wolfe on the political dance-card and his Governor's-Mansion-with-the-air-conditioned-bedroom dream began to fade.

No member of the media called Wolfe (or has called him, despite his many subsequent Nay votes), this a big disappointment, "The Watchdog of the Treasury." The quality of journalism, Wolfe thinks, fell off sharply just about the time Alf Olerude cashed in his chips.

Charisma be dammed. Wolfe was re-elected with a solid majority in 1954, it's only the governor serves four years, handily defeating another sacrificial lamb put up by the Democrat-Farmer-Labors, Alf Olerude's write-in vote dwindling: District 33B after all had not elected a Democrat of any variety since the Civil War. He assumes he'll be elected again in November but won't launch his '56 campaign until after the Fourth of July. There's a permanent "Strudel For District 33B State Representative Campaign Committee" now, Annie is the chairman, dormant between elections but ready to spring into action.

Wolfe no longer campaigns in his bib overalls. He has two suits in addition to his old blue serge, a new blue serge and a green pinstripe plucked from the rack at a Big Suit Sale at Sears, and a purple tie festooned with tiny embroidered loons, the Minnesota state bird, on it. He wears one of his suits, he's partial to the green pinstripe, to the Sunday service at the First Lutheran Church in Hayfield he attends regularly. This is killing his mother, a former Burns girl who tried to raise him Catholic, dragging him off to Mass every other Sunday when he was a kid and an adolescent. Other Sundays his father dragged him off to a Lutheran place of worship and on Christmas and Easter, which he dreaded, he got dragged off to both. The old lady still harps on his going to Mass, or not going to Mass, but Wolfe opted for the Lutherans early in his first campaign. Old Dobermann figured the DFL candidate, whoever he was, would get most of the Catholic vote so they might as well offer the Protestants, of whom there were more anyway, a full-time Lutheran. The agnostics, if any, which is what Wolfe sometimes wishes he were, were left up for grabs.

Like a redneck with a strong left arm and smoke who in ten years in the Major League acquires a certain polish, Wolfe in three sessions up at the Legislature has acquired by osmosis a certain sophistication. Not much but some. He also, once he got onto it, introduced some bills. Getting onto this was not hard. He read some State Statutes and bills drafted by other legislators. The trick was to load them with gobbledygook. Lawyer talk.

Around 60 percent of the sitting legislators after all were failed lawyers and a number of others failed Law School before turning to public life. Wolfe drafted his bills at the Strudels' kitchen table, chewing his pencil, Annie helping with the spelling. If adopted they would have slashed taxes, slashed the Welfare Department bureaucracy and welfare payments by half, eviscerated the state payroll, slapped a freeze on wages paid surviving state employees etc. But the goddamn Democrat-Farmer-Labors, clinging to control in the state House though losing the Senate by two seats in '54, which pretty much halted lawmaking, shot those bills down in committee.

And only once in those three sessions, late in the last ('56) session, did Dollar Dobermann request, or order, an Aye vote. In fact, that session was legally, technically, over, but the clocks in the House and Senate chambers were covered, this a traditional ploy, so nobody in theory knew what day or what time it was while the so-called leadership cobbled up haphazard compromises on various matters and the good old per diem rolled in.

Wolfe, slumped at his little desk on the House floor at 11 p.m., was calculating his extra per diem when a page brought him a telegram. "Senate Bill 808 comes up you vote Aye repeat Aye Dobermann." The maximum count for the minimum charge, Wolfe noted, and at 2 a.m. when SB 808 came up for a vote with a clutch of other bills, he voted Aye. For the first time. Which might have rated a mention in one of the newspapers' Capitol Roundups but was overlooked in the usual frenzy accompanying the session's delayed adjournment.

In the morning, curious, on his way to catch the Jefferson bus to Hayfield, Wolfe stopped at the House clerk's office and found a copy of SB 808, a law once Governor Diptill signed it, which one of the bureaucrats in the clerk's office said the skinny was Diptill promptly would, and discovered that, minus the gobbleydegook, effective August 1: (1) The state's several hundred home-based village Justice Courts will cease to exist, replaced by Village Courts in "suitable facilities" provided by the village(s) concerned. (2) The JP Courts' presiding elected justices-of-the-peace, who collect fees in lieu of salaries, will be terminated, jobwise, and replaced by Village Court judges paid $1500 per annum elected to two-year terms. (3) Governor Diptill will appoint the first Village Court judges, pending the November election.

All the goddamn Democrat-Farmer-Labors, naturally, embraced SB 808, it was another way to spend money, and Wolfe for a time was sorry, except he was following orders, he'd voted for it. He also wondered why Dollar Dobermann wanted he should vote Aye on it?

* * *

He still wonders. But more to the point, Wolfe Strudel thinks this bright May morning while mushing around in red rubber overshoes in his barnyard, up to his ankles in mud and pig shit, dumping slops in his pig trough, it looks like Hayfield Justice-of-the-Peace Jane Klamatty's days are numbered. That's a pleasing thought. Gotdamn Klamatty, she's been the Hayfield JP forever. Years and years anyway. She's a tough old bird. Likes to call herself "The Law West of the Winatchee." Meaning the Winatchee River. But she doesn't know much about the law. In Wolfe's opinion. Twice in disputes over fence lines she found for that crook, old Jerry Hennessey. Wolfe will be glad to see Klamatty and her Justice Court gone.

Unless, a miserable possibility, Governor Diptill appoints Klamatty the Village Court judge. Diptill is on record as saying "Politics will play no part" in those appointments, but the skinny is he'll appoint Republicans if warm and breathing. As well he should, exhibiting some party loyalty. But is Klamatty a Republican? Wolfe doesn't know. She's never been active in politics, far as he knows. But in the privacy of a voting booth, he suspects, she's a goddamn Democrat-Farmer-Labor. Her late husband after all worked for the government. He had a rural mail route.

What he'll by god do, Wolfe decides, is write Governor Diptill. Confer first with old Dobermann, of course. Then write Diptill.

Chrissake, they're both Republicans though Diptill sometimes exhibits suspicious liberal tendencies. Write, cite party loyalty, tell Diptill this Klamatty is incompetent, knows nothing in regards to fence line law, recommend somebody else. Who? Well, Win Hooter the druggist's boy Elmer, who just passed the Bar Exam on his third try. Elmer has an office over the drugstore but no known clients, $1500 per annum no doubt look pretty good to him.

That decided and the slops poured, Wolfe opens the barn door. Forty prime 500-pound Spotted Poland China swine and an old 700-pound boar, all of which Wolfe selected earlier, charge from the barn and plunge their snouts in the trough. Pushing, shoving, grunting, snorting, squealing, they remind Wolfe of his fellow lawmakers at the spreads (booze, shrimp, booze, crab legs, booze, a few loose women, booze) the lobbyists lay on at the St. Paul Hotel when the Legislature is in session.

Spotted Poland Chinas are a popular big pig breed in the Middle West. White with black spots (or black with white spots), they grow fast and produce large litters and there are several other breeds among their ancestors.

The slops these swine are gobbling up are extra slops. The idea is to put a little extra fat on them for their trip to the B&P Meat Packing plant in Fairbow. Gloomy Toomey will be along late in the afternoon with J.P. (Whip) Rahilly's livestock rig, a used '44 International tractor and beat-up slatted trailer, to load these pigs and forty more Spotted Poland Chinas old Jerry Hennessey is shipping. It's not that far to Fairbow but they want to be first in line at the meat plant in the morning, when the prices per cwt. the B&P pays tend to be higher. They'll spend the night in the truck between coffee breaks at a nearby diner, jammed in the cab, sleeping fitfully, listening to old Hennessey snore. But sharing the truck with Hennessey and his pigs, sharing the cost, is a big saving. Half a load or a full load, Rahilly Trucking charges the same.

Whip Rahilly is the business agent for the Teamsters Local in Winatchee Falls. Some think the one-truck trucking business he runs on the side is a conflict of interest but Whip runs it anyway.

Gloomy Toomey does most of the work and all the driving. Whip is busy making life miserable for Winatchee Falls capitalists. Dollar Dobermann and other capitalists would like to see Whip Rahilly taken out and shot but the goddamn National Labor Relations Board frowns on that. Maybe, Wolfe thinks, he should draft a bill, ban the goddamn NLRB in the Great State of Minnesota. But the goddamn Democrat-Farmer-Labors would shoot it down.

The pigs clean the trough like the lawmakers clean the buffet table at a lobbyist's spread (nothing left but the melting ice sculpture) and settle in the mud and manure in the barnyard. The old boar emits a satisfied grunt and Wolfe, though little given to anthropomorphism, surveys him with a certain fondness. The old boar was a good old boy in his day, fathering numerous large healthy litters, but he's slowed down now (rather like Wolfe before Wolfe got into politics) and there's a feisty young boar, go about 500 pounds, itching to take the old boar's place in the scheme of things. The old boar will soon be ham, sausage, pork chops, etc.

The pigs dig into the trough like members of the Legislature at a spread laid on by a lobbyist.

So it goes, Wolfe thinks. Squinting against the sun, he surveys with a certain fondness his daughter Apple plodding down the long driveway. The big yellow school bus is rolling down

Hennessey Hill, so named for Hennessey's grandfather, the original homesteader.

* * *

The bus seats forty-four students and it's close to full. Just the Strudel kid and five more little bastards to pick up, the driver thinks. The driver is Wade Cummins, twenty-four, a lanky young fellow with a GI haircut wearing olive-drab GI pants, a denim shirt and sunglasses, two years in Korea with a Army Postal Unit, a student these days at Winatchee Falls Junior College, soon to be a famous novelist. He's getting As in Creative Writing anyway and has in hand thirty ill-typed pages of a somewhat fictional work called "The Yellow Bus." A searing work based on the nine months Wade has been driving the goddamn school bus. A work that will shatter the shaky theory he first heard at his high school commencement, to wit: "Our young people are our great nation's most invaluable asset."

Wade looks in his rear vision mirror. Two young people, Mary Hennessey and Elsa Gruber, both ten, supposed to be seated, are standing, pulling each other's hair. "You two back there," Wade bellows, captain's orders. "Sit down! Or I'll throw you off the bus!" That's the ultimate threat and the combatants sit on opposite sides of the center aisle and stick their tongues out at each other.

Wade sighs. Twelve more days, school will be out and he'll be finished with the little bastards. He's got a summer job waiting at the Cornbelt Foods Inc. canning plant in Winatchee Falls, once the pea-pack starts the middle of June. He'll have two weeks between jobs in which to really get to work on "The Yellow Bus," holed up in his room in his parents' house, whacking away on the old Underwood he bought used when he began Creative Writing. Pithy phrases trickle through his mind, but driving the damn bus takes precedence. He hits the brakes, they need adjusting, halts the bus in the right lane at the foot of Hennessey Hill, extends the red STOP arm, starts the warning red lights mounted fore and aft flashing and looks at his wristwatch. School starts at 8 a.m., he's behind schedule and the goddamn Strudel kid as usual is poking down her driveway like she thinks she's winning a race with a hare.

He could honk the horn or lower his window and yell, though he's not supposed to swear with kids on the bus, "Hurry the hell up, Apple!" But Apple Strudel, he's learned over the months, has but one speed: slow. Apple marches to a different drummer as the saying goes. A slow drummer: about a thump a minute. And there's a whiff of cigarette smoke in the bus.

Wade looks in his rearview mirror, spots a curl of smoke at the back of the bus. Billy Hennessey, no doubt, he steals smokes from his big brother Jerry. Smoking on the bus is of course forbidden, a cardinal sin. But who cares, twelve days to go, and there is a car behind the bus, rolling down Hennessey Hill. It will have to stop, the STOP arm extended, warning lights flashing. Apple reaches the end of the driveway, which, pierced by a metal culvert, spans the ditch beside County Road K. She's been told a thousand times, Stop and look both ways, but that went in one ear and out the other, and the goddamn car, Wades notes with near panic in the rearview mirror, is crossing the center line into the left lane and it's tearing along. It's not going to stop!

It's a large brown automobile and it sails by the bus, STOP arm extended and warning lights flashing be dammed, Apple invisible beyond it, and disappears over the low hill with no name just ahead. Leaving Apple Strudel sprawled in the new knee-high weeds in the ditch beside County Road K.

Wade Cummins just about pees in his pants. He leaps from his seat, yells at his passengers, "Stay put!" and jumps from the bus, looks neither way, crosses County Road K at a gallop and drops to his knees in the weeds beside Apple, dead or alive but badly injured as the case may be. Her eyes, however, are open though somewhat glazed, and her fat legs are threshing around in the weeds.

"Oh jeezuzz!" Wade gurgles. "Are you hurt, Apple? Did that goddamn car hit you?"

"Nuh," Apple says. "I jump. It dint hit me. My lunch."

"Oh jeezuzz! I guess we thank our lucky stars then, Apple!" Wade figured his driving record was shot. Not his fault but he was in charge, the bus and the little bastards and Apple's old man, the State Representative, a real asshole, would skinned him alive no doubt, Apple was dead or injured. "C'mon, I help you up." He helps Apple up.

"My lunch," Apple says. "I drop it."

"Don't worry. We'll find it, Apple. But we got to hurry up or we be late for school."

"There." Apple spots her Mickey Mouse lunch bucket in a tangle of weeds. "And my jacket."

Wade grabs the lunch bucket and Apple's pink vinyl jacket and puts them in her hands. "C'mon, Apple. We got a get on the bus."

"Nuh, wait." Apple shakes her vinyl jacket. "My flute. I can't find my flute. It must fell out my jacket. Case, too. I got a find them. I got a turn them in. This the last day turn them in."

"Oh shit! Awright, we'll look." Which they do, poking through the weeds while time ticks by, but do not find the flute or its case. It's 7:50, five more little bastards at two stops waiting for the bus. "We got to go, Apple! Come on, get on the bus."

"Nuh. I got a find my flute. I got a turn it in or my Pa kill me."

"No! You can look for it after school. Turn it in tomorrow. Chrissake, Apple, come on! Or I drive off and leave you!"

Wade grabs Apple's arm and propels her across County Road K and into the bus, where all the little bastards, jumping and talking at once, want to know what part of Apple was hit?

"Shut up!" Wade bellows. "Sit down!" This babble subsides. Wade retracts the STOP arm, kills the flashing red lights and starts the bus. They'll be late to school. He'll have to explain that to the Consolidated School principal, grouchy old Dr. Kermit Kammerfuss, and report the near miss that left Apple in the ditch, minus her goddamn flute. Kammerfuss, Wade's heard, is an Ed.D., nothing special as degrees go, but he likes to be called Doctor. He'll no doubt want the guilty driver, whomsoever that may be, apprehended and prosecuted. Drawn and quartered preferably. Few crimes after all in the Great State of Minnesota are considered more heinous than passing a school bus with STOP arm extended and warning lights flashing. But Wade got only a glimpse of the guilty vehicle. "Big brown car" won't satisfy Kammerfuss. He'll have to question Apple and the other little bastards, perhaps get a better description, though that's not likely.

It's 8:10, two more Grubers and three Shanahans, males and females, aboard, when Wade pulls the big yellow bus into the parking lot behind the Consolidated School on Hayfield's south side, kills the engine, stands blocking the door and asks the little bastards, all eager to disembark, "Any you kids get a look at that car went by the bus and almost hit Apple? Did you, Apple?"

"Nuh," Apple says. "I owny seen it was car." The rest likewise babble "No." Or, half of them, "No, I was sit the other side the bus."

Wade, his gloomy surmise as to their observational skills confirmed, opens the door and forty-two little bastards erupt from the bus and race across the parking lot, bound for their various classrooms, all itching to be the first with a news flash for their teacher. "Car went by the bus it was stop the bottom Hennessey Hill and almost kilt Apple Strudel!"

Apple, marching to her different drummer, exits more slowly. She's been crying: tears stain her cheeks. "I supposed and turn my flute in," she whines. "Mister Burcholtz gonna kill me, I ain't got it." Chester Burcholtz is the Music teacher and Band Director.

"Don't be silly, Apple," Wade says. The momentary sympathy he felt for Apple when on his knees beside her in the ditch, afraid she was dead or badly injured, has evaporated. "You just tell Mister Burcholtz what happened. He won't kill you. Hurry up. You're late for class awready."

And here comes little bastard No. 43, Billy Hennessey, a skinny little kid with dirty ears who needs a haircut, wearing bib overalls and a denim shirt and torn sneakers, his skimpy lunch in a greasy paper sack. He's always the last little bastard off the bus. Billy hates school, plans to major in Auto Shop when (and if) he makes it to ninth grade, dreams he'll be a long-haul over-the-road truck-driver wheeling a big Peterbilt and a double-bottom, two trailers in tandem, when he grows up.

"C'mon, Billy," Wade says. "Get the lead out. You're late for class awready."

"Who gives a shit?" Billy, he's a cocky foul-mouthed little bastard, says. "You want a know some'pin, Wade? I seen what kind a car it was fuckin near hit Fatso. Fifty-four Buick Roadmaster four-door. Color they call Desert Dawn. License start eight-eight-eight. I dint see the rest it."

"What! You saw all that!" Little bastard must have eyes like an eagle, bless him. "You sure, Billy? That car must been going fifty sixty miles an hour." Billy says fuckin right he's sure. "C'mon then! I got a tell the principal what happen, bus was late. You come with me. We tell him what you seen."

"No! I don't want a go the fuckin principal's office!" Billy's been there before, several times, most recently when caught smoking in the boy's john, suspended a day for that, his parents informed, whacked ten times then with the old man's razor strap. He still smokes in the john, but uses a stall, pretends to be taking a poop, smoke alone in the absence of a cigarette, which he flushes down the john if need be, insufficient evidence to convict.

"You come with me, goddamn it!" Wade says. There's no point to not swearing in Billy's presence, on or off the bus. "Or I'll tell Doctor Kammerfuss you are withholding information. Tell him you were smoking on the bus too." Wade could pass along the information regarding the suspect vehicle but he'd rather it came from Billy, case it turns out Billy's often vivid imagination is at work.

They go into the sprawling single-story Consolidated School's administration wing, Billy reluctant but left with no choice. Dr. Kammerfuss is busy, the school secretary says, so they wait a few minutes, then she says they can go in and they go into the principal's private office.

"What did he do this time?" Kammerfuss, scowling at Billy, says. He's a large pear-shaped man in his fifties with a broad pale face and thin brown hair combed over a growing bald spot, wearing a brown suit, a bowtie and spectacles, married, three kids, from somewhere in Iowa originally. A former high school math teacher selected from among three finalists by the Consolidated District Search Committee, he moved to Hayfield and bought a house when school started. He earned the "Doctor" he likes to be called in ten summers of grad school at Iowa State, with numerous credits in Driver Education.

"Nothing, this time," Wade Cummins says, and explains. "I had the bus stopped the bottom Hennessey Hill, STOP arm extended, warning lights flashing. The whole nine yards. I was waiting for the Strudel kid. Rep Strudel's kid. I always have to wait for her. Then a car came tearing down Hennessey Hill. Didn't stop. Didn't even slow down. Went right by the bus."

"My god!" Kammerfuss says. "Went right by! Passed a school bus with STOP arm extended and warning lights flashing!"

"Yessir. And the Strudel kid, she was the edge the road and she had a like jump out a the way or this car prolly hit her. She fell in the ditch there. She's wasn't hurt but she was pretty scared. I had a calm her down like. That's why the bus a few minutes late."

"The car. You recognize the car?"

"No. But Billy here. Tell Doctor Kammerfuss what you saw, Billy."

"I seen it was a Fifty-four Buick Roadmaster," Billy says and adds the details (Desert Dawn, half a license number) while Kammerfuss takes notes.

"Are you sure about all that, Billy?" Kammerfuss says. "You must only have had a glimpse of that car." Billy sticks his lower lip out, he's a stubborn little bastard, and says Yeah he's sure. "All right. You can go, Billy. Tell your teacher I excused you, you're tardy."

Billy scoots from the office and heads for the boy's john for a quick smoke. Kammerfuss the old goat might said thank you but he didn't, but that's about what you'd expect, a fuckin principal.

"I'll call the Sheriff's Department," Kammerfuss says. "Tell them what happened and give them Billy's information. For what it's worth. You think the little delinquent might be making things up? Or lying? That wouldn't surprise me." Well, the car was brown, Wade says. "In any case, we have to pursue this. Apprehend the driver. Prosecute him, or her, the full extent of the law. My god, passing a school bus with STOP arm extended and warning lights flashing! And almost hit the Strudel child, you say?" Wade Cummins nods, ruefully, and Kammerfuss emits a low moan. "Her father, member the Legislature, he's if you'll pardon the expression a pain in the ass. Fought consolidation, you know. He'll blow a gasket, he hears his child had a narrow escape. And I suppose he will?"

"Yeah, prolly," Wade says. "She prolly tell him. Kids on the bus prolly tell their folks. Everybody prolly know it pretty soon. Strudel kid lost her flute too, she jump in the ditch, and bawl about that. Said she supposed to turn it in today."

"Her flute? Today? No, the rental instruments were turned in last week. Supposed to be. There was a man here from the music company, Mister Hossman, picked them up."

Wade shrugs. "Strudel kid might forgot, last week. We look for her flute. I help her. We look all through the weeds in the ditch. But we dint find it."

"Never mind that," Kammerfuss says. A lost flute is a minor matter compared with Rep. Strudel's probable wrath. "I don't think I know the Strudel child." Kammerfuss knows but a handful of his students, the troublemakers. They come and they go so why bother, get acquainted?

"Big girl," Wade says. "Big for her age. Fat. Not real bright, I don't think." This rings no bell with Kammerfuss. "Well I guess I better get going." Wade rides an old Harley he parks in the garage behind the school where the buses are maintained the sixteen miles to (and from) Winatchee Falls. "I got a ten o'clock class."

"No, you stay right here while I call the Sheriff's Department," Kammerfuss, reaching for his phone, says. "They might want to talk to you."

* * *

At just about this same time, 8:30 a.m., Harold E. (Hoss) Hossman, a big man staring at fifty, 6-2, 250 pounds, the last thirty fat, wearing a wrinkled tan suit and a blue tie embroidered with musical notes, sitting in his '54 Buick Roadmaster, angle-parked in front of the Municipal Liquor Store on Hayfield's Main Street, they still angle-park in this one-horse town, lights another Lucky. And finds, to his dismay, his big hands are still shaking.

Well, no wonder. But he did not, he's pretty sure, actually hit the dumb kid headed for the goddamn school bus, crossing the road without looking either way. Did not at any rate hear or feel anyway the thump of steel on flesh. And the glimpse he got of the kid in his rear vision mirror, sprawled in the weeds in the ditch beside the road, he or she was still moving. His or her legs were kicking. A near thing though. But the goddamn school bus made a sudden stop, popped its STOP arm, red lights flashing. He had no choice but to swerve and pass the goddamn bus. It was that or impale the Buick on its rear end. Granted, his thoughts at the time were elsewhere, dwelling on the erotic enthusiasm displayed by the little wench he picked up last night in the Pow Wow Lounge at the Dobermann Hotel, hustled back to his room in the Moon Beam Motel and screwed until dawn, then drove home, that a big apartment building on Winatchee Falls' west side.

Margie Bremer. Said she was in real estate. Short, plump but firm, great set of jugs, liked to talk dirty. A one-night-stand now high on Hoss Hossman's long list of one-night-stands, with a matinee promised following a lunch at Winatchee Falls' best restaurant,

Manny's Steakhouse, which the Diptill Music Co. will pay for. The company pays the expenses Hoss pads while on the road sucking up to Music teachers and School Band Directors and foisting rental musical instruments on unsuspecting students in September, half the rent applied to purchase, collecting those instruments in May if no purchase is forthcoming.

Passing a school bus with STOP arm extended and red lights flashing though! Jeezuzz! That is a terrible crime in Minnesota! Next thing to first-degree murder. Or vehicular homicide anyway, of which Hoss Hossman once many years ago was found to be not guilty. But nobody on the bus, or the dumb kid, could have got more than a glimpse of his Roadmaster in the second or so the whole thing happened. One or more kids or the bus driver might come up with "big brown car." Desert Dawn, the dealer called it. But there are lots of "big brown cars."

Sucking his Lucky, Hoss comes to the conclusion no one will ever know it was him passed the goddamn school bus with STOP arm extended and red lights flashing. He got away clean, the goddamn school bus far behind him on County Road K when he zipped by the new Consolidated School on Hayfield's south side, then was held up by a slow Milwaukee St. Paul & Pacific Railroad freight train chugging across Main Street on the MSP&P's Main Line. Dangerous crossing, Hoss thought. No barricades or red lights. Just two X-shaped Railroad Crossing signs. But the natives, he guessed, all know the crossing is there and the times the trains come through. Whatever, that was no skin off his ass and Hayfield, he remembered, has a Municipal Liquor Store. The freight on its way west, he found the Muny, that's what the locals call it, and parked in front of it.

The Muny is a squat one-story stucco building with a single window and scant identification. Just a sign in the window. Liquor On-Sale Off-Sale. And another sign someone inside just stuck in the window, Open. Hoss Hossman gets out of his Buick. He got away clean but he needs a drink. Calm his nerves.

"Double Jim Beam straight up, soda on a side," Hoss, his big butt on a bar stool, says. The Muny is a long narrow establishment with a linoleum floor and bare walls, dim compared to the bright sunshine outside. A dusty blind, closed, covers the single window: local drinkers prefer privacy. The rest of the clientele, two old codgers in bib overalls humped over beers at a table near the silent jukebox, spotting a stranger, eye Hoss with suspicion.

"Comin' up," the bartender, a heavyset man in his mid-forties with a face full of broken veins, wearing Sears work pants and a T-shirt advertising Hamn's Beer, says. Waiting, Hoss surveys the softball and bowling trophies and famous athletes' photos on display between the bottles on the back bar and finds among the latter, surprise, his photo. Hoss Hossman, circa 1929, potential All-American, from the waist up, in his Land Grant U football jersey, the No. 33 he once made briefly famous, looking fierce, snarling at the world, a football tucked in his left elbow, straight-arming an invisible tackler, his signature scrawled across the jersey. One of those posed shots beloved by the LGU Athletic Department, which provided, forged, the signature.

But that was then, this is now, and the years since (Hoss thinks, momentarily, though he seldom dwells on this) have been a long slow slide downhill. The bartender delivers the double Beam and says Fifty cents. Hoss digs into his wallet, finds Margie Bremer's business card and drops a $5 bill on the bar. "See you got my picture there."

"Yah? Which one?" The bartender, puzzled, surveys the photos.

"One next the Southern Comfort. Number Thirty Three."

"Hoss Hossman?" The bartender turns and stares at Hoss. "Holy smoke! Hoss Hossman! You was Hoss Hossman?"

"I still am, for chrissake." Hoss swallows half his double. "Long time ago, that picture was took."

"Well I'll be dammed!" the bartender burbles. "Hoss

Hossman!" Then studies Hoss. "You put some weight on. Since then."

"Few pounds. I got a start working out one these days. Get back my playing weight." Hoss has been saying this for twenty years. Both his former wives and other wives, not his, often whined, right in the middle of an act of love, that he "weighed a ton." His present wife, the former Louella Diptill, used to too but doesn't any more, mainly because they seldom engage in an act of love these days. Margie Bremer, though scarcely half his weight, did not.

"You from up The Range, wasn't you? I mean 'riginally."

"Yeah. Chisholm. My old man was a foreman, the mines. That work never interest me."

"I seen you played a few times," the bartender says, reverently. "Me and some us, we was in high school, we allas drive up a couple times a year, see a game. Hey! I seen that game, I think it was Indiana, you run for like two-hunnert yards!"

"Two-hundred-and-eight. On thirty-two carries." Hoss sometimes forgets his car keys but remembers all his statistics and is suitably modest. "Indiana wasn't much a team though, that year."

"Still, jeezuzz, two-hunnert yards. Two-hunnert-and-eight. That was the year you was gonna be a All-American, wasn't it? S'posed be, I mean."

"Yeah. Supposed to be. Year I was a senior. But I tore up my knee and missed two games." Hoss swallows the rest of his double. "We finish second, the conference, and they pick some kid, I think it was Michigan he played, First Team. And some other kid, I forget where the hell he played, Second Team. I was All-Conference."

"Shit. They ought to of pick you, Hoss, them All-Americans!" All this was more than a quarter-of-a-century ago but it rankles a true fan still. "I never unnerstant how they pick them All-Americans. Hey, lemme buy you a drink, Hoss. Old times sake. Same thing?" Hoss nods. The bartender pours Hoss a generous double and a short Beam straight up for himself. "You play pro awhile too, dint you?"

"Yeah. Couple years with the Packers." But Hoss was too slow for the pros, soon overweight, banged up his knee again, was put on waivers, left unclaimed and released and the long slow slide downhill began. But that's not this friendly bartender's business. "Thanks for the drink. What's your name?"

"Marv Gruber. I'm the manager here. I mostly work nights but my day guy, he got some kind back trouble, he had a go to the Chiro there in Winatchee Falls. What you been up to since you played pro?"

"Oh, this and that. Selling mostly."

Selling heavy equipment, sand-and-gravel, office supplies, Yellow Pages ads, liquor, beer, billboard space, fencing, radio commercials, autos (new and used), trading on his fame on the gridiron initially but that soon faded. And he wasn't (isn't, might as well face it) much of a salesman. He hated, still hates, sucking up to potential customers. Also, while the years slowly rolled downhill, married and divorced, twice each. Missed The War with his bum knee, three years at Douglas Aircraft in Long Beach, California, instead: pretty good years in which he riveted many a Rosie the Riveter.

And monuments. He was selling monuments at the Anderson Monuments Co. in St. Cloud, the company called them monuments, what they were actually were tombstones for graves hewed from the granite blasted out of a nearby quarry, on straight commission, fifteen percent against a stinking $50-a-week-draw, the end of the line, the last stop on that long slow slide, when he met Louella Diptill. Six years ago, come next week.

Louella was looking for a massive tombstone for her parents, the late Marcus Diptill Sr. and his wife Freda, her mother, both recently laid to rest in the Lutheran Cemetery in St. Cloud. Where, Louella said, Marcus when still in his teens first took an interest in musical instruments and several times revived the First

Lutheran's ancient pump organ when it looked about ready to expire. Subsequently, just turned twenty-one, this also Louella's story (which if he hears it one more time, Hoss thinks while sipping his Beam in the Muny, he will kill Louella with his bare hands) Marcus Diptill founded the Diptill Music Co. in St. Paul. Stocked with a single used piano.

Hoss heard this story while Louella looked at tombstones. She was a tall rawboned woman in Hoss guessed her middle forties with a big bosom and shapely legs, wearing a good dark suit and numerous rings but no wedding band. That missing band roused Hoss' interest. He turned on the charm, which he can when he wants to, listened with apparent interest to the story of Marcus Diptill Sr's. rise to fame and fortune with appropriate grunts and eventually sold Louella, his commission a welcome $300, a $2,000 "custom-made" tombstone: a raw chunk of granite that weighed a ton on which the Anderson Monument Co's. skilled craftsman would sandblast Marcus Diptill (1878-1950) & His Wife Freda (1880-1949) in large Gothic letters (and numerals) surrounded by, Louella had a sketch, vines, cherubs, trumpets and musical notes. Hoss also got Louella's phone number so as to keep her posted as to the progress of this work.

"Fact," Hoss said. "I'm down in St. Paul a lot weekends. I got friends there. I could give you a ring with a progress report like. Next time I'm down there?"

"Why don't you do that," Louella said, and Hoss did, two weekends later, phoned Louella, said the tombstone was "coming alone fine" and wondered if they might if Louella cared to have a drink some place? They had this drink and several more and eventually dinner at the University Club, Louella's favorite watering hole, and she, though Hoss voiced a faint protest, picked up the tab. Hoss took a cab to the club because his car at the time was a beat-up '48 Ford two-door, the fenders rusted through, but he was wearing his best suit and had his charm turned to high.

Louella came in her '48 Lincoln. Hoss drove her home in the Lincoln, her home a huge stone monstrosity a block away on

Summit Avenue built by the late Marcus Diptill Sr. before the federal income tax in his bracket soared to a crippling ten percent. They had a nightcap in this monstrosity, the maid was in bed and so in fairly short order were Hoss and Louella. Their coupling in Hoss' opinion was a 3 on a scale of 10 (but a 9 if you counted Louella's money) and Louella seemed to find it exhilarating. Hoss after all had had a lot of practice. Louella's sexual experience was limited. She had, she eventually confided, "slept with one or two people" when she was in the Service (a Second Lieutenant in the Women's Army Corps, 1943-45) and was "for a while after the war" married to then divorced from a member of the St. Paul aristocracy. But none of those gentlemen apparently was any great shakes in bed. She said virtually nothing about the ex-husband and Hoss did not pry. What did he care?

Whatever, Louella slept with Hoss thereafter, almost every weekend, while the craftsman blasted away at the tombstone and Hoss made various excuses, a grandmother's funeral, his bum knee acting up, in order to avoid his Saturday stint at the Monument Co.

Hoss also met Louella's only sibling, her little brother Marcus Jr. Louella called him Marky and with Marcus Sr. planted, awaiting the tombstone, Marky was dumping the Jr. He was a two-term Republican state senator when he wasn't running the Diptill Music Co., married, no children, and his wife was dying, some kind of cancer. Marky was thirty-nine. "Five years younger than Louella," he once blurted out, revealing a state secret. He was a Land Grant U grad and, though only twelve at the time, remembered Hoss' exploits on the gridiron, those golden days, and still was impressed by those exploits. Marky was (and is) a wild-eyed LGU sports fan with season football and hoops tickets and still wears his raggedy old maroon-and-gold Golf Team letter sweater now and then,

It was Marky's idea Hoss quit the Monument Co. and join the Diptill Music Co. Which Hoss did, quitting the Monument Co. before he was fired, and three months later, the tombstone with the trumpets, vines and musical notes in place, Hoss and Louella were wed in the Summit Avenue First Lutheran Church. As good a place as any, Hoss guessed: he'd had little experience with places of worship. The ceremony was followed by a reception for 300 at the University Club.

But all that, Hoss thinks while Marv the bartender draws two beers for the old codgers, was then. This is now. Louella was a loving wife for awhile, bought Hoss a decent car, a '51 Olds 88, and a decent wardrobe, while he learned the music business, doing a year in the warehouse where the rental instruments and band uniforms are stored and eighteen months in the main downtown store and an outpost in one of the malls, selling instruments, pianos and guitar lessons before he went on the road, his "territory" a dozen Southern Minnesota counties. Marky by then, his dying wife dead, was the governor, at home in the renovated Governor's Mansion, and Louella, replacing him, was president and CEO of the Diptill Music Co. She still is and also the president these days of the Business & Professional Women's Twin Cities Chapter.

It was Louella's idea Hoss go on the road with a "territory" and a new car every other year. She figured his former football fame would open doors, impress principles and coaches in the schools in his "territory," and she knew coaches often had a significant say in purchasing decisions regarding school band uniforms. But Louella was wrong about the fame. A few weary old principals and weary old coaches counting the days to their retirements dimly remember Hoss and his gridiron exploits, but most of both species were (and are) far younger and never heard of Hoss. The school band uniform sales and instrument rentals in Hoss' "territory" are mostly repeats and his instrument sales are flat. He's drummed up scarcely any new business and recently "lost" (that Louella's sneering term) two high school bands, instruments and uniforms, to the rival Bailey Music & Uniform Co. in Minneapolis.

Hoss would like to give the whole thing up. Give somebody else his goddamn "territory" and do something else for the Diptill Music Co. Something to do with public relations, for instance. Whatever that may mean.

But Louella is a stubborn bitch. She often berates Hoss these days for his perceived failure to suck up or suck up enough to the music teachers and school band directors in his "territory." She treats him like common help and snarls he's just plain lazy, which he sometimes is. She also, now and then, calls him a "goddamn slacker," this a reference to his defense work at Douglas Aircraft while she was shuffling personnel files in a WAC unit at Fort Des Moines. Louella also now suspects, Hoss suspects, Hoss is "fooling around," screwing other women he encounters while traversing his dozen counties Monday through Friday. Which he is, but what the hell. Yet Louella will not relieve him of his "territory," though recently warning or perhaps threatening him, thus: "You better get your big butt in gear, Buster, and get some new uniform orders, or else."

Or else what? Hoss, sipping his Beam in the Hayfield Muny, doesn't know (or much care, truth be told) but he does have an appointment, 10 o'clock, with the Band Director at the Hayfield Consolidated Elementary School. Chutney Buckholder, some name like that, a jerk in Hoss' opinion. They'll look at the full-color illustrations in the new Diptill Music Co. band uniforms catalog and, a waste of time, discuss piping, epaulets, buttons and prices. Wasting time because Buckholder or whatever his name is can't by himself buy anything that costs in excess of $10. The school principal, the superintendent, the school board, a snarled bureaucracy Hoss does not fully understand, must approve all purchases in excess of $10. Nevertheless, he'll go see Buckholder. And pick up the rental instrument, a goddamn flute, not purchased, a dumb kid forgot to turn in a week ago.

Fucking instruments! Fucking uniforms! The Diptill Music Co., old Marcus sniffing an opportunity while the Roaring Twenties roared, already doing pretty well renting instruments to inept kid musicians, jumped into the school band uniform business in 1927, and this business, though flat throughout The Great Depression, now produces close to 40 percent of the bottom line. Or so Hoss overheard Louella telling the accountant. She does not share that sort of information with Hoss. Louella no longer is a sharing person. Diptill Music has had a lock on the Land Grant U Marching Band's uniforms (140 gaudy maroon jackets with gold epaulets, yellow pants with broad maroon stripes, yellow shakos) since 1935. It used to have, until the Bailey Co. came along, a similar lock on half the state's high school bands, which is also largely equips with rental instruments, and it's moving fast to lock up the new bands springing up in the consolidated schools. Not fast enough though, if you listen to Louella.

Louella also is Marky's official hostess these days at goings-on at the Governor's Mansion, mainly receptions and state dinners for visiting VIPs and big contributors to Marky's ongoing war chest. Louella often drafts Hoss for these affairs, makes him haul extra chairs from the basement etc. and watches him like a hawk, less he get his hands on more than one cocktail. Hoss generally manages to slip away though, Louella busy being the official hostess, and make himself a drink at the bar in a little room behind the dining room, or join the help and the caterer's staff in the kitchen, where he keeps a jug of Beam stashed. There's a cute little maid-of-all work and waitress just joined the Mansion staff, Belle Something or a name like that, blonde and bold and busty, he first met her a week ago during a reception for Young Republican chairman, he'd like to pop, he ever gets a chance.

"One more?" Marv says.

"Why not?" Hoss says. "Here, I pay for this one. Have one yourself."

"No. Thanks. But I got a like pace me, I be here all day. What kind of team, you think, the U gonna have this year?"

Hoss shakes his head. He still follows LGU football, reads the sports pages, skeptical of their rosy forecasts. "Lousy. Be lucky they finish fourth or fifth, the conference. Defense might not be so bad but they got no offense."

"I see they recruit a couple Color kids though. Finally. From South Carolina or someplace. One a them supposed to be a pretty good running back."

"Ricky Harris. But he ain't very big. Hundred-and-eighty. And those Color kids, they don't like and play it gets cold. There's snow on the ground. They ain't used to that."

"Yeah, ain't that the troot," Marv, resigned to another lousy season, LGU whipped 49-0 by Michigan, 52-6 by Ohio States or scores like that, says. "I don't follow basketball much. I never played it. I played football, high school. Played guard. Hoops, you touch some guy, your little finger, the goddamn whistle blows."

"Right. Game for girls, I allas thought." Hoss finishes his drink. He's put eight ounces of whiskey in his belly (Marv pours a generous shot) but he ate a big breakfast and he's a big man, he can carry his liquor. It's 9:45 on the clock on the backbar. "I got a get going. See a guy the Consolidated School. You got some mints, I freshen my breath?" Marv produces Lifesavers. "Thanks. Been nice talkin' to you, Marv." Hoss drops a dollar tip and departs.

Outside, blinking in the sunshine, Hoss wonders: is it smart, going to the school after passing the goddamn school bus with STOP arm extended, etc.? That no doubt was where the goddamn bus was going. But, emboldened perhaps by eight ounces of whiskey, Hoss decides he better keep his appointment with Buckhead. And pick up that goddamn flute. Or Louella will have a fit.

"Hey," Marv, addressing the old codgers, says. "You know who that was I was talkin'?" The old codgers do not. "Hoss Hossman! He just about the best football player the U ever had!"

The old codgers evince no interest. Marv sighs. But he has something to tell other customers as the day rolls along. "You know who was in here? Hoss Hossman!" A few diehard fans may remember Hoss and go away impressed.

※ ※ ※

"I seen it!" Billy Hennessey says. "I seen the car hit Fatso Strudel! Almost hit her. It was goin' out the parking lot we went out for recess!"

"Are you sure, Billy?" Miss Wendy Bauer, twenty-two, a prim young woman winding up her first year in a classroom, surrounded by a two-dozen sixth-graders, says.

"Yeah, Billy seen it!" the two-dozen chirp and squeal. "He seen it we was on the bus and we went out for recess he seen it again! He write the license number with a stick in the dirt out the playground!"

"Yeah, I'm sure." Billy says. He's getting pretty tired of that question.

"All right, Billy," Wendy Bauer says. Apple Strudel's brush with death has had the whole school in a quiet uproar all morning. "We'll go tell Doctor Kammerfuss. The rest of you, sit down and study Maine's principal crops." The sixth grade is working its way through the forty-eight states' principle crops. "And don't act up!"

Minutes later, Kammerfuss though reluctant bestows a little praise in his office. "Well, Billy, I guess we have to hand it to you this time. You're sure now, the numbers you wrote in the dirt in the playground we looked at, eight-eight-eight-seven-oh-two, are correct?" Billy rolls his eyes. "Well, yes, I'm sure they are correct. You did the right thing, Miss Bauer, bring this to my immediate attention. I'll call the Sheriff's Department. I believe if they have the license number they can identify the driver. Or who owns the vehicle anyway."

"I seen the guy drivin' it too," Billy says.

"What!" Kammerfuss says. "You saw him! Who was it? I mean do you know?"

"No. I just seen him was all. Big galoot."

Trust this little delinquent, Kammerfuss thinks, raise one's hopes then dash them. "But visitors are supposed to check-in. I'll find out." A muffled scream and a loud crash interrupt him. "My god! What?"

"My class!" Wendy Bauer squeals "I left them unattended! Just so I could bring Billy." Never ever leave students unattended is Kammerfuss' First Law, reiterated at every faculty meeting.

"That's all right then, Miss Bauer," Kammerfuss says. "But you better get back there." Wendy gets back there, Billy tagging along behind her, and Kammerfuss picks up his phone.

* * *

At 11 a.m., State Highway Patrol Trooper Lionel Redhardt (also known as Dog Food, there's a dog chow called Red Heart, by young bucks he's ticketed in his four-county patrol territory) is sitting in his maroon patrol car, a '55 Ford with the big engine and heavy duty suspension, parked in one of his favorite hiding places, the radio turned off, all he was getting was static. A muscular fellow, 5-10 and 195 pounds, just turned forty-two, based in Winatchee Falls, with a round red face and a GI haircut under his Smoky The Bear hat, he's munching a Milky Way and patiently waiting. It's warm in the Ford, parked in the sun, not air-conditioned, and Trooper Redhardt, all buttoned up in his maroon uniform with the Sam Browne belt, a Colt pistol on his hip, is perspiring. Patiently perspiring. Ten years on the Highway Patrol, he's learned patience.

This favorite hiding place is behind a billboard a mile out of Hayfield on County Road O, a two-lane blacktop that, ten miles to the east, crosses the state highway that, six miles to the north, slices through Winatchee Falls. The billboard advertises sparkplugs. It depicts a tomato red racing car allegedly equipped with these sparkplugs rounding a turn at high speed while thousands cheer on a track that might be the Indianapolis 500 Speedway. All of which, Trooper Redhardt has discovered, seems to send a powerful subliminal message to young bucks leaving Hayfield in '52 Chevys or whatever, bound for Winatchee Falls' bright lights. A surprising number at any rate on passing this billboard promptly wind up their Chevys or whatever and blaze east on County O, the posted speed limit 65 mph, at speeds in excess of 80 mph. Closely pursued, caught and ticketed by Trooper Redhardt.

But the young bucks, Trooper Redhardt fears, may be getting onto him. He's been patiently waiting for forty-five minutes but all the eastbound traffic, he's an excellent judge of speed, was doing less than 70 mph. He might as well quit his hiding place and patrol County O awhile before breaking for lunch, a hot pork sandwich with extra pork for a peace officer at Bonnie's Café in Hayfield.

But hold the fort! A big brown (Desert Dawn) Buick Roadmaster just ripped by the billboard, eastbound on County O at close to 80 mph.

Trooper Redhardt stuffs the rest of the Milky Way in his face, starts the Ford, pulls out from behind the billboard in hot pursuit and, five miles down O, meanwhile clocking the Buick at 85 mph, pulls up behind this joker and cranks up his siren and the flashing red Mars lights on the Ford's roof. The Buick accelerates momentarily (is this joker thinking high-speed chase!) then slows, pulls off the blacktop onto the shoulder and halts. Trooper Redhardt pulls up behind it, shuts down his siren and cautiously, one hand on his Colt, approaches the Buick's driver-side window. A fellow trooper recently was shot at but missed by an irate motorist in Turkey County and you never know. The Buick's window is closed: goddamn heap probably has air-conditioning. Trooper Redhardt makes a cranking motion and the driver rolls the window down. He's a big man with a battered face, wearing a wrinkled tan suit.

"See your driver's license, Sir," Trooper Redhardt says. "Just take it out and give it to me." He could, he figures, take this guy, big as he is, push comes to shove, but that's unlikely. The guy, squirming, digs a wallet out of his hip pocket, extracts his driver's license and hands it over. Hossman, Harold E., b. 4.4.07, sex M, 6-2, 230, eyes Blue, Summit Avenue, St. Paul, address. Must be a rich bastard. "You know you were going eighty-five, Sir? In a sixty-five zone?"

"I was?" Hoss Hossman, evincing surprise but no particular contrition, says. "No, I dint. But I just had this buggy tuned-up and the way she runs now. Well, no, I dint."

That's an excuse or lame explanation Trooper Redhardt's heard a hundred times. And this driver it's clear is an arrogant sonofabitch. So what he ought to do is give the big galoot a ticket, 85 in a 65, and haul him into Justice-of-the-Peace Jane Klamatty's Justice Court in Hayfield. Klamatty is a tough old bird, death on speeders and DWIs, probably sock this rich bastard with a $50 fine. Trooper Redhardt and JP Klamatty have an on-going arrangement: he hauls them in and she socks it to them. Justice is swift in Klamatty's Justice Court and it's seldom encumbered by lawyers, a species Trooper Redhardt detests. Not much longer though, perhaps. That new law. Klamatty's court will vanish August 1, replaced by a Hayfield Village Court. Klamatty of course may be the Village Court judge. If the governor appoints her. Trooper Redhardt does not entirely understand this. All he knows for sure is the goddamn State Legislature, which did not approve funds for a Highway Patrol pay boost, screwed things up. Again.

But Trooper Redhardt's immediate problem is what to do with this big arrogant galoot in the Buick? Haul him before Klamatty, that'll take thirty minutes, more if Klamatty is fiddling around in her garden and they have to wait while she dons her jurist's robes. She's a stickler for that. Then this big galoot might plead not guilty. Screw things up. Besides, it's getting onto lunch time, Trooper Redhardt's stomach is growling, a Milky Way is no food for a grown man, and he's fulfilled his semi-monthly speeding ticket quota the Highway Patrol insists does not exist.

"What I ought a do, Sir," Trooper Redhardt says. "Is give you a speeding ticket, eighty-five in a sixty-five, and take you right to court."

"Well, I hope not," Hoss says. "I figure you maybe just give me a warning ticket? Like I said, I dint realize." And wonders: should he mention he is Governor Marcus Diptill's beloved brother-in-law? Or tickle this cop's square jaw with a $20 dollar bill? Neither, he decides. Hoss though a lousy salesman became while selling or not selling a fair judge of character. This cop, he judges, wouldn't care if he were Governor Diptill's secret lover and if he saw a $20 bill probably charge Hoss with attempted bribery. "But I guess you got to do your duty, Officer."

Trooper Redhardt chews his lip. "Okay. What I am gonna do, Sir. I am gonna give you a ticket, eighty-five in a sixty-five, you can plead guilty and pay by mail." Redhardt writes this ticket and hands Hoss a copy. "You mail this in, Sir. With your check. You got ten days, do it. Address on the ticket. Fine and costs be twenty-eight bucks. And you take it easy now, Sir. Watch that speed."

"Yeah, sure." Hoss stuffs the ticket in his shirt pocket, starts the Buick, pulls onto the blacktop and drives off at a sedate 50 mph.

Trooper Redhardt returns to his Ford and updates his daily log (1115, Hossman H.E., Tag 888-702, mail-in 85/65) and gives the radio a try. The Highway Patrol band is still full of static. He switches to the Winatchee County Sheriff's band and gets Millie Stokes, the dispatcher, four-by-four.

"All units. Highway Patrol too, you're listening. Be on the lookout for a brown fifty-four Buick Roadmaster four-door. Tag number eight-eight-eight-dash-seven-oh-two. Registered to the Diptill Music Company up in St. Paul. Apprehend on sight. The Winatchee County Sheriff's Department has issued a John Doe warrant for the arrest of this party on suspicion of passing a school bus with stop arm extended and warning lights flashing. Vehicle was last seen departing the Consolidated Elementary School in Hayfield at approximately ten-forty-five this date."

"Sonofabitch!" Trooper Redhardt squeals. He starts the Ford, racks in onto the County Road O and, his lunch forgotten, cranks up his siren and lights and at 95 mph blazes by a farmer on a tractor hauling a load of hay. He had this suspect! No John Doe now. But let him go! Goddamn big galoot! Goddamn big galoot didn't say anything about passing a school bus with STOP extended. Didn't say he was fleeing, 85 in a 65, avoid prosecution either. But he can't be far ahead. Trooper Redhardt will catch him before he reaches Winatchee Falls and disappears therein.

Unless. There is road work ahead. Repairs to the bridge over the Winatchee River. One-way traffic there. Trooper Redhardt tops a low rise and wouldn't you know it! The dumb flagman on duty at the bridge has the one-way open to westbound traffic.

Trooper Redhardt hits his brakes, grabs the handset hung from his radio and triggers the send button. "Highway Patrol Unit Ten to Winatchee County Sheriff. Suspect vehicle your last communication proceeding." Then pauses. He'd like to collar the big galoot himself. "I am in hot pursuit."

* * *

Apple Strudel gets off the outbound school bus at 4 p.m. and pokes around for a while in the weeds in the ditch beside County Road K, looking for her flute. She does not find it and gives up when Gloomy Toomey arrives in Whip Rahilly's big rig, tractor and slatted trailer. Gloomy wrestles the rig onto the Strudel's driveway, leans from the cab and asks Apple, "You want a ride up to your house?"

Apple climbs into the cab. She's been told a thousand times, Never ever get into a car (or a truck) with a strange man and Gloomy by any criteria is pretty strange: a short little man with a monkey face and few teeth, wearing grimy denims and a large filthy Western "cowboy" hat. Gloomy is said to be "not all there" but he holds a Class B Commercial driver's license, proof some of him is "there." And Apple knows him more or less, so it's okay she gets in his truck.

Gloomy drops Apple off at the house on his way to the barnyard and her mother, Annie, charging from the house, embraces Apple in a bear hug.

"Oh Apple!" Annie babbles. "I heard! You almost were kilt! A car went by the school bus and almost kilt you! Doctor Kammerfuss phoned me. From school. He said he didn't want I should worry, I heard some wild story from somebody got it all wrong. Are you all right? Are you sure?"

"Mmm. I wasn't hurt none," Apple says. "Just scairt some. But I lost my flute when I jump in the ditch! I never turn it in and Mister Bucholtz, he was pretty mad. He bawl me out and the man was there and get the flute. He was pretty mad too. He said I got a mail it in. But I lost it!" Tears well up in Apple's eyes. "I look and I look in the ditch. But I dint find it."

"We'll find it, we'll find it," Annie says. "Don't cry, Apple. "You're not hurt. That's the main thing. I dint tell your Pa yet, you almost were kilt. He'll have a fit! And he's busy, those pigs he's shipping. Don't say anything about your flute. I'll help you look for it. Where's your jacket?"

"Jacket?" Apple is momentarily confused. "I guess I left it to school. I forgot it. I want a go watch them load the pigs."

"All right, go watch," Annie, cancelling Lecture No. 1102 about not forgetting things, says. Apple after all was almost killed. "Don't say anything to your Pa, you were almost kilt. We'll wait'll he gets home tomorrow. Here, give me your lunch bucket."

Apple did not forget her lunch bucket. Annie takes it into the house and Apple ambles down to the barnyard. Gloomy has the slatted trailer backed up to the gate and a ramp in place and Wolfe Strudel, armed with an electric cattle prod, sweating and swearing, Gloomy helping with the swearing, is driving forty Spotted Poland Chinas up the ramp into the rig. The pigs are grunting and squealing, reluctant to get into the trailer. They're pretty smart, may guess they're on their way to the slaughterhouse. The old boar casts a baleful look at Wolfe. But Wolfe jams them in, close to 8,000 pounds of pork-on-the hoof. Gloomy barricades them in the front half of the trailer, removes the ramp, throws it in the trailer and closes the trailer's rear doors.

"We got a go get Hennessey's pigs now," Gloomy says. "He told me he shippin' a big old boar too. Then we got a go in a Hayfield and I gas up."

Wolfe grunts and tells Apple, "Go the house. Help your Ma. Tell her I be home around nine o'clock the morning." He climbs into the rig with Gloomy and they pull out of the barnyard.

* * *

It's close to 5 p.m. when the fourth mosquito starts feasting on Hayfield Justice-of-the-Peace Jane Klamatty, a short plump woman in her early fifties with a firm jaw and short dark hair tinged with gray, busy pulling the first weeds in the vegetable garden behind her small white frame house a block off Main Street across the alley behind Win Hooter's Drugstore. She decides to call it a day, the damn mosquitoes are out, take a shower and change, and goes into her walkout basement, dropping her gloves and garden tools at the door. There is a small official looking sign, black on white, on this door: Justice Court. There is a similar larger sign in her front yard: Justice Court Arraignments 10 a.m. Mon/Sat Appointments Phone 3713 Entrance In Rear.

Half the basement is Klamatty's Justice Court. The furnace, water-heater, washing machine and her late husband's tools and workbench are in the other half. She sits at her desk, her "bench" when court is in session. Just for a minute, catch her breath. Her current boyfriend, Webster R. (Web) Allen, no boy actually, a Winatchee Falls lawyer in his middle fifties, will be along at 7 o'clock to take her to dinner at the Fish House on Lake Winatchee.

Web Allen is Klamatty's fourth boyfriend in the seven years she's been a widow. Or more accurately the fourth in five years. Devastated, lonely and celibate, she had no boyfriends in the two years following Cedric Klamatty's swift death at forty-three, the medical profession helpless when confronted by leukemia. She was sorry then they'd had no children: there was something wrong with Cedric in that department. But she was (and is) all right for money. Her little house is paid for. She has Cedric's postal pension, he had a Rural Route for twenty years, the GI insurance he got when caught in the up-to-thirty-eight Draft he spent six months in the Stateside Army, eighty acres of good bottomland her father left her, which a sturdy young farmer works on shares, and her Justice-of-the-Peace business. It was the Justice-of-the-Peace business, Jane Klamatty often thinks, dispensing justice, privy to the bad luck, bad judgment and terminal stupidity besetting other people, kept her going through those two lonely years.

And brought before her in mid-February a lawyer she'd not seen before, a thin gentle bony medium-sized man with blue eyes and graying hair who gave his name as Webster R. Allen and said he was associated with Schott & Schott in Winatchee Falls. He was in her court representing Clyde Dobermann, a Winatchee Falls aristocrat, old Hein (Dollar) Dobermann's only offspring, apprehended by (who but?) State Trooper Lionel Redhardt and charged with, this a first in Winatchee County, operating a snowmobile on a public highway, to wit, the shoulder on County Road O, while Under the Influence. Allen moved for dismissal on grounds the evidence was insufficient. She denied that as a matter of course and Dobermann, a big soft man in his early forties wearing ski clothes and sunglasses though he did not look like a skier, pled not guilty. She released him on $50 cash bail, trial set for March 1. He dropped a $50 bill on her desk and went merrily on his way followed by Trooper Redhardt and Allen picked up his overcoat.

"You must be new around here," Klamatty, she was curious, said. "You've not been in my court before."

"Pretty new," Web Allen said. "I joined Schott and Schott the first of the year. I was in practice in Wisconsin before that."

"How come you drew Clyde today? Slick Riordan usually represents him. You know Riordan?" S.L. (Slick) Riordan is a slick pompous Winatchee Falls lawyer with ties to the Dobermann cartel.

"Yes, I know Riordan. He's in Florida. Vacationing. This snowmobile thing came up, Dobermann's father called Mister Schott. Old August. I gather we do quite a lot of work for Dobermann Enterprises. August asked me to represent Clyde at his arraignment."

"How the devil is old August anyway. I've not seen him in years. Is he still practicing? He must be close to eighty. They still call him First Shot? And his son, what's his name, Birdshot?"

"Eighty-one. Yes, August is still practicing. Fiddling with wills and estates anyway. He forgets things but his secretary. You know Mabel Murphy? She remembers for him."

"I know Mabel. It must be forty years she's been with August. I never thought what's his name, Birdshot, was much of a lawyer."

"Junior. Well, he's more like the office manager, the firm. Incidentally, my client, Clyde, thinks, he's not sure, Trooper Redhardt charged him once before with a DWI. Eight or nine years ago. In Winatchee Falls. Charge was dismissed, Clyde says."

"Probably was. Clyde is more or less above the law in Winatchee Falls. In view of Dobermann Enterprises' standing in the community. But I think Redhardt was up north, the Hibbing Patrol District, until four or five years ago. You know they call Clyde's father, his name is Hein, Dollar Dobermann? In view of his main interest in life. He have his fingers in anything new these days?"

"Yes, I knew that. Matter of fact, he has. You understand I'm not talking out of turn, lawyer-client privilege. It will be announced today. Brochures and contracts came off the press yesterday. Checked by me, no loopholes therein. There'll be a story and a full-page ad in the newspaper. Everlasting Rest Gardens. A wholly-owned Dobermann Enterprises subsidiary. A non-denominational ecumenical final resting place for one's loved ones. Perpetual care guaranteed."

"You mean a cemetery!"

"Yes," Web Allen said. "The Protestant cemetery in Winatchee Falls is just about full. Or has no plots left anyway. But not to worry. Dobermann owned, owns, thirty acres south of town just off the highway. East of the highway with a nice rising slope so one's loved ones, or loved ones high on the slope anyway, can watch the sun set. There are stone pillars and a wrought iron arch spells Peace and Everlasting Rest Gardens at the entrance. And a tasteful little building. The Sales Office and there's a non-denominational chapel in it. The plots, six feet by eight, are not cheap. Six-hundred-ninety-five to nine-ninety-five at the top of the slope."

"Leave it to old Dobermann!" Klamatty said. "Buy it by the acre. Sell it by the foot. Is he actually selling some of those plots?"

"Well, they won't be on the market officially until tomorrow. But he's sold some. August bought two. Adjoining. One for Elaine. His wife. You know she's not at all well? Some kind of cancer."

"Yes, I heard. Is she in the hospital?"

"No, at home. With three private nurses and I guess it's a housekeeper. My client Clyde Dobermann is the Everlasting Rest Gardens subsidiary president and sales manager. Just so named. Speaking of whom, again. I understand Clyde's had one or two previous brushes with the law in Winatchee Falls and in those cases he was granted continuances. I'll be requesting a con—"

"Not in my court, counselor. I'll deny it. Clyde's had a dozen previous brushes with the law. He goes to trial March first in my court."

Web Allen shrugged and smiled. He said he'd "heard something" about "The Law West of the Winatchee" and surveyed Klamatty's courtroom. "So this is it." Klamatty was still curious, wondered how this Allen had landed with Schott & Schott, but guessed it was none of her business. And Allen said he'd enjoyed their chat but had to go, said goodbye and went.

Klamatty, catching her breath, surveys her courtroom. Cedric, who was handy, built stairs beside the house so people do not have to go through the house to reach her courtroom. He also made her gavel and paneled her half of the basement with plywood long before the leukemia got him. There's a ratty old rug on the concrete floor, two church pews Cedric salvaged when the old Lutheran Church (there's a new one now) burned down and, behind her desk, two tall green metal file cabinets stuffed with Justice Court files dating to 1870. She inherited the files when though only thirty-two, defeating old Tom Clancy, she first was elected JP in 1936. After Clancy went a little bit loopy and, there being no Winatchee County Juvenile Detention Center at the time, sentenced a dozen juvenile Halloween pranksters (who, granted, had put two geese with goose dysentery in his new Studebaker, an $1100 automobile) to 90 days in the Winatchee County Jail. Justice perhaps but that enraged all the pranksters' parents and relatives, enough to swing the election.

Well, JP Klamatty thinks, she's had a pretty good run since. Twenty years. And only twice, she recollects, Cedric was still alive, was she roused in the middle of the night by young people, a male and a female wishing to marry who'd seen jolly old Justices-of-the-Peace perform that ceremony in films. One pair unquestionably were drunk and none of them had had the blood tests for social diseases, found negative, required by the Great State of Minnesota. She sent them packing and as far as she knows they never did marry. Not each other, that is.

Twenty years. The end may be near though. Leave it to the Legislature to do something stupid. Replace perfectly good Justice Courts with expensive (by Hayfield standards) Village Courts. There is of course a chance Governor Marcus Diptill will name her to the Village Court bench. But Diptill is taking his own sweet time, appointing Village Court judges. He's named a few and some according to the JP grapevine were serving JPs. Some were not. All those named according to the grapevine were "political," meaning they were known Republicans. But nobody knows what Jane Klamatty is. She eschewed politics on becoming a jurist.

Whatever, it's time she took her shower and checked her liquor supply. She'll offer Web Allen a drink before they head for the Fish House. Where they may encounter Clyde Dobermann: he frequently dines there. Who, if they do, probably will buy them a drink. One thing you have to give Clyde: he does not hold grudges.

Clyde, accompanied by Web Allen (Slick Riordan was still in Florida chasing tarpon), came to his trial March 1 in a $100 suit and sunglasses. The state was represented (reluctantly, it was clear) by Assistant Winatchee County Attorney J.J. Doodle, a thin man in his-mid thirties with a permanent sour expression. Web Allen moved for a continuance, denied, and Doodle called his one witness, Trooper Redhardt, who went on a great length as to the "erratic manner" in which he observed Clyde on a snowmobile "in and out the ditch and all over the shoulder on County Road O," before halting him and "detecting a strong odor of intoxicating liquor on his breadth." Web Allen moved for dismissal on grounds this testimony without corroboration was insufficient to sustain a conviction (at which point Trooper Redhardt was heard to growl, "Fuckin lawyer!"). Denied. Allen moved for dismissal on grounds the Minnesota DWI law did not specifically cite snowmobiles. Denied. And he moved for dismissal on grounds snowmobiles were a relatively recent addition to the transportation spectrum, it wasn't Clyde's snowmobile anyway, it belonged to a friend, and Clyde though sober was not familiar with its operation. Denied.

"Court finds defendant guilty," Klamatty said. "Fines him one-hundred dollars and sentences him to thirty days in the County Jail."

"Hot damn!" Trooper Redhardt, a big grin splitting his face, said.

Web Allen, expressing horror and amazement, threw his hands up in a lawyer's gesture of despair and said, "Defendant will appeal forthwith."

"Sentence stayed pending appeal," Klamatty said. "Bail continued. Court stands adjourned." And banged her gavel. "Court would like to discuss with defendant's counsel the matter of an appeal."

J.J. Doodle and Trooper Redhardt (muttering, "Goddamn lawyer!") left, Clyde Dobermann went merrily on his way and Klamatty and Web Allen had coffee in her kitchen and began to get acquainted.

They'd both, they learned, lost a spouse to cancer, pancreatic in Web Allen's case (or his late wife's case), which seemed to establish between them a certain rapport. Neither, they also learned, would ever rest in a Dobermann Enterprises' Everlasting Rest Gardens plot. Both are Catholics (more rapport) and that ground is not hallowed (blessed) in the eyes of the True

Church. She was "raised Catholic" anyway, Klamatty said, and Web Allen said he was a convert but "kind of a backslider." Klamatty said the technical term was "fallen away."

Web Allen also said he was "getting a sense of the Law West of the Winatchee." Which seemed to him to resemble in many ways Judge Roy Bean's Law West of the Pecos.

"I'll give you some advice," Klamatty said. "File your appeal with District Court Judge Lamar Kelly. Crazy Kelly. He's a bleeding heart and close to the Dobermanns. Tell me, I'm curious. How'd you get connected with Schott and Schott, you were practicing in Wisconsin?"

"West Cork," Web Allen said. "Little town on the Mississippi. You know it?" Where it is, Klamatty said, she has an aunt lives in Plum City. "Right up the road. Well, my wife died. My law partner retired, he was seventy and a widower and went off to Arizona with our office girl. She was sixty-five. I could not find another girl who could spell. I took some time off and went to the ABA convention in San Diego. I'd only ever been to one of those. I ran into old August there, at the bar. The bar bar. We got to talking and it turned out we'd both been temporary colonels in the Quartermaster Corps. In different wars. August still calls his The Big War. We traded a few war stories. I told August I'd been a prosecutor, assistant county attorney, and a defense attorney and August said he was looking for a trial lawyer, he was getting too old for that, and he was willing to pay for one. Said Schott and Schott was one of Winatchee Falls prestigious law firms. Which I guess it is. And promised me a partnership if things worked out. My girls were gone. Barbara's a stewardess with Northwest, based in Detroit. Becky married a boy she met in college. He's with the National Park Service in Montana. I was ready for a change. I accepted August's offer, closed my practice, sold my house and here I am."

"And so you are," Klamatty said.

Web Allen then expressed the hope that his client Mister Dobermann's current brush with the law would not make a big splash in the public prints. Klamatty said she couldn't promise that, her court proceedings as he well knew are a matter of public record and Trooper Redhardt was known to have a big mouth. Web Allen shrugged, said it was time he was leaving, got into his overcoat and, at the door, wondered would Jane Klamatty like to have dinner with him some evening?

Klamatty said she would and, Web Allen scarcely out the door, took a phone call from her friend Eddie Devlin, a reporter who often puts her name in the Bugle Call, Winatchee Fall's daily-except-Sunday newspaper. He had "information," Devlin said, from a reliable source he could not reveal, that "a well known Winatchee Falls citizen had another brush with the law." Klamatty confirmed that but never did see a "Falls Man First County Snowmobile DWI" story in the Bugle Call. She did not expect to: Dobermann Enterprises has a lot of clout in Winatchee Falls.

Web Allen and Jane Klamatty have had several dinners at the Fish House and Manny's Steakhouse in Winatchee Falls and drinks in those places and elsewhere since March 1 and been to bed together half a dozen times. There's been no talk of any more permanent arrangement and that's just fine with Jane Klamatty. She has her own life: her little house, her garden, two female cats, bridge once a week with three female friends, golf in season every Wednesday (Ladies Day at nine-hole Hayfield Golf & Country Club) with those same females (they shoot, not counting every stroke, in the low 110s). And a cleaning lady, her principal extravagance, Mims McNeely, who comes in once a week, a widow with a son who drives a Co-op Dairy truck and a sultry daughter, Little Nell, a waitress in St. Paul these days.

* * *

Both her cats, starving, are meowing. One was ripe the first time she went to bed with Web Allen and a nearby tomcat was howling high Cs, which they both thought funny and appropriate.

Replevy for a Flute | 73

Klamatty goes up the stairs from her courtroom into her kitchen, feeds the cats, showers, dresses in a good dark suit and high heels and finds her Jack Daniels is just about empty. She leaves her house, walks through her garden, crosses the alley to Win Hooter's Drugstore, buys a pack of Kools from Elmer, a lawyer helping out between clients, and steps out onto the Main Street sidewalk. The Muny is a block up Main Street beyond Bonnie's Café. A livestock rig, its trailer jammed with grunting pigs, is pulling out of the Standard Station beyond the Muny and in the near distance a train is tooting its whistle. That will be the MSP&P's Omaha Flyer passenger, westbound, which sails through Hayfield, crossing Main Street at 40 mph at 5 p.m. each day when on time, this often the major event of the day. The Flyer also comes through at 5 a.m. when on time, eastbound to Milwaukee, its whistle an unreliable alarm clock, but only a handful of early risers see it then.

The livestock rig goes by Klamatty, trailing a strong odor of pig shit, J.P. Rahilly Trucking in flaking paint on its cab door, and rolls on down Main Street and the Omaha Flyer's yellow diesel locomotive, a Baldwin Hercules 303, emerges from behind the Archer-Daniels-Midland (ADM) elevator with its whistle emitting a panic-stricken shriek and its locked wheels sliding, screeching, on the Main Line tracks and plows straight through J.P. Rahilly's livestock trailer.

(The engineer aboard, one James Watts of Wyville, Wisconsin, later a witness at several personal injury suits, testified that the instant he saw the livestock rig he knew it was not going to stop at the Main Street crossing. And he did what he could. Slammed his throttle into reverse, grabbed the whistle cord and held it, dumped sand and hit the airbrakes. But a lot of good any of that did.)

The Flyer (locomotive, baggage car, four coaches, dining car and a Pullman sleeper, eight-hundred tons of steel, green plush and oak paneling, ninety-four passengers and four crew aboard), whistle wailing, wheels screeching, plows through the trailer full of pigs with a resounding crash, ripping it from the rig's fifth wheel, turning it all in an instant into kindling, the eighty pigs aboard flying every which, and rolls on though slowing, strewing wreckage along the Main Line track, wreckage and pigs dead and alive, whole and in bits and pieces, all those alive squealing like banshees, before grinding to a stop, the last Pullman just beyond the crossing. The rig's cab, just clear of the crossing when the Flyer went through the trailer but flung sideways, slowly topples over, driver side up.

("What it was like," old Seth Crowder, one of the village octogenarians who, perched on the freight dock outside the old MSP&P Depot, like to watch the Flyer go through, said later. "It was like that goldurn rig just explode pigs! And kindling!" And the decibels this produced, according to Vern Lake, another old-timer with a long memory, "Was like the noise the cyclone went through the south edge of town in Ought-Nine made!")

Two dozen Spotted Poland Chinas, one of them a 700-pound boar, survive the crash. They are still mobile at any rate, though perhaps badly damaged psychologically. They race off squealing in a dozen directions. The boar lost his right ear in the collision and the left one is torn. He pounds up the middle of Main Street, trailing blood.

Klamatty and the octogenarians are eyewitnesses to this disaster. So, dawdling on Main Street, are a dozen other citizens. All these people, Klamatty forgetting the Jack Daniels, race down to the crossing. Two dozen more alerted by the Flyer's whistle and screeching wheels, the awful noise a livestock trailer turned into kindling makes and the squealing pigs, erupt from the Muny Liquor, various stores along Main Street, the Hayfield State Bank & Trust and Ford Deal's (Get a Deal With Deal!) Ford garage and dealership. These citizens also race to the crossing. Many will later claim they saw the disaster but in fact they only see its aftermath or fallout. Which is bad enough for those with queasy stomachs.

"What it was like it was like that goldurn rig just explode pigs!"

Pigs and bloody bits and chunks and parts of pigs rain down for a time and all the pigs not actually decapitated squeal like violated divas. There also are muffled cries from the passengers aboard the Flyer flung from their seats by its sudden deceleration. Some press horror-stricken faces against the Flyer's windows. The Hercules 303 sighs like a weary long-distance runner. The engineer, Watts, and his firemen, badly shaken, slowly descend from the Hercules, their striped overalls covered with blood. Half a Spotted Poland China came flying through the firemen's open window immediately following the collision.

Gloomy Toomey, dazed and shaken, sticks his head out of the open window on the driverside door on the rig's cab, casts a bewildered look at the place the trailer used to be, then slowly hoists himself out of the cab. Standing spread-legged on the door, he helps Wolfe Strudel and old Jerry Hennessey, both likewise dazed but intact, climb from the cab. All three drop onto Main Street and Hennessey, grabbing a piece of rope he finds at his feet, plunges through the assembled spectators, bawling, "My boar!" and sets off at a limping run up Main Street in pursuit of the huge boar with the missing ear. Wolfe Strudel (likewise bawling "My boar!") plows through the spectators in hot pursuit of Hennessey,

At which point the whistle goes off at the village utility (water and electric) plant, a series of ear-splitting blasts set off by Harry (Baldy) Conroy, the assistant superintendent on duty, who, by nature unstable and Hayfield's Civil Defense director, mistaking the awful noise he heard for a bomb, assumes Soviet aircraft to be overhead and World War III underway. Baldy was expecting that since September 23, 1949, when President Harry Truman told Americans a "recent atomic explosion" had been detected in the U.S.S.R. Meaning the goddamn Russians had The Bomb.

These blasts, also the local tornado warning, rouse and scare half to death everybody else in Hayfield, including Leonard Wyncoop, retired from the ADM elevator and the Volunteer Fire Department chief, half asleep in a chair outside the Fire Hall on the far north side of Hayfield.

Wyncoop leaps from his chair, races into the Fire Hall, grabs his chief's hat, starts the old 1924 red LaFrance pumper the department bought used a year ago, cranks up the siren and awaits his volunteers, of whom there are ten. They'll drop whatever they are doing and race to the Fire Hall, that's the drill, grab their firemen hats, rubber boots and yellow slickers and the old LaFrance will roll with Wyncoop at the wheel. Roll where? Well, into the village. Fire, tornado, whatever, Conroy wouldn't blow the Light Plant whistle for nothing. Would he?

The sextons puttering around in the new Lutheran church and the Catholic church, St. Bartholomew's, hearing the whistle and the fire engine siren, unclear as to what these may mean but no matter, start tolling their bells.

Neither the noise the trailer turned into kindling made or the whistle, siren and bells rouse Wilbur Flatley, asleep in a hammock in his backyard behind the MSP&P Depot after working a long shift preparing machinery for the upcoming pea-pack at the Cornbelt Foods canning plant in Winatchee Falls. But a jagged piece of angle iron torn from the livestock trailer, whizzing by Wilbur's head, slashes the rope on his hammock and Wilbur, who fell asleep reading an Aliens From Outer Space Invade Earth story in Astounding Tales, his favorite magazine, wakes when he hits the ground. Wakes and is startled to find a large white creature with black spots tearing through his yard, emitting grunts, some strange foreign tongue. The Aliens From Outer Space are here! Wilbur charges into his house, grabs his old shotgun, hustles his wife and two children into the basement and, breaking the glass, pokes the shotgun he forgot to load out a basement window, prepared to sell his life (and his wife's and children's) dearly. Until the phone rings and his wife goes up and answers it and comes back.

"That was Ma," Mrs. Flatley says. "She says there just been a awful accident down the Main Street crossing. She seen it from her window. Omaha Flyer hit a truck and there's dead people all over. She says we should take the kids and go see it." Which they do, Wilbur still thinking Invasion and lugging his 12-gauge, doubtful as to Ma's veracity.

They reach the crossing (Ma was right, more or less) along with Village Constable Marlin Poole, roused from his late afternoon nap by the whistle, the bells and the siren, and Constable Poole promptly takes charge.

"Stand back! Clear the area!" Constable Poole, a big man in his forties with a military background, bellows. He shoves a few spectators, mainly small boys, clear of the crossing, then leaps from harm's way when the huge boar with the missing ear comes tearing down Main Street pursued by Hennessey and Strudel. The boar skids to a stop, front feet braced, just short of the crossing, squeals, turns on a dime with change to spare, eludes Hennessey, eludes Strudel and goes tearing up Main Street.

At which point the Custer Women's Relief Corps' Hayfield Troop, a dozen buxom women in the Corps uniform (long white dress, blue cape, white stockings, blue go-to-hell cap), Troop Leader Celestial Vanderhoeven in the lead, waving a drum major's baton and counting cadence, marches out of Second Avenue North onto Main Street with its flags, Old Glory and a 7th Cavalry pennant, flying. And there encounter the 700-pound boar with the missing ear.

    The CWRC was founded following the massacre at the Little Big Horn. Its purpose was to aid and assist 7th Cavalry widows and orphans and there soon were Troops all over the nation's northeast quadrant. Most have since disbanded. All the widows are dead and if there are any orphans left they are up in their eighties and in nursing homes. No matter. The Hayfield Troop clings to life. This mainly is due to Celestial Vanderhoeven, a big woman with no offspring reluctantly approaching fifty. Her husband Cleveland is the Hayfield State Bank & Trust president, as was Celestial's daddy, the late J. Gaither Featherstone. Celestial, like Constable Poole, has a military background. She wangled a direct commission in the Women's Army Corps in 1942, trained other WACs at Ft. Oglethorpe and often was heard to express in the Officers Club the hope that the Army would one day come to its senses and equip selected WAC units with heavy tanks. She holds a more or less permanent seat on the five-member Village Council and chaired the fund drive for the Volunteer Fire Department's new (used) LaFrance pumper. She also led the battle against the Municipal Liquor Store, finally approved by village voters, 298 to 287, following three recounts. Celestial lost that one but she doesn't lose many. She also runs with a iron hand the Hayfield Garden Club and Lutheran Ladies League, yet finds time to golf in season with Jane Klamatty's Wednesday foursome. She belts long but erratic drives and is prone to improve her lie.

    Celestial's mother and grandmother also commanded the Hayfield CWRC Troop but there still were 7th Cavalry widows and orphans in their day. The Troop under Celestial's guidance (since 1946) is a more general disaster relief organization. It competes with the Red Cross and the Salvation Army in bringing aid and assistance to local victims of fires, floods etc. This competition is often acrimonious. The Troop also marches in local parades and that's what the ladies are doing, practicing for Hayfield's upcoming Memorial Day Parade, when they march onto Main Street. And encounter the huge boar.

"Whoa there!" Celestial, whacking the boar with her baton, bawls. She might as well whacked it with a flyswatter. The boar goes through the Custer Women's Relief Corps like a 700-pound bowling ball, leaving in its wake scattered across Main Street six large female bodies in long white dresses, including both the flag-bearers. There are screams. Hennessey and Strudel, chasing the boar, dodging Celestial's baton, leap over these bodies but not all of them. They trample some, producing more screams promptly drowned out by the siren on the old LaFrance pumper, which rolls by at 20 mph, its top speed, Wyncoop at the wheel, eight volunteer firemen, two are out of town, clinging to it. And encounters the boar.

The boar squeals and makes a sharp left turn. The old LaFrance swerves, Wyncoop pumping its worn brakes, misses Hennessey and Strudel and the women scattered in the street and Celestial, sensing an opportunity, swings her baton at Chief Wyncoop. The Volunteer firemen are famous for smashing china and soaking Oriental rugs while fighting fires (or false alarms) and they smashed a year ago, the day her furnace was smoking, the matched china her mother left Celestial.

The baton catches Wyncoop in the chops, smashing his dentures. He loses his grip on the steering wheel. The pumper veers across Main Street, jumps the curb, spilling several firemen, and decapitates the hydrant outside the Muny. A geyser erupts, drenching all nearby and producing a flood that rolls down Main Street.

Wyncoop is moaning, a handkerchief clamped to his bloody mouth. The firemen spilled from the pumper scramble to their feet. Those still aboard jump off and Assistant Chief Wardell Wartburg, sensing an opportunity, waving his trusty fire axe, bawls, "Fire might be in the Muny! Follow me, men!"

But Marv Gruber, the Muny manager, racing back to the Muny from the wreckage at the crossing when he heard the pumper's siren, blocks the door. "Oh no you don't!" Marv says. "You jokers swipe goddamn near a case whiskey, time my cooler overheat! Go on down the crossing there. You maybe steal a pig. Have yoursells a barbeque."

The Volunteer firemen, disappointed, give up on the Muny and turn to inspect the LaFrance. It's in a bad way, the right front wheel badly bent, half the wooden spokes broken. Chief Wyncoop is still moaning, moaning he needs a doctor or a dentist.

"Shit!" Assistant Chief Wartburg says. "We prolly have and get it towed back the Fire Hall." He surveys the crowd at the crossing, by now roughly half the village population. But this crowd is dispersing, retreating to the sidewalks in the face of the six-inch flood rolling down Main Street, and there doesn't seem to be a whole lot else going on down there. Numerous pigs, some more or less eviscerated, lie about, moaning like Chief Wyncoop. Constable Poole, ankle deep in the flood, is herding several small boys fascinated by these pigs to safety on the sidewalks. Gloomy Toomey, two men in bloody striped overalls and another in uniform, the Flyer's conductor no doubt, appear to be arguing beside the tipped over cab, while the flood laps at their ankles. But that's about all and Assistant Chief Wartburg males a command decision. "Let's have a drink first. Put them axes away, boys." Reluctantly, the volunteer firemen toss their axes on the pumper, Wyncoop's still moaning but he'll survive, and follow Wartburg into the Muny.

Marv Gruber is phoning Harry Conroy. "Goddamn it, Conroy! Shut that goddamn whistle off! Get your ass over here and turn off a busted hydrant!"

Up the street, blowing her whistle, waving her baton, Celestial Vanderhoeven is rallying her Troop. Most of the Custer Women sent flying or knocked flat by the boar are back on their feet and old Doc Street, Harley Street, Hayfield's general practitioner, a skinny little man in a shiny black suit, twenty years a widower, is attending to the two still down, Eve Benson and Moira McCaffery. But they're sitting up, pawing at their torn skirts lest some male, God forbid it's a Volunteer fireman! glimpse their thighs.

Wilbur Flatley's wife's mother, old Mrs. Bjork, who saw the Flyer hit the trailer from her apartment upstairs over Henry Hank's Hardware but mistook the pigs for human beings, her sight's not what it used to be what with the cataracts and all, phoned Doc Street with this startling news right after she phoned her daughter, and Doc was on his way to the Main Street crossing, trotting along with his little black bag, when he came upon the Custer Women scattered across Main Street. A scene that, just for a minute, he took to be an historical reenactment of the Massacre at the Little Big Horn. Then he set to work. Doc's pushing eighty and he's not cracked a medical book in fifty years but he's still pretty spry.

To Doc's surprise, considering the boar weighed 700 pounds and was covering ground somewhat faster than the old LaFrance pumper, most of the Custer Women, most of them well-padded, though briefly traumatized, escaped with abrasions and contusions. Eve Benson, who was carrying the 7th Cavalry pennant, may have a dislocated shoulder, and Moira McCaffery, carrying Old Glory, probably, has a broken thumb. But both, like all the Custer Women, are made of stern stuff and soon are on their feet. All the Custer Women run down by the boar look a mess: hair awry, stockings torn, dirt all over their white dresses. But those who lost their caps find them and volunteer flag-bearers replace Eve and Moira, who say they'll stop by Doc's office later, Doc should hurry on down to the crossing, he may be needed there. Celestial, blowing her whistle, waving her baton, soon has the Troop organized or reorganized and prepared to march. They'll call off the rest of the practice, however, Celestial says, return to her big old house for refreshments and practice again tomorrow. "Two o'clock! Be on time! Ready, march! One-two! One-two!"

Battered but unbowed, the Custer Women march off up Second Avenue and Doc Street, rolling up his pants legs, exposing his skinny white shanks, splashing through the flood, trots down to the crossing with his little black bag.

The spectators there, four deep on the sidewalks in view of the flood, most of the excitement over, are beginning to disperse. Names have been taken: Gloomy Toomey's, the engineer's, the conductor's, those of several octogenarians thought to have witnessed the collision, though two refused to give their names on grounds they don't want to get involved.

Doc Street finds Jane Klamatty and asks, "Anybody hurt?" There might be some on the train, Klamatty says. Doc climbs aboard the Flyer, where he finds and sets, more or less, two broken wrists and treats sundry contusions and abrasions, nothing serious. Three passengers pay him a total of $16. The rest seem to think the MSP&P will, or by god should, cover their medical costs.

Ford Deal arrives with his big tow truck, negotiates a $5 charge with Gloomy Toomey, hooks onto the tractor on the rig and calls for volunteers. Constable Poole and a dozen strong men respond, splash through the flood and push and shove and swear while Deal guns the hoist on his tow truck and eventually the cab rises, slowly, and crashes down on all its wheels. The passenger side on which it fell when it toppled over is banged up, the side mirror smashed, and the windshield is cracked.

"Rahilly is gonna shit," Gloomy says, gloomily. "Flyer smash his trailer and you charge him a arm and a leg, tip it up. Get a deal with Deal, my ass!" Then climbs into the tractor, starts it up and drives away, bound for Winatchee Falls with his bad news. Deal gets busy loading the wheels that were on the trailer into his tow truck.

Doc Street descends from the Flyer and surveys the battered shattered moaning pigs lying about. "We must put these poor creatures out of their misery," he says. "There are more too, up the track."

"Right!" Constable Poole, who just about has had it with the small boys, says. "I'll go get my piece and shoot them."

"Me too. I help you," Leonard (Len) Steckle, the butcher who runs the Hayfield frozen meat locker, says. "I go get my deer rifle." Wilbur Flatley likewise volunteers but discovers he forgot to load his shotgun.

All the small boys present promptly tell their parents, if present, they want to stay and watch this humanitarian operation. "Watch old Poole and Steckle shoot the smashed-up pigs." But most of these small boys are removed, still whining, by various parents. It's getting on to supper time and the crowd is beginning to break up. Half a dozen lucky small boys, no parents present, stick around but are soon disappointed. Constable Poole and Len Steckle return, armed, Constable Poole, a former Navy cook, with the Colt .45 he bought off an Infantry sergeant in Manila late in The War and smuggled home. He makes the small boys left sit on the freight dock at the old MSP&P depot and they really can't see much from there.

The MSP&P crew gets back aboard the Omaha Flyer. The whistle toots and the Flyer, delayed one hour and ten minutes, the Hercules 303 snorting, departs, bound for Omaha.

The last spectators slowly depart and old Mrs. Bjork, Mrs. Flatley's mother, up in her apartment over Hank's Hardware, picks up her phone. Never mind she's half blind and half a shut-in, old Mrs. Bjork is the Winatchee Falls Bugle Call's Hayfield Correspondent. Paid a nickel per published inch, she mails the Bugle Call a weekly report on Hayfield residents' goings and comings, two or three badly typed pages single-spaced she whacks out on an ancient Underwood. She dredges up much of this news by phone but also, using her walker, gets up to Bonnie's Cafe most days (in good weather) and gleans more there. And now and then, as now, she phones the Bugle Call with a hot news tip. There won't be anybody at the Bugle Call at this hour but she'll phone Cadence Snorkel II, the Editor & Publisher, at home, and he may or may not reward her with a 50-cent bonus for this hot news tip.

Jane Klamatty in her wet pumps, she did not entirely escape the flood, and Doc Street in his wet shoes walk up Main Street together, Harry Conroy got the broken hydrant shut off and the flood has subsided, and go into the Muny Liquor. Doc says he needs a little libation "in view all the excitement, most excitement I had since Winnie Kimball had her twins and the little buggers breeched."

The Muny is jammed, full of witnesses or near witnesses to the recent disaster, all talking at once, exchanging various versions and much misinformation as to the disaster. Horace Greeley Trudd, editor and publisher of the weekly Hayfield Star & Shopper, a skinny old man with wild white hair wearing baggy pants and ink-stained shirt, is taking notes. Marv Gruber is still on duty, staying on in view of the crowd to help Lyman Arkey, the night bartender with the bad back. The Volunteer firemen are working up a head of steam at two tables pushed together, jammed with empty beer bottles. Chief Wyncoop, a bloody handkerchief in one fist, beckons Doc and Doc, libation in hand, briefly examines the smashed dentures wrapped in the handkerchief. His professional opinion is the chief will have to see a dentist.

Old Jerry Hennessey comes up in, puffing. He accepts a drink, a straight shot, on the house in view of his narrow escape when the Flyer hit the livestock rig. Trudd, taking a page from the instruction book issued teenage TV reporters, asks Hennessey, "What did you think, Jerry, you seen that train was going to hit that truck you were in?"

"There wasn't no time, Horace," Hennessey says. "Think a goddamn thing." He also says, "That crazy Strudel. He runnin' all over town like a chicken with its head chop off lookin' for live hogs he thinks prolly his." Then Hennessey, using the Muny phone, calls home and tells his oldest son, Young Jerry, come and get him with their pickup.

Constable Poole comes into the Muny. "Get your crew together, Wyncoop," he says. "We got a police up the boards and stuff scattered all over down by the crossing there. Some the rest you citizens can volunteer too."

Chief Wyncoop hesitates. He's inclined to think he outranks Constable Poole in the village hierarchy. But half his firemen are rising, other volunteers are coming forward and cleaning up the mess left by the collision is after all a civic duty. "Thum on, men," he says, rising, his mouth full of gums. "Folloth me."

Klamatty buys a fifth of Jack Daniels and goes home, stows the Jack Daniels and finds dry shoes. Web Allen will be along shortly. Somewhere in the distance along the MSP&P's Main Line a pig squeals, followed by the heavy boom of Constable Poole's .45 and the sharp crack of Len Steckle's deer rifle.

2.

It's another sunny May day, 10 a.m. the morning after the Omaha Flyer hit J.P. Rahilly's livestock rig, when JP Jane Klamatty, wearing her black robe, a judicial mumu, comes down the stairs into her basement courtroom and Constable Poole, her bailiff, in uniform, Sears work pants and a pressed blue denim shirt, a tin star on the shirt, bawls, "All rise!"

JP Klamatty is not at her best this bright morning. Though pleasantly sated following a lively time in bed with Web Allen (in the course of which her phone rang three times but they let it ring), she did not sleep much after Web left at midnight. A few surviving Spotted Poland Chinas, for one thing, lost and confused in Hayfield, no doubt hungry, missing their evening slops, were still squealing at intervals, shattering the night's silence. Then her phone rang again, she answered it and the party calling, ranting and raving and spluttering, was State Rep. Wolfe Strudel. Ranting and raving and spluttering, as near as she could determine, about a stolen boar, a goddamn school bus and an attempt on his daughter Imogene's life.

"I just got home," Strudel spluttered. "My wife Annie drive in a town and get me. I was chase all over town tryin' find some my pigs but I never but that gotdamn Hennessey got one them and I run in a Flatley works the canning factory and he tell me his mother-in-law tell him a guy in a car went by the school bus it was stopped and gotdamn near hit my Imogene and my wife

Annie tell me the gotdamn school tell her that too and I want a know who and he ought a be lock up! By got—"

"Strudel," Klamatty said, finally. "Calm down! My court is not in session at one o'clock in the morning! Come and see me in the morning, when it is." And hung up, but did not, having had some previous experience with a litigious Strudel, sleep much thereafter.

Nevertheless, the wheels of justice must turn. JP Klamatty, at her desk (her bench), surveys those present as they rise from the former church pews. They number eight in addition to Constable Poole and might be, Klamatty thinks, she's a movie fan, a call at Central Casting. She bangs the desk with her gavel. "This court is now in session." All present sit. "First case. That's you, Ev. Stand up. Constable has charged you with disorderly conduct. Let's hear the particulars, Constable."

Everett (Ev) Geisel, nineteen, a sullen local nere-do-well in greasy levis and a dirty T-shirt, a gas station jockey by trade but currently unemployed, stands, slouching. He is not represented by counsel but who cares.

"Your Honor," Constable Poole says. "I catch Ev here pissin'. I mean pee. I mean urinate in public last night. Around eleven. Right after me and Steckle shot the last hog we found. He come out the back door the Muny. Ev, I mean. And I catch him in the act in the alley there with his dingus sticking out."

"What about that, Ev?" Klamatty says. "You aim to plead guilty?"

"Well, jeez," Ev whines. "You ever been in that can in the Muny, Jedge, you prolly piss. I mean pee in the alley there too! That can's a healt menace! But, yeah, okay." Ev's been through this before. "Gilly, I guess."

Klamatty bangs her gavel. "Fined five dollars and costs. Be eight dollars, Ev." Reluctantly, Ev pulls eight grimy $1 bills from his pants pockets and reluctantly hands them over. "What were you doing in the Muny anyway? You're not old enough to go in there."

"Jist buyin' a six-pack Coke was all. Can I go now?"

"Get out of here." Ev, glaring at Constable Poole, departs. A six-pack pack of Coke is a likely story. She'll have to talk to Marv Gruber, Klamatty thinks, about serving minors. Talk to Marv again. The Muny could lose its license, serving minors. Celestial Vanderhoeven would like that. The move to establish the Muny split Hayfield like a knife gutting a fish and a good many citizens still think the Muny the first step on the Road to Perdition. But her talk with Marv can wait. "Next case."

"I believe, Your Honor," Assistant Winatchee County Attorney J.J. Doodle, rising and assuming a lawerly pose, gripping the lapels on his seersucker suit while Winatchee County Deputy Sheriff Ernie Rommel, in uniform, propels the defendant forward, says. "You are familiar with this case. Mister Sam Hutch here, charged with the taking of indecent liberties upon the person of a female not yet of the age of consent, pled not guilty at his arraignment and was held for trial."

"Oh yes," Klamatty says. "I remember Mister Hutch. The Ding Dong Man. Are you ready for trial, Mister Hutch? Do you have a lawyer?"

"Nuh," Mister Hutch, a scrawny specimen in his late twenties wearing stained white coveralls, the garb the Winatchee County Jail issues its inmates, says. An entrepreneur with the weary carnival that pitched its rides and games on Main Street during Hayfield's annual Pioneer Days two weeks ago, held without bail since in the ancient Winatchee County Jail in Winatchee Falls, the carnival departing without him, Mister Hutch was hauled back to Hayfield, the jurisdiction in which the alleged indecent liberties allegedly were taken, by Deputy Rommel. "Ah ain't got no money git no lawyer. But Ah giss Ah am ready and git this thang ovuh wit."

"Very well, Mister Hutch," Klamatty says: why clutter things up with a defense counsel. "Proceed, Mister Doodle. Let's have a witness chair, Constable."

Constable Poole gets busy, sets up a metal folding chair beside Klamatty's bench, and Doodle calls his first witness, Elmira Hostetter, a pudgy girl, fifteen, with acne, wearing tight purple slacks and a pink blouse. Her father, George Hostetter, a large man in Sears work clothes, the ADM elevator manager, propels her to the witness chair.

"Just tell us, Elmira," J.J. Doodle says. "What happened the time you met Mister Hutch and afterwards. Don't you be bashful now."

"Well, what happen," Elmira, blushing the color of her blouse, says. "I went the carnival and there was this game there he was runnin' was like a thermomometer like and you hit a thing with a sludge-hammer and if you hit it hard 'nuff a thing went up the thermomometer like and hit a bell and made a noise like ding dong and you win a prize."

"When you say he, Elmira," Doodle says. "Do you mean Mister Hutch here?"

"Yeah, him. We talk some and he say he the Ding Dong Man and try it so I hit the thing with a sludge-hammer and it went up the thermomometer like and hit the bell and made a noise like ding dong. I guess everbody was watch was pretty surprise. Three times I done it and the Ding Dong Man, he give me three stuff animals."

Then, Elmira testifies, she hung around for awhile and watched several puzzled young bucks fail to ring the bell even once and around eleven o'clock, when the Ding Dong Man closed the game in view of Hayfield's curfew, "He ask me I want a see his trailer. Where he live."

Elmira pauses and George Hostetter flexes fingers the size of bananas with which no doubt he'd like throttle the Ding Dong Man.

"So Mister Hutch," Doodle says. "Took you to his trailer. You were just curious was all. Isn't that right, Elmira? You just wanted to see his trailer."

"Yah, I guess. It was pretty messy though. And we hardly in it and he stick his hand up my skirt I was wearing. And pinch me like. Up there."

"And he said something," Doodle says. "You told me he said something. What did Mister Hutch say, Elmira? Don't be bashful now."

"Well, he say," Elmira, blushing the color of her purple slacks, says. "You rang my bell, baby, I help you some. Now lemme rang yours. Then another fella I seen the carnival come in the trailer and he say, Chrissake, Ding Dong, you be get your ass in a wringer foolin' with that jailbait. I guess her age tonight. She's fifteen. And the Ding Dong Man take his hand out from up my skirt then and I left and went home and told Pa what the Ding Dong Man done. I had a tell Pa somethin' because I supposed and be home by ten o'clock. And Pa, he call Constable Poole."

"Thank you, Elmira," Doodle says. "Prosecution rests, Your Honor. Or I can call Constable Poole should the court wish to hear testimony regarding the defendant's arrest?"

"We'll skip that," Klamatty says, or rules. "Let's move along. What's your story, Mister Hutch?"

"Well, shee-it!" Mister Hutch, evincing no repentance, says. "Young lady here rang ma bell but Ah help her. Ah reckon it owny fay-uh, I rang her'n. But Ah dint do nuffin' a her."

"Did you," Klamatty says. "Put your hand up her skirt and pinch her? Up there? Propose sexual congress? Under the law, Mister Hutch, those are indecent liberties."

"Whad? Ah nevuh say nuffin' 'bout no Congress. Ah fum Alabam, Jedge. Ah nevuh hee-uh nuffin' 'bout no in-decent libertees befoh. Mebbe yawl c'n tell me, Jedge. They any decent libertees a fella c'n take, this part the country?"

"No, there are not. Not in this jurisdiction. Did you, Mister Hutch, put your hand up the young lady's skirt? And pinch her? Up there?"

"Well, yeah, prolly."

"Court finds you guilty, Mister Hutch." Klamatty bangs her gavel, justice West of the Winatchee swift and sure. "Ninety days in the County Jail. Credit for time served."

George Hostetter, Deputy Rommel and perhaps Elmira, it's

hard to tell about Elmira, evince glee and depart with poor Mister Hutch the Ding Dong Man, handcuffed, shocked, surprised and dismayed, seventy-six days in the County Jail infested with bedbugs (with credit for time served) confronting him.

"There is another case, Your Honor," J.J. Doodle says. "Parties be here shortly. I'll just step out and have a cigarette."

He does that and Justice-of-the-Peace Klamatty bangs her gavel. "Next case. That's you, Mister Strudel. Matter involving a pig."

Wolfe Strudel, fidgeting throughout the previous proceedings, springs to his feet with Elmer Hooter in tow and old Jerry Hennessey slowly rises. Old Jerry is a lanky weary son of the soil in his fifties with a wad of tobacco in his cheek, wearing faded bib overalls, a denim shirt and work shoes stained with manure. Strudel is all dressed up in new overalls and a fairly clean white shirt and Elmer is wearing slacks, a sport coat and a yellow bowtie.

"Judge," Strudel snarls. "I want the constable arrest Hennessey here forthwith. What we talk about last night. That charge I tell you I am gonna file. Grand larceny. Hennessey that sonofabitch swipe my boar! The one should a won a blue ribbon up the State Fair."

"Your boar, my ass!" Hennessey says. "That's my boar and you know it Strudel. You asshole."

"Order in the court!" Constable Poole bawls.

Klamatty bangs her gavel. "Settle down! Both of you! Watch your language!" Strudel and Hennessey subside, though rumbling like dormant volcanoes. "I heard your version of all this, Mister Strudel, you phoned me the middle of the night. Now I want to hear Mister Hennessey's version. What happened, Mister Hennessey, after the Flyer hit Mister Rahilly's livestock rig."

"Well, what happen," Hennessey, shifting the chaw in his cheek, says. "Was all the hawgs wasn't kilt or tore up when the goddamn train hit us was runnin' ever which way. You seen that, Jedge. But I climb out the rig I seen my boar runnin' up Main

Street and he look okay. So I grab a piece rope must fell off the rig and lit out after him. I chase him up Main Street and back and up Main again, which was when he knock them Custer Women over like they was tin pens, and through the park there and up and down some more streets and through some yards. Mel Barnes' yard for one. Mel was up a ladder, whitewash his garridge, and my boar knock it out from under him, the ladder, but Mel warn't hurt none, just cover with whitewash, he land on the grass. He finally run out a wind, my boar run out, I was pretty near run out too, and I corner him finally down by the stockyard. There was a gate open one the pens and he run in it and I shut the gate. I leave him there 'cause I dint have my truck." Old Hennessey, normally a taciturn man, runs out of wind, pauses and shifts his chaw. "That's he is now. I went and look, make sure Strudel dint steal him. I come in my pickup and I go get him and take him home, we're done here."

"You can't do that, Hennessey!" Strudel squeals. "He ain't your boar! He's my boar! You try that and you be in real trouble! I seen it was my boar runnin' up Main Street and I chase him. Chrissake, I was right behind you, Hennessey. Yellin' you was chasin' my boar! Then I step on a gotdamn ball some goddamn kid leave in the park and turn my ankle. But I limp down the stockyard and I seen you put my boar in a pen there."

"He ain't your boar, Strudel," Hennessey says. "I seen your boar. What was left him. Up along the track there tore in half. I heard you behind me. Squawkin' it was your boar. But I knowed it was my boar. So I dint pay you no attention. I wouldn't even be here 'cept you call me up this morning bellerin' it's you boar and you was gonna take me in a court."

"Please the court," Elmer Hooter squeaks, his first contribution to these proceedings. "My client Mister Strudel will move for an injunction in order to prevent the removal of the uh said boar from the uh location cited. And like he uh said, a warrant, arrest Mister Hennessey." But Elmer is not well versed in the Law West of the Winatchee.

"Don't be silly, Elmer," Klamatty says. "Sit down and be quiet." Elmer sits down and pouts. "It appears to the court that what we have here is a situation the court has found to be not uncommon in this agricultural community. A dispute as to the ownership of a particular livestock. But don't you people cut notches or something in your pigs' ears? Like cattle brands. So you know who owns a particular pig?"

Yes, Hennessey and Strudel, reluctantly agreeing on one thing, say. But the boar in dispute, Hennessey says, "His right ear was tore off when the goddamn train hit us. That's the one with the notch we calls the litter notch. Tells you what litter he was in. Left ear is tore up some too. But that don't matter. Chrissake, I know he's my boar. I know the way his spots look and where they are."

"Spots on that boar you tryin' steal," Strudel screams. "They the spots on my boar! You think I don't know the spots on my boar look like?"

"Yah, you prolly don't, Strudel!" Hennessey says. "You half-ass farmer! You up the goddamn Legislature there half the time, screwin' things up!"

Klamatty bangs her gavel. "Shut up, both of you! What about the other pigs that survived the collision? Is there any dispute between you two as to their ownership?"

But only the boar in dispute, it turns out, survived to trigger a dispute. Most of the rest of the pigs aboard the rig were either killed instantly or "tore up so bad," Hennessey's description, Constable Poole and Len Steckle had to shoot them, put them out of their misery. Steckle, Hennessey says, working late into the night, collected the carcasses and is going to have a Big Fresh Pork Sale at his butcher shop, which may lead to further litigation, but that's not presently before the court. Perhaps a dozen pigs that did survive may still be at large though more likely they're locked up by now in sundry sheds and garages, pork chops awaiting somebody's platter.

"I get them thiefs arrested too," Strudel says. "They got any my Chinas and I find out. I catch a couple mine finally out by the school around eleven o'clock."

"You catch a couple they might be my Chinas," Hennessey says.

Klamatty bangs her gavel. "Those pigs are not before the court. Can either of you offer any proof the boar down at the stockyard is your boar?"

"Yah," Hennessey says. "I tell you the spots on my boar look and they is on him. There's a big black one on his right shoulder look like a football and some little ones on his rear end. And he know his name. Chubby. He come when I call him."

"Jeezuzz!" Strudel says. "I never heard anybody got a China it's got a name! Mine got a black spot look like a football too. Like the one down the stockyard look. And I got a pitcher, my boar! My wife Annie took it with her camera, we had him up the State Fair."

"You better get you eyes examine, Strudel," Hennessey says. "You think you seen a spot on my boar down the stockyard look like on your boar."

Klamatty bangs her gavel. "Enough! The court is going to continue this matter pending proof of ownership of this boar. You both get your proof together, whatever it is, and I'll see you. Let's see." She consults her calendar. "Week from today. Same time." Hennessey and Strudel grumble but acquiescence. "Meanwhile, as to the care of this boar. Can you two work that out?"

Neither Strudel nor Hennessey think they can, both stating the other to be incompetent. There's also the knotty question of where the boar will remain until its legal owner is determined. The court rules the stockyard is as a good a place as any. The stockyard just east of the village adjacent to the Main Line belongs to the MSP&P but was abandoned years ago when trucks grabbed the livestock transport market. Its wooden pens and fences are warped and weathered gray. Pre-pubescent Hayfield kids, mostly boys, play in it and have tried several times (but failed) to set it on fire. The court also rules the two claimants will take turns, day each, slopping the boar.

"That's a court order," Klamatty says. "You two do it or I'll hold you in contempt. And fine you. Or put you in jail." Confronted with this example of The Law West of the Winatchee, Hennessey and Strudel grumble they'll do it.

"My client Mister Strudel," Elmer Hooter, rising, sticking his oar into these turgid waters, says. "Feels Mister Hennessey should be required to post bond. In the event he fails to comply with the aforesaid court order or attempts unilaterally to take possession of the aforesaid swine."

"Him too then, by god!" Hennessey says. "I got to do that, Strudel got to."

"Hell I do!" Strudel says. "I'm a member the State Legislature! Took a oath, uphold the law!" A member of the Legislature, he clearly feels, is entitled to certain feudal privileges in any dispute with a serf the likes of Hennessey.

Klamatty bangs her gavel. "Sit down, Elmer. Shut up. The court will not require bonds. Constable Poole in addition to his other duties will keep an eye on the damn pig." Elmer sits and pouts, his first case is not going well, and begins to think about his fee, figuring it in the quarter-hour segments he learned about in Law School. "This matter is concluded, the time being."

Hennessey departs, grumbling. They hear his noisy old Dodge pickup with a broken muffler, parked in the alley behind Win Hooter's Drugstore, drive away.

"That other matter I mention last night on the telephone," Strudel says. "Car went by the gotdamn school bus and almost kilt my kid. Apple. What the hell is goin' on with that? I call the sheriff but all they know is some guy name Hostman, some name like that, prolly done it. And they lookin' for him but they ain't find him. What the hell's the matter anyway, our law enforcement?"

"I can't help you with that, Mister Strudel," Klamatty says. "I've got an arraignment coming up. Eleven-thirty. Any minute now. It's a Highway Patrol case. Trooper phoned and requested it. But I don't know if it has anything to do with that school bus incident. All I know about that is what you told me. You are welcome to stay though. See what this Patrol case is all about."

Strudel gives this offer some thought but rejects it. "No. I got to mosy around town. See I can find some my Chinas wasn't kilt or that gotdamn Steckle shoot and steal or some thief hiding. You let me know, huh, you hear anything, that school bus thing?"

She will, Klamatty says, and Strudel and Elmer leave, cutting through her garden. No doubt, she surmises, Strudel loves Apple and fears for her safety, but missing Spotted Poland Chinas hold a higher priority. And there are people coming down the outside stairs beside her house: she can see their feet through her basement window.

Three people. They and J.J. Doodle push through her basement door. Trooper Redhardt in uniform looks pleased and, often the case, truculent. Web Allen looks mildly embarrassed: he was after all in bed with the presiding judge earlier this day. J.J. Doodle looks unhappy and a large man, a stranger in a wrinkled tan suit clutching a manila envelope, looks angry and disgusted.

Klamatty bangs her gavel. "Court is now in session. I take it, Trooper, this is the arraignment you requested."

"Yes, Your Honor," Trooper Redhardt says. "This guy here, Harold E. Hossman, the defendant in this matter, which I now identify for the court by pointing my finger at him, is charged by me with passing a school bus with STOP arm extended and warning lights flashing and recklessly endangering. Right out south town here yesterday morning. And I give him a mail-in speeding ticket yesterday, eighty-five in a sixty-five. So long's we're here, that too."

Recklessly endangering Apple Strudel then? Sounds like, Klamatty thinks, foreseeing breakers ahead, but maintains her composure. "Defendant state his name, please." Hoss states his name. "Are you represented by counsel?"

"I represent Mister Hossman," Web Allen says.

"Do you wish to enter a plea, Mister Hossman?" Klamatty says. "Or two pleas?"

"Well," Hoss says. "The speeding thing, okay, guilty. That school bus thing. Not guilty."

Klamatty bangs her gavel. "Defendant fined twenty-eight dollars including costs, the speeding thing." Hoss digs $28 from his wallet and slaps the bills on Klamatty's desk. "As to the school bus thing. Will defendant want a jury?"

"No, Your Honor," Web Allen says. "Defendant waives his right to trial by jury. Confident that he will receive justice, he prefers Your Honor hear this case." Though rolling around in bed together within recent memory, Klamatty and Web Allen are very proper when court is in session.

"Let's set a trial date then," Klamatty says. But Web Allen has a personal injury suit (woman who slipped on something spilled on the floor at the Princess Café and fell and suffered a whiplash) going to trial in Winatchee County District Court, and J.J. Doodle whines, "Our office was only apprised of this case this morning and we'll need time in which to uh consider it." Trial is set for Friday, June 15, 10 a.m. "Any recommendation as to bail, Mister Doodle?"

"Leave to the discretion of the court," Doodle says.

"Fifty-thousand dollars," Trooper Redhardt says.

"Fifty-thousand dollars!" Web Allen, expressing horror and amazement, says. "That's ridiculous! This is traffic case. A misdemeanor."

"Gross misdemeanor," Trooper Redhardt says. "Passing a school bus with STOP arm extended and warning lights flashing. Defendant might be a risk, flight avoid prosecution, too. I call the Patrol chief, Colonel Wood, and he said fifty-thousand dollars. He said Mister Hossman might be kind a special case. But Patrol won't show him no favors."

"Colonel" Dedrick (Ded) Wood, the Patrol chief, is a rare holdover Democrat-Farmer-Labor in Gov. Marcus Diptill's administration. His actual title is Patrol Commander, but he rose to lieutenant-colonel (temporary in grade) in the Military Police in WWII and prefers "Colonel." His real expertise is public relations. His name is frequently in the newspapers and he regularly shows up in uniform in photos featuring Important Persons visiting the state. It's a rare week he doesn't hold a news conference at which he reports some Patrol triumph: a DWI sweep,say, that netted thirteen alleged miscreants. Or more recently a gallant young Trooper's high-speed run to International Falls in Koochiching County with a pregnant woman, halted when, her time upon her, the gallant young Trooper though he'd never done that before assisted in the live birth of a healthy nine-pound baby boy. The mother, unfortunately, was a 250-pound Red Lake Reservation Native American forty-two years of age with a history of spectacular deliveries. "Colonel" Wood would have preferred a white female in her mid-twenties with her first child. But you can't have everything.

"Special case?" Klamatty says.

"Mister Hossman," Web Allen says. "Is Governor Diptill's brother-in-law. Mister Hossman's wife is Governor Diptill's sister. But that has no bearing on the case before the court. There also are some suspicious circumstances in regards to Mister Hossman's arrest. I'll bring those up at trial. Further, it please the court, Mister Hossman is a highly respected St. Paul businessman. I respectfully suggest the court release Mister Hossman on his own recognizance."

Klamatty bangs her gavel, a kind of automatic response under the circumstances. No bearing on the case! Is Web Allen insane! It's Governor Diptill who, he ever gets off his duff, will name (or not name) Jane Klamatty the new Village Court judge! And this Hossman is Diptill's brother-in-law! There are ramifications here, wheels within wheels, and three ancient maxims hopscotch through Klamatty's head. Give and take. You scratch my back and I'll scratch yours. One hand washes the other. All three, she surmises, apply in the present situation. But she needs time in which to think this through.

"The court," she says. "Finds fifty-thousand-dollars bail excessive. Is Mister Hossman prepared to post bail in the amount of one-hundred dollars?" Mister Hossman is. He slaps five $20s on Klamatty's desk and she bangs her gavel. "This matter is concluded, pending trial."

Trooper Redhardt expresses disappointment but holds his peace. "See you this guy goes to trial, Judge," he says. "Or else before, I nab another guy rips by a school bus with STOP arm extended and warning lights flashing." With that departing shot, he departs.

J.J. Doodle says he'd like to "discuss this case" with Web Allen prior to trial. Web Allen says they'll do that and Doodle departs and Web says, "There is another matter, Your Honor. Mister Hossman wishes to request the court for a Writ of Replevin in order to recover a musical instrument."

Queried by the court, Hoss explains. The instrument is a flute valued with case at $89.95, property of the Diptill Music Co., rented by and to a student at the Consolidated School last September, supposed to have been returned to the Diptill Music Co. or its agent a week ago, and again yesterday, no subsequent purchase of said flute with case forthcoming, and no flute with case either.

"We go through this a lot, Judge," Hoss says. "Kids lose the instruments they rent or something. I had a kid over Elgin lost a tuba. Or he might sold it. But I don't have the time, track those instruments down. We learn by experience, best way to handle these situations is replevy the instrument. That turns them up sometimes. Or if it don't, company gets the value thereof anyway. This particular flute." Hoss digs into his manila envelope and extracts a form. "This our standard rental agreement. We had a argue with that dumb state cop, me and Mister Allen here, before he let me go back my motel and get it. This particular flute with case was rent by a kid name Strudel, Imogene."

"Let me see the rental agreement," Klamatty, foreseeing more breakers ahead, says." Hoss hands it over. It's boilerplate, full of legalese, appears to be ironclad, said instrument if not purchased to be returned without fail in its original condition no later than etc., etc. "All right, Mister Hossman. I've a strong feeling we are opening a can of worms here, but the court will grant your request." She digs from her desk and prepares three Writs of Replevin in decinet, the legal purpose of which is to obtain for plaintiff immediate repossession of personal property legally acquired but illegally retained by defendant or in the alternative monetary compensation equal to the value of the personal property when acquired by defendant, and hands Hoss one. "Constable Poole will serve Mister Strudel. You'll probably hear Mister Strudel then, you're within ten miles of here."

"Thanks, Judge," Hoss, stuffing his writ in his manila envelope, says. "Well, I'm ready for some breakfast, that's okay with you, Mister Allen? I mean you wait for me, twenty minutes? I dint eat the breakfast they give us, the Jail. It look like cornmeal mush with drain oil. There a good place eat here? Hey, I buy you breakfast, Mister Allen."

"Bonnie's Café," Klamatty says. "On Main Street. Go through my garden and across the alley and through the drugstore and turn right. It's right up the street."

"You go ahead," Web Allen says. "I had breakfast. I'll pick you up at Bonnie's."

Hoss departs and Klamatty bangs her gavel. "Court's adjourned. Let's have some coffee. I want to talk to you, Web! Why the devil didn't you tell me beforehand, this Hossman is Governor Diptill's brother-in-law?"

"I didn't have a chance," Web Allen, settled in Klamatty's kitchen, says. "I didn't know myself until I picked him up at the City Jail. It's been a wild morning, Jane. The story I got from Hossman, Trooper Redhardt arrested him late yesterday afternoon and popped him in the City Jail. Hossman phoned his wife in St. Paul. The phone call he was entitled to. He didn't need the phone, he told me, once he got her. It's only ninety miles. He could hear her yelling. Then Missus Hossman called August. And yelled, I guess. August has done some work for the Diptill Music Company. Replevys, probably. I was in court and August forgot to tell me this when I got back to the office. But he did leave a note. Mabel Murphy found it and phoned me this morning. Woke me up. All it said was I should pick Mister Hossman up at the City Jail and represent him at his arraignment. It was Hossman told me he was Diptill's brother-in-law. He said he told, I quote, That goddamn dumb State Cop that too. End quote. But Trooper Redhardt apparently was not impressed."

"What did Hossman say about school bus thing?"

"Jane! That's privileged information. Lawyer-client relationship."

"Come off it, Web! I've got the governor's brother-in-law in my court, charged with a terrible crime and it's the governor who is going to appoint me, or not appoint me, Village Court judge!"

"My client says he might have passed a school bus with STOP arm extended and so on. But if he did, the school bus came to a sudden stop. With no warning. And if there was a child getting on the bus, my client has no recollection of him. Or her."

"Her. I'm almost sure. State Rep. Wolfe Strudel's daughter Imogene. They call her Apple. Do you know Strudel?"

"No. Well, I know who he is. A Republican, right? I shouldn't think he'll make a big thing out of this, it's the governor's brother-in-law might be involved. So alleged. Oh! My client's replevin! Is that the same Strudel?"

"One and the. And you don't know Strudel. He's a maverick Republican. He thinks Diptill is a spendthrift. Soft on Welfare. And Apple, you'll pardon the expression, is the apple of his eye. Or pretty close. Right behind his pigs."

"Speaking of which," Web Allen says. "There was something on the radio this morning and the cops were talking about it. Train hit a truck full of pigs here yesterday?"

"Yes. But no one was injured. Not much anyway. Nobody

local. Never mind that. What am I going to do with your client Mister Hossman? Considering who he is and who his brother-in-law is and what's going to happen to my future in the judiciary. Counsel me, counselor."

"All right," Web Allen says. "Believe me, I've been giving this a lot of thought. The logical assumption is Governor Diptill would rather not see his brother-in-law convicted of this terrible crime. Rather not see it come to trial even. Bound to reflect on him and his Administration if it does. Or so many will say. The only question really is ought the court to dismiss the charge naming Mister Hossman as of now, then await Governor Diptill's appointment to the Village bench? Or hold Mister Hossman hostage so to speak and get the appointment first? My advice, grounds politicians are not to be trusted, is get the appointment first."

"Let us hope," Klamatty says. "I can't dismiss, Web. No way! Passing a school bus with STOP arm extended! Damn near hit the Strudel kid! All that will be common knowledge before the sun sets. I dismiss, Strudel will bring the rope and the locals will lynch me. Later, maybe."

"How about this then?" Web Allen says. "Assuming for the moment my client Mister Hossman did pass a school bus with STOP arm extended and so on and there was a child. The child was not hit. We are not talking personal injury here and I doubt the county can prove my client passed a school bus. Who saw him, if he did? Kids on the bus and the driver perhaps. But only for an instant. No identification really. No reliable witnesses. The court, therefore, following a fair trial and due deliberation will find Mister Hossman not guilty. Pleasing Mister Hossman and his brother-in-law, Governor Diptill, and they and Hayfield's new Village Court judge will live happily ever after."

"You're sure," Klamatty says. "That's the way Diptill will see it?"

"I can't think of any other way. Potential stain on the family name and the Diptill Administration erased. Following due process. No favors sought nor granted. No political fallout. I don't of course know much about Minnesota politics."

"You don't have to know much. Just your name is Olson or Johnson or Swenson or Carlson and you are not actually behind bars, convicted of molesting small children, you probably can get elected to just about anything. Except on the Iron Range. The Range elects Democrat-Farmer-Labors in or out of jail."

"My client Mister Hossman aside," Web Allen says. "Will politics play a part in this appointment? What are you anyway, it comes to politics?"

"Politics probably will. I'm an Independent."

"Neither fish nor fowl then. I quote old August. He's got a lot of pithy sayings. You know, Jane, you could in Mister Hossman's case simply take cover and recuse yourself."

"On what grounds? More coffee?" Klamatty pours more coffee.

"Fornicating with counsel."

"I hope you're joking! There is nothing everybody in town would rather know than that I am fornicating with somebody. Well, they're pretty sure I am. But they don't know who. No, I've got Mister Hossman in my court and I'm going to hold onto him. But will Governor Diptill, he's not very bright, understand the situation? Will he even know it exists?"

"Oh I'm sure he'll know it exists. Knows now, probably. Mister Hosssman said his wife would tell Marky. That's what he calls the governor. Marky. My impression, Mister Hossman is expecting a gubernatorial pardon before the sun sets."

"Well, sure. What are brothers-in-law for anyway?"

"It might be helpful though if someone who has the governor's ear apprised him of the situation. And explained it. You know anybody might do that? Old Hein Dobermann perhaps? My understanding, he is, or was, a power in the Republican Party. Or no, I guess not. I doubt old Dobermann likes you much since you tried to put his son in jail. Speaking of whom. I hope you weren't disappointed when Judge Kelly upheld my appeal. Finally. Set aside young Mister Dobermann's conviction. Did you get Kelly's findings?"

"Yes. Last week. They made no sense to me. Didn't surprise me though. Crazy Kelly. How'd he ever get to be a judge anyway?"

"Couldn't cut it as a lawyer be the first step."

"Anyway, seems to me I recommended Kelly. Trooper Redhardt was disappointed. I told him forget it, Clyde Dobermann leads a charmed life. In Winatchee Falls. He said he knew that. He said he nabbed Clyde once before on a DWI. His first arrest. He was just out of the academy and the Highway Patrol was breaking him in in the Winatchee Falls Patrol District. Charge was dismissed though. Insufficient evidence. Trooper Redhardt by then was stuck in the Hibbing Patrol District."

"Long arm of the law then," Web Allen says. "Came up a little short. But getting back to my present client, Mister Hossman. I wonder if August might know somebody who knows somebody who knows somebody close to Diptill? Wasn't August active in the Republican Party, he was younger?"

"Yes. He was the county chairman preceding old Dobermann's reign. Won't hurt to ask him. You said something in court about suspicious circumstances in regards to Mister Hossman's arrest. What is that all about?"

"A long story I got from him. I'll bring it up at trial. If we get that far. You heard Doodle. He wants to discuss the case and we will. My impression, the County Attorney is not wild about prosecuting this case. In light of Mister Hossman's family situation. Wouldn't surprise me, Doodle moves for a dismissal."

"He does, I'll deny it," Klamatty says. "I want Mister Hossman in my court. Until Diptill appoints me Village judge. Or appoints somebody else. In which case, off the record, following a fair trial, Mister Hossman is going to be in deep doo-doo."

"Well! That's clear enough! Okay, I'll move for a continuance for Mister Hossman. I probably would anyway. Maybe two. We'll leave Mister Hossman to twist in the wind as they say. Until Governor Diptill comes to his senses and appoints you Village Court judge in and for the Village of Hayfield."

"Bless you, Sir! But Mister Hossman might like to get this over with."

"Mister Hossman," Web Allen says. "Is the client. I am the lawyer. I call the shots. That's another saying old August frequently shares with me. Once you're appointed, Mister Hossman will take his chances with The Law West of the Winatchee. Or throw himself upon the mercy of the court. There is one other thing. I would hope Mister Hossman's situation will not make a great big splash in the public prints. Or on the air. If it does, I'm afraid Marky, that's Governor Diptill, will have to say for public consumption, Let justice prevail. Which is not to say justice might not be tempered with mercy."

"Forget it," Klamatty says. "I won't say anything. Neither will Doodle or Ravitz, he's the County Attorney. They're Republicans. But Trooper Redhardt knows the whole story and he's got a big mouth. Before the sun sets, never mind the public prints, half the county will know I have the governor's brother-in-law in my court. Charged with a terrible crime."

The phone rings in the living room. Klamatty answers it, talks and returns to the kitchen. "Speak of the devil. That was a public print. My friend Eddie Devlin at the Bugle Call. He said he heard from a source he can not reveal I had Governor Diptill's brother-in-law in my court this morning. Charged with a terrible crime."

"Oh hell! What?"

"I lied. I said I could not confirm that and gave Eddie another story he can have some fun with. I don't like to lie to Eddie. He's good about putting my name in the paper. But somebody else, no doubt, will fill him in on Mister Hossman."

"No doubt. But the chap owns the newspaper, Clarence Snorkel? I'm sure he's a Republican."

"Cadence. Of couse. He's a publisher. But sometimes Snorkel gets the idea he's a journalist with a duty to inform the public. If this is one of those times, Mister Hossman's story will be in the Bugle Call. The Associated Press will pick it up and Mister Hossman and his brother-in-law will be all over the Twin Cities newspapers too."

"We'll leave it to Marky to deal with that then," Web Allen says. "It really doesn't change the situation. Tell me, it's not my business but do you really need this Village judgeship, Jane? Moneywise, I mean."

"No," Klamatty says. "I could manage without it. But fifteen-hundred a year would be nice. And what would I do all day, I didn't have a court? Besides, I like dispensing justice. West of the Winatchee. For instance, the story I gave Eddie Devlin. A big boar survived the wreck yesterday. Jerry Hennessey, he farms out south of town, chased it and caught it and put it in a pen in the old stockyard and he says it's his boar. But our friend Strudel, even now perhaps chewing up a Writ of Replevin, says it's his boar. I am going to have to decide whose boar it is and, frankly, I am going to enjoy the challenge that will be. I've asked both of them for proof of ownership. Whatever that may be. Are there blood tests, I wonder, for pigs? Like in paternity suits?"

"I don't know. Those tests aren't always definitive anyway. I could look for some case law."

"Well, sure, if you have time. Or the court will flip a coin, it comes to that. More coffee?"

"No. I better go get my client and hide him. No interviews." Rising, bestowing a light kiss on Klamatty's cheek, Web Allen departs and collides at the kitchen door with Mims McNeely, Klamatty's once-a-week cleaning lady, a thin loquacious woman with gray hair in a bun, a terrible gossip, a fountain of local information and misinformation, which she promptly begins to dispense.

"Jew hear, Missus Klamatty! The Strudel kid, Apple! Oh, pardon me, I dint know you had company." But the company is gone. "Apple was almost kilt yesterday! Guy driving a car went right by the school bus it was stop and almost kilt her!"

"Yes, I know, Mims. I know all about it. The driver, I mean the State Patrol thinks he was he driver, was in my court this morning."

"Who was he? Anybody local?" Mims has other homes to clean this day and other homemakers to keep abreast of the news.

"No. He's from St. Paul." And Governor Diptill's brother-in-law but that will all come out soon enough and Mims has other news.

"I tell you 'bout my Little Nell? New job she got?" No, Klamatty thinks, but you will. "My Little Nell is workin' for the guvner now! In that great big house his up in St. Paul! She's like a maid and a waitress some the time. She was workin' a waitress, y'know, up the Atlectic Club there in St. Paul. Where all the big wheels eat. Them lobbyists and members the Legislature and the guvner, sometimes. My Little Nell wait on the guvner a few times and I guess she make a good impression. Well, you know my Nell. Anyway, a fella works for the guvner come and see her, the Atletic Club, and offer her a job, the guvner's big house, and she took it. She miss the tips, she says, but they dint amount a whole lot anyway and the pay and hours is better and she gets some benefits like. State benefits. She ain't Civil Service exactly but."

"I'm glad to hear that, Mims. Good for Little Nell. I'm sure she'll do well. Now I have some work to do. Court work. I'll be downstairs."

Klamatty escapes to her courtroom and Mims though disappointed, this report regarding her Little Nell just an outline, unlimbers Klamatty's vacuum cleaner and starts banging it against the furniture.

Indeed, Klamatty knows Little Nell McNeely, a former Hayfield High cheerleader who dropped out in her junior year to become the waitress at Bonnie's Cafe. After, local lore has it, introducing half the Hayfield Wolverines football team to the joy of sex and, though a minor herself, once charged by the parents of the starting left tackle with contributing to the delinquency of a minor. Case dismissed in view of Nell's tender age. Bo Mangle, the football coach and civics teacher, wanted Little Nell locked up. Bo thought high levels of testosterone the first step to success on the gridiron and blamed Little Nell for the Wolverines' dismal 1-8 season. And now by golly Little Nell is employed by the governor of the Great State of Minnesota! Only in America, Klamatty thinks, where upward mobility is open to all, and starts leafing through. "Booth's Judicial Manual." But there's nothing in "Booth's" about swine whose ownership is in dispute.

* * *

Web Allen enters Bonnie's Café: a counter with eight stools, a grill behind it, four tables for four, four booths and an overhead fan slowly stirring greasy air. Hoss Hossman is not there. "Big guy said his lawyer be along?" Bonnie, a buxom woman busy at the grill, says. "That's you, he went up the Muny." Web Allen goes up the street to the Muny, finds Hoss sipping whiskey while listening to the bartender's garbled version of the Great Collision, hauls Hoss out of there and they start for Winatchee Falls in Web's '55 Olds 98.

"That asshole state cop," Hoss says, as they go by a billboard advertising sparkplugs on County Road O. "Like I told you. I know the bastard let the air out my tires, my car was parked in front the motel there. I dint see him do it but he was there, I come out the motel. Grin all over his goddamn face. And arrest me. Cuff me! I was about ready and stuff the sonofabitch in a dumpster in front the motel there. But resist arrest. I know there no future in that. What I am gonna do, though. I am gonna ask Marky, get that assholt transferred the hell-and-gone up the North Woods someplace."

Further along, beyond the bridge work on County O, Hoss says, "What are my chances, you think, you're the lawyer, this goddamn school bus thing?"

"Hard to say," Web Allen says. "I'll be talking to the county attorney who was there today. We might work something out. Or we might not. I'll move for a continuance, we're back in court. Postpone your trial. You're in no hurry, are you?" No, Hoss says. "This whole thing might die on the vine if we give it time. In view of your connection with the governor. It doesn't, I'll move for a dismissal. Court might grant it. Are you and the governor pretty close?"

"Yeah, pretty close. Me and Louella, my wife, and him, she's his sister, we usually have breakfast together Sundays. Louella tells him how and be governor. She's older'n Marky, five years. I guess she allas boss him around. Louella, she's runnin' the company now Marky's the governor. Marky, he's a real sports nut. Remembers me from when I was playin' football, LGU. I damn near was a All-American, y'know. Long time ago."

"Is that right? Tell me, I doubt its important, but what were you doing out in the Hayfield area at seven-thirty in the morning?"

"I had a go pick up another goddamn instrument a dumb kid forgot and bring his school. Clarinet. Out by Dexter. Kid lives on a farm and his old man said I got a be their place seven o'clock, get the clarinet. Else the whole fuckin family be out in a field, farming."

"You and I will have to confer too. Before we go back into court. Some day next week. You phone me Monday and we'll set up a time."

"There gonna be anything' about me, the goddamn school bus thing, in the goddamn newspapers? Louella prolly kill me, it's in the goddamn newspapers."

"I don't know. We can't control that. But I'm told the trooper has a big mouth. You should know too. The child you did not almost hit is State Representative Strudel's daughter. The defendant in your action to replevy. We get into a dismissal, he'll raise an uproar."

Hoss shrugs. "You say court, you mean the old bird wears the black robe is allas banging that wooden hammer? Yeah, I know, gavel." Web Allen nods. "She's kind a old but a nice set a jugs, what I could seen. I wouldn't mind poppin' her some day."

"I wouldn't plan on that," Web Allen says, and gives Mister Hossman, client though he be, something to think about. "She can be tough too. She likes to put people in jail. You're not out of the woods yet." They ride the rest of the way to the new Moon Beam Motel on Winatchee Falls's south edge in silence.

"Got a take a shower and shave," Hoss, climbing out of the Merc, says. "Get the goddamn jail smell off me. Call a garage, get my tires that asshole vandalized fixed. Got a call my goddamn wife. Bring her up to date. Listen her bitch and scream."

* * *

The new Moon Beam Motel is a long two-story stucco building parallel to the highway, forty units, the stucco cracking, erected in 1948, parking in front of it. The old Moon Beam was a long low frame building rather like a hog barn popular with persons engaged in illicit sex.

Hoss inspects his Buick, parked in front. It's sitting low to the ground, all four tires flat. Hoss inspects the right rear then the rest. The party or parties who let the air out (well, he knows who the goddamn party was) also pulled and absconded with the valve stems. Hoss swears and goes into the Moon Beam's miniscule lobby: a counter that's the front desk, a cigarette machine, two soft drink machines, a pay phone, a 12-inch TV with rabbit ears tuned to a soap opera behind the counter.

"Mister Hostman," the young fellow with pimples who seems to be the day and night front desk clerk, says. "Are you checking out? Check out time is noon, y'know."

"No," Hoss says. "Later," and goes up to his room, which overlooks the parking lot, or would if the drape was open. The double bed has not been made. Hoss calls the front desk and complains. Do Not Disturb sign was on your door, Pimples says, You want the maid make it now? "Forget it," Hoss says, and orders a six-pack of Hamns. The new Moon Beam does not sell beer (or liquor) but Pimples' little brother will go and get a six-pack at the beer joint up the highway and deliver it, adding a $1 delivery charge and expecting a tip.

Hoss strips, showers, shaves, gets into clean clothes and stuffs his clothes with the jail smell in his suitcase. The six-pack arrives. He pops one, lights a cigarette and sits on the unmade bed. It's a tangle of blankets and sheets, one pillow on the floor.

What a difference a day makes, Hoss, drinking his beer, thinks. Is that an old saying? If not, it is now. He just made it up. Less than twenty-four hours, he was rolling around in this bed with Margie Bremer, Realtor. After she picked him up in her sky-blue '56 Cadillac with fins like a rocket ship. No sense, she said, they both drove and she had to show a house. Afterwards. After their lunch, a good lunch in that downtown steak place. He had Margie for dessert.

They then took a shower together and she left to show the house. Hoss had an appointment with the Winatchee Falls High School band director, Ludwig Bock: they were going to look at band uniforms in the Diptill uniform catalog. He went down to get into his Buick, found the tires flat and that asshole state cop waiting, handcuffs at the ready, yapping about a warrant and the goddamn school bus.

Hoss sighs, pops another beer, counts his money, $18, where the hell did the rest of it go, and gets busy. He finds the local Buick dealer, T.J. Hanrahan Auto Sales & Service, in the Yellow Pages, phones T.J. Hanrahan Auto Sales & Service and inquires of the female with whom he is speaking, Will T.J. Hanrahan Auto Sales & Service take a check? A Diptill Music Co. check, good as gold.

No, the female says. T.J. Hanrahan Auto Sales & Service's policy, written in stone, is All Parts & Labor Strictly Cash. Hoss expresses surprise and dismay at some length and the female finally says he can talk to her dad. T.J. himself. Who, an old man by the sound of him with a voice like a broken muffler, finally convinced there is a Diptill Music Co., in business since 1921, says he will "just this once and don't tell anybody" take a check not to exceed $20 and will send a man out.

This man is a skinny kid in his late teens with a tow truck. Hoss meets him in the parking lot. The kid inserts new valve stems, inflates the tires with the compressor on the tow truck and gives Hoss a bill. Parts, valve stems (4) @ 25 cents, Labor $12.40, Total $13.40. Hoss gives the kid a Diptill Music Co. check for $13.40, goes back to his room, pops another beer, lights another cigarette, phones Winatchee Falls High and eventually is connected to Mr. Ludwig Bock in the Band Room.

"Mister Bock? Harold E. Hossman here. Diptill Music. Say, I want to apologize, I missed our appointment yesterday. Something came up."

"Yeah, I guess," Bock, he's got a fluty voice, says. "Heard you were arrested. In jail. Went by a school bus was stopped.

"Where the hell you hear that?"

"Oh news gets around," Bock, he sounds like he's smirking, says. "My wife's sister's husband's brother's sister's husband, he's the constable out to Hayfield. He told Bonnie, that's his wife, he saw you in court and that news came right up on the line pretty fast."

"Yeah, well. There ain't nuthin' to that. Dumb state cop got it in for me is all. It gonna be dismissed. You can ask my lawyer. What I'm thinking is we set up another appointment? Like this afternoon?"

"No, not today. I'm busy. We're rehearsing for our Commencement. I really don't know. The man from the Bailey Company was in Wednesday. I know we've always dealt with Diptill. But Bailey has some awfully nice uniforms. And they're a little bit cheaper."

"Price almost always negotiable, Mister Bock. How about some day next week then? Believe me, you be doing yourself a favor, you take a look at our catalog."

"Well, maybe. Middle the week maybe. Give me a ring Monday."

"Monday be fine, Mister Bock. I'll give you a ring. Been nice talking to you." Hoss hangs up, Bock is another asshole, pops another beer, lights a cigarette, takes a deep breath and makes the call he's been putting off, long distance through the Moon Beam switchboard to the Diptill Music Co., office of the president, which puts him on hold for some minutes.

Then Louella, she has a loud commanding voice, says, "Yes? Who is this?"

"Lou? Harold."

"Where are you?

"I'm still in Winatchee Falls. Listen, everthing is under control, Lou, that bus thing. I got a hell of a lawyer from that law firm I guess you call. He'll get that thing dismissed, he says. I had a put up a little bail was all. Another thing, you be happy and hear. I just about got a uniform order wrapped up here. Winatchee Falls High School. Forty, fifty uniforms. I got to see the band director again next week. I guess he has to get the okay is all, the superintenent or whoever, spend the money."

"I want to see that in writing, Harold. You say bail. You were in court, then?"

"Yeah. Well, Justice-the-Peace court, they call it. Little dump they call Hayfield. Bunch of hicks. I got their attention though. I told them I was Marky's brother-in law."

Which is the last thing Hoss says for what seems to be a very long time while Louella rants and raves and swears, the thrust of all that how could be so stupid, such an idiot, dragging Marky's name into it and Marky up for re-election, a great many things on his mind, the last thing he needs an idiot for a brother-in-law, and of course it will all over the goddamn newspapers and the TV, bad enough he's besmirching the company name and the family name too, the Diptill name, sawdust for brains, etc., etc.

This concluding with, "Get your big butt up here! You and I are going to have a talk with Marky. And his advisers."

Hoss follows orders, throws the rest of his stuff in his suitcase and goes down to the front desk to check out. "Got to charge you for another day, Mister Hostman," Pimples says. "On account of you dint check out before noon." Hoss opens his mouth, prepared to cut Pimples down to size. "But I ain't gonna charge you that double occupancy you had up your room Wednesday night." Hoss shuts his mouth, writes another check on the Diptill Music account and departs.

* * *

In the Winatchee Falls Bugle Call newsroom overlooking Broadway, upstairs over the Ad and Circulation Departments, Eddie Devlin, thirty-five, a Bugle Call reporter since 1948, and others on the news staff (Ralph Haney, the managing editor, Pearl Mulch, the Society Editor, Ken Crackers, another reporter) and Cadence Snorkel II, Editor & Publisher, are hastily at 2 p.m. checking the first copies off the press for glaring errors and possible grounds for libel. This done, no grounds for libel or errors so glaring they'll require a "Clarification" in a subsequent Bugle Call discovered, Eddie reads three of his contribution to the day's news:

Train, Truck Collide in Hayfield

A Milwaukee St. Paul & Pacific Railroad passenger train and a semi-truck carrying some 80 swine bound for market collided late yesterday afternoon in Hayfield, sixteen miles southwest of Winatchee Falls. Several passengers aboard the train, the MSP&P Omaha Flyer, suffered minor injuries. They were treated at the scene by Dr. Harley Street of Hayfield. Three persons in the truck escaped with minor bruises.

A witness to the collision told the Bugle Call the three were District 33B State Rep. Wolfe Strudel, who farms near Hayfield, Gerald R. Hennessey, also a Hayfield area farmer, and Francis Toomey, 46, of Winatchee Falls, the truck driver. The semi rig was said to be owned by the J.P. Rahilly Trucking Co. of Winatchee Falls.

Nearly 40 swine were killed instantly in the crash and about 30, all badly injured, had to be destroyed. A dozen survived the crash and were rounded up later. About half the swine were owned by Strudel and half by Hennessey.

The witness told the Bugle Call the train hit the trailer portion of the semi-rig at the Main Street crossing in Hayfield. There are no barriers or warning lights at the crossing. Railroad officials and the Winatchee County Sheriff's Department are investigating the crash.

Not much of a story, considering the devastation the collision wrought, and no byline: the Bugle Call has a rule, one byline per day per reporter. But it was pretty much a second-day story (with no fatalities) the way the Bugle Call saw it. Radio station KWIN, tipped off by Horace Greeley Trudd, Editor & Publisher of the weekly Hayfield Star & Shopper, who considers the Bugle Call a competitor, made a big thing of the collision on its 10 O'clock News last night and its 6 O'clock News this morning. So all the Bugle Call did, this Cadence Snorkel's decision, was cover its ass, so to speak. Snorkel never did get old Mrs. Swenson's hot news tip. He was tied up at a Winatchee County Republican Committee meeting and his wife, who did get the hot tip, forgot to mention it. The Bugle Call would not have sent a reporter all the way to Hayfield anyway, on overtime, for anything less than a triple ax murder. The Bugle Call does not pay overtime, but grants compensating time off, and that's the same as overtime, you look at the bottom line, which is where Snorkel looks at it.

St. Paul Man Charged With Passing School Bus

Harold E. Hossman, 49, of St. Paul, was charged today before Justice-of-the-Peace Jane Klamatty in Hayfield with passing a Hayfield Consolidated School school bus with stop arm extended and warning lights flashing early yesterday.

Hossman pleaded not guilty and was released on bail, with trial set for mid-June. The charge was filed by State Highway Patrol Trooper Lionel Redhardt of the Winatchee Falls Patrol District.

There were reports that Hossman is connected through marriage to Gov. Marcus Diptill but Justice-of-the-Peace Klamatty told the Bugle Call she could not confirm that report.

Cadence Snorkel knows this Hossman is Governor Diptill's brother-in-law. He discussed this story at length with Ralph Haney before Eddie wrote it. But Snorkel did not have the idea he was a journalist and told Eddie, "Don't make anything out of it, he's the governor's brother-in-law."

Train, Truck Crash Sparks Dispute: Who Owns Pig?

By Edward T. Devlin, Bugle Call Reporter

A collision late yesterday in Hayfield between a Milwaukee St. Paul & Pacific passenger train and a livestock truck heavily loaded with swine has left Hayfield Justice-of-the-Peace Jane Klamatty with a knotty legal problem.

Most of the swine aboard the J.P. Rahilly Trucking Co. rig were killed instantly in the crash or so badly injured they had to be destroyed. An 800-pound prize Spotted Poland China boar, however, survived in good health and its ownership is now in dispute.

Both District 33B State Rep. Wolfe Strudel and Gerald R. Hennessey, Hayfield area farmers, claim they own the prize boar and both came before Justice of-the-Peace Klamatty today for an adjudication hearing on the matter.

Justice-of-the-Peace Klamatty took the matter under advisement and set a subsequent adjudication hearing for a week from today, at which time Strudel and Hennessey have been directed to present proof of ownership.

"The court," Justice-of-the-Peace Klamatty told the Bugle Call, "has not yet determined exactly what will constitute proof of ownership, beyond a reasonable doubt, but will be considering precedents regarding similar disputes."

The prize boar and the other swine aboard the truck were bound for the B&P Meat Packing Co. in Fairbow. Hennessey, following a lengthy chase, caught the boar following the collision. Pending Justice-of-the-Peace Klamatty's decision, it will remain confined in the abandoned MSP&P stockyard in Hayfield, while Strudel and Hennessey take turns feeding it.

This story is not, Eddie feels, representative of his best work, but he did get Klamatty's name into it (her name in the paper) five times. Seven, counting the Hossman story. That will please Klamatty. And she in turn often apprises Eddie of odd cases he turns into humorous little features. He scratches her back and she scratches his, so to speak.

The reason this story is not his best work is Eddie has other things on his mind. For one thing, he has to hustle over to Connor's Men's Clothing, Winatchee Falls' premier haberdasher, and buy a new suit, his first new suit in eight years. A new suit in which to wed Evylee Haber nee Hanrahan in.

Eddie still considers the durable dark blue pinstripe he bought eight years ago for his old friend Chesty Bennett's funeral (Chesty killed and buried in Germany late in The War but dug up later, returned to the U.S. and buried again in the Catholic Cemetery outside Hayfield, his mother's hometown) his new suit. But Evylee made it clear during a post-coital discussion the night they became engaged (or Evylee decided they were engaged) she wasn't going to marry anybody in an eight-year-old suit. Or a suit off the rack at Sears or Ward's either. A new dark medium-weight flannel at Connor's will run Eddie $54.95, but so it goes. Besides, he loves Evylee. She's a spunky little girl, well, woman, Eddie's age, twelve years a war widow, Archie Haber Jr, USMC, killed at Iwo Jima. And Evylee, Eddie's pretty sure, was somewhat disappointed with her engagement ring, a diamond just visible to the naked eye he's buying on a year-long Installment Plan. So he'll buy a new suit at Connor's.

The wedding is set for Saturday June 3, 2 p.m. at Holy Redeemer, The Rev. Bernard Griffin officiating, followed by a reception at the Winatchee Falls Golf & Country Club, where Eddie used to caddy in his teens. This reception will be his parents', Hack and Ceil Devlin's, first trip to the Country Club. Ceil bought a new dress for the occasion. Hack got his suit cleaned and pressed. Both are pleased Eddie is getting married, finally. They were beginning to wonder and worry about him, thirty-five and still single. And Ceil would like grandchildren. But may be disappointed. Evylee says they'll "still have to be careful." She's not sure she wants children at her age. Her old man, T.J (Slippery) Hanrahan (a.k.a Hanrahan Auto Sales & Service), though given to expressing his opinion on many subjects, has not expressed an opinion on this subject.

T.J., Eddie is pretty sure, is not wild about the upcoming nuptials. Or more accurately, he's not wild about Eddie for a son-in-law. That's the impression Eddie got anyway the three times he had dinner with the Hanrahans, once at their home, twice at the Country Club. But he may be wrong. T.J. is pushing seventy, a lanky old man with a raspy voice, bristly eyebrows and high blood pressure. Few things please him. He lived in Wisconsin, he often says, he'd "by god vote for Senator Joe McCarthy!" He's pretty sure Eisenhower is "one of them goddamn closet Commies!" And he hates the press because the Bugle Call sometimes screws up his car ads. But T.J. loves his only offspring, Evylee, no doubt about that, wants the very best for her, may think Eddie better than no husband at all.

In fact, T.J almost offered Eddie a job, this over the rare prime rib at the Country Club, which T.J. is not supposed to eat in view of his high blood pressure, but eats anyway. "I'd by god give you a job, Devlin," T.J. said. "Selling, my Used Lot, I thought you could cut that. But I don't think you could cut that. You're not aggressive enough. You're not cut out for the car bidness, close a deal, get that name on the dotted line, a conditional sales contract."

T.J. of course is footing the bill for the reception. He also came through with $600 for a week's honeymoon on Mackinac Island. He also grit his teeth and, violating every ethic in the Auto Dealers Code, took Eddie's ancient '46 Ford on a trade-in and sold Eddie a used '53 Pontiac Sunbird at what he claimed, though probably lying, was "his cost," $995. And T.J. made the down payment, $2000, and co-signed the mortgage on their new house, a three-bedroom "ranch home" with attached garage in Haber's First Subdivision, a good location across the Winatchee River from the Municipal Golf Course, priced at $16,000, but Art Haber Sr. took $1,000 off that because Evylee was his former daughter-in-law and all.

The monthly payment, property taxes and insurance included, and utilities, still will exceed by a few dollars the 25 percent of Eddie's $80-a-week at the Bugle Call he read somewhere should equal one's housing costs. But Evylee plans to go on working part-time at Hanrahan Auto Sales & Service. There's also a possibility Art Kealey, the Bugle Call's veteran Sports Editor, sixty-eight, crippled with arthritis, may "hang it up." If Art retires, Eddie is pretty sure, he's been the acting Sports Editor days Art was laid up with his arthritis, he will become the Sports Editor. Full-time, at $90-a-week. Any case, Eddie is sure, T.J. Hanrahan will not let his darling daughter starve.

Eddie sometimes wonders exactly how he got into all this. It seems to have been Evylee's idea more than his in retrospect. It popped up when, after trying to seduce her on and off for years, he did, on the evening of St. Patrick's Day, and Evylee said, "I guess we're engaged now." But of course he loves Evylee. They have had though careful quite a lot of fun in bed since then and now no doubt will have more. And it probably is time he got married. Or he'll soon be a certified old batch. Whatever, it's too late now for second thoughts and, all things considered, he could do worse than T.J. (Slippery) Hanrahan for a father-in-law.

Eddie folds his Bugle Call, stuffs it in his coat pocket, says so long to Ralph Haney, struggling with the spelling in a Garden Page story concocted by Pearl Mulch, goes down the stairs from the newsroom, through the Ad Department, where Cadence Snorkel III, the Ad manager, is frowning at a Sears display ad (Men's Stripped Shits $2.39) fresh off the press, emerges onto Broadway and heads for Connor's Men's Clothing.

* * *

In Hayfield, late in the afternoon, Jane Klamatty, one eye on the dark clouds building up in the western sky beyond the village water tank, is weeding her garden, which could use some rain. There is, borne on the light wind that is blowing, the faint unpleasant odor of dead spoiled meat. Two badly injured swine crawled under the loading dock outside the old MSP&P depot and died there and efforts to remove them have failed. Constable Poole, however, is supposed to be throwing lime on them.

Klamatty's garden work is interrupted when Len Steckle's son Tommy, eight, cuts through her garden with a bundle of handbills. He hands Klamatty one, fresh off the job-press at the Hayfield Star & Shopper, the ink still wet, no union bug, and what it says is Steckle's Butcher Shop & Frozen Locker Service is having a GIANT FRESH PORK SALE! 3 DAYS ONLY! Ham, Ribs, Chops & Sausage, 19 to 29 cents a Lb!

So that's why the lights were on all night in Len Steckle's Butcher Shop & Locker Service following the Great Collision. Klamatty sighs. Barring the unlikely possibility that Steckle paid Strudel and Hennessey for the carcasses he collected, more litigation is bound to ensue. But she won't worry about that now. And wonders: is Web Allen pursuing the hunt for somebody who knows somebody who knows somebody close to Governor Marcus Diptill?

* * *

Web Allen is. He's conferring with old August Schott in the Schott & Schott offices in the First National Bank building in Winatchee Falls.

Old August as befits the senior partner has a big corner office, the walls festooned with plaques and citations attesting to his many civic endeavors when younger, and a big desk awash in papers he is prone to mislay. Mabel Murphy is in her tiny adjoining office, the door closed, typing something, in bursts. Her new electric sounds like a distant machine-gun.

A tall gangly old man is old August, with snow-white hair, cataracts and thick spectacles on a great beak of a nose. Some think he resembles the actor, C. Aubrey Smith. He walks with a cane now and comes late to the office most days in a good dark three-piece suit, he has a closet full of those, with an Elk's tooth on his watch chain.

"Always liked Klamatty," old August says. "Tried a case or two in her court. Years ago. Something to do with fence lines. She's pretty high-handed sometimes. Way she runs her court. Interprets the law. But I always liked her. Klamatty Jane, we used to call her. You know, that Western gal. Calamity Jane. The one was quick with a six-gun. Shoot the feather off the Indian on a buffalo nickel."

"I believe that was Annie Oakley, Sir."

"Who? That's a free ticket, an Annie Oakley. Who are we talking about?"

"Jane Klamatty, Sir, the justice-of-the-peace in Hayfield," Web Allen says and explains, again. Klamatty has in her Justice Court a Schott & Schott client who happens to be Governor Marcus Diptill's brother-in-law. He is charged with a terrible crime, passing a school bus with STOP arm extended and warning lights flashing, a gross misdemeanor, and Klamatty, ordinarily, given her reputation, would slap this client with jail time and a stiff fine if guilty, which he probably is. "But she will, I have her word for this, temper justice with mercy if the governor appoints her the Village Court judge there. In Hayfield. That new law."

"What new law is that?" August says. Web Allen explains SB 808 effective August 1. "Strange business. Typical, those confounded Democrats. Another way to spend money. Get the picture though. Clear enough. Brother-in-law is a hostage then. Be dammed! Klamatty's no fool! Man named Hesssman, I think. Yes. Believe I spoke with his wife recently."

"Hossman. Yes. His wife retained us. I am representing Mister Hossman in this matter."

"Interesting situation," old August says. "Clear case, you scratch my back, I'll scratch yours. Well, not you and me. But you know what I mean."

"Yes. And one would think that's the way Governor Diptill will see it. But Jane, I mean Justice-of-the-Peace Klamatty, would feel more comfortable with the situation if she knew someone who knew someone who knew someone who could and would explain the situation to the governor. Just in case. But she doesn't know anybody fits those specifications. She wonders if you."

"Good thinking. My opinion, Diptill's a lightweight. Has but one oar in the water half the time. Soft on Welfare. Yes, I know some people. Attorneys. In Minneapolis. Or St. Paul. Twin Cities anyway. Two in particular. Gave Diptill campaign contributions, I think. Don't remember their names. Offhand. But Mabel will find them. I'll give them a ring. Make a note of that right now." Old August scribbles himself a note. "Tell them tell Diptill appoint my friend Annie Oakley or the brother-in-law goes to the slammer!"

"Klamatty, Sir. Jane Klamatty. I know she'll appreciate your help. How is Missus Schott feeling?" That's a ritual question old August hears twenty times a day.

"Not so good," old August, removing his spectacles and rubbing his eyes, they're suddenly a bit damp, says. "Not good at all. Matter of days, her doctor thinks. Be a blessing really. Morphine seems to be wearing off."

3.

Klamatty, on her phone at 8 a.m. Friday, May 23, Jerry Hennessey on the line. "Don't come to court today, Jerry. Strudel won't be there. He just called me. He has to go to St. Paul, he said. Some kind of meeting, some committee he's on up the Legislature."

"That goddamn Strudel!" Hennessey says. "It's his day feed my boar!"

"He knew that, he said. He said you feed it today he'll feed it tomorrow and Sunday. Then you'll be even."

"Why'd he wait the last minute, tell you? I got my day all arranged so's I could come to court. Now I got to arrange it all over again."

"I don't know, Jerry. But you know Strudel. It's a wonder he let me know at all. How is the boar doing anyway?"

"It ain't the boar! It's my boar! Awright, I guess. Might lost a little weight. That goddamn Strudel don't know how and feed it good, I don't think. When are we gonna be in court then? I got field work to do. I got to arrange my schedule."

"Well, there are some things I want to look up, Jerry. And study. Laws and other cases pertaining to disputes regarding livestock ownership. That will take me a while. I'd like to put your case and Strudel's off until the middle of June. The fifteenth, say. That's a Friday."

"Oh f'chrissake, Jedge! That's my boar! I know that and you know that. Should anyway. It's a pain in the ass, drive in a town ever other day and feed it. Whyn't you just tell Strudel go take a flying. Awright, you know what I mean."

"I can't do that, Jerry. I don't know who, which of you, owns the damn boar. Get your field work out of the way and I'll see you on the fifteenth. Ten o'clock."

Hennessey, risking contempt of court, says something that sounds obscene and hangs up and so does Klamatty. There is, she thinks, a chance the litigants will grow tired of trips to town to feed the boar and agree to some kind compromise settlement. A slim chance. They're both stubborn as goats. Web Allen to date has found no pertinent case law but he's still looking.

* * *

House District 33B State Rep. Wolfe Strudel lied. There is no committee meeting up in St. Paul. Instead, wearing his best suit, he is reporting at 11 a.m., following a thirty-minute wait, for an audience with old Dollar Dobermann in Dollar's office on the Dobermann Hotel mezzanine.

"Sit," old Dobermann, puffing a big cigar, says. Wolfe sits. "Cigar? No, you don't smoke. All right, you wanted to see me. Make it snappy. I'm busy."

"Yessir," Wolfe says. "It's about that Senate bill, eight-oh-something, the one there won't be any more damn justice-the-peaces the first August but there be village judges. The one you tell me vote Aye and I did. There's a justice-the-peace out to Hayfield, woman name Klamatty, be out a job then. But she prolly like and be the village judge, the governor point her, and that ain't a good idea, I don't think. I want a tell the governor that. Write him a letter. One thing, she don't know a gotdamn thing about fence lines. Twice we was in court, me and a guy name Hennessey is my neighbor except he ain't much a neighbor. They strips land in two my fields Hennessey claim was his land I put the fence where it belong. Klamatty give them him. Three-foot strip one time. Two-foot strip the other time. And I think she prolly give Hennessey a boar now is mine I was gonna sell, the B&P, but got loose and run, that train hit the rig he was in, and that gotdamn Hennessey catch it and claim he is his."

Old Dobermann raises one hand like a cop halting traffic, Strudel's problems bore him, and Wolfe subsides. "That's all taken care of, Strudel. I know all about Klamatty. Crazy woman tried to put my son in jail. That's why I told you to vote Aye on that Senate bill. The one establishes village courts. I thought the vote in the House might be close. My son did not go to jail. Should have maybe, but that's my business. I kept it out of the goddamn newspaper and Judge Kelly cleared him. Finally. I had to remind the old coot. He mislaid the appeal. I want that woman, Klamatty, out of there. And she will be. I talked to Milo Bumshoot, the State Chairman. He'll talk to the governor. Anything else on your mind?"

"Well, Klamatty, you know," Strudel says. "She got a guy in her court now. Sonofabitch claims him and the governor is brother-in-laws. Sonofabitch went by our school bus, it was stop. Damn near kilt my girl Imogene. I like and kill the sonofabitch and I figger Klamatty prolly gonna let him off."

Old Dobermann halts traffic again. "Harold Hossman. There was something in the goddamn newspaper. I know all about him too. Bumshoot said the governor is aware of that situation and if he has to he'll say he wants justice served. That situation won't help Klamatty. Anything else? I'm busy."

"No. Well. There's a young fellow I like and see be the Village Judge out to Hayfield. Elmer Hooter. His dad runs the drugstore. Elmer's a lawyer. Just starting out. He went to Law School."

"Good for him. I don't recollect there are any minimal requirements for a Village Judge in Senate eight-oh-eight. Leave it to the goddamn Democrats to screw things up. But I suppose a law degree is something the governor might consider. All right. Write the governor. Recommend this Hooter, that's your pleasure. Don't mention Klamatty. That's taken care of. There's something else I want to talk to you about too, Strudel. But not yet. I'll let you know when."

Old Dobermann turns to the papers piled on his desk and Wolfe, sensing this audience to be over, mumbles his thanks and departs.

4.

"All rise," Constable Poole bellows. All rise from the former church pews. Justice-of-the-Peace Klamatty bangs her gavel, her court is in session, and surveys the usual suspects: Strudel (all dressed up for this occasion in clean bib overalls and a white shirt), Elmer Hooter (sports coat, bowtie), Hennessey (in smelly bib overalls, manure on his shoes, chaw in his cheek) J.J. Doodle (in his trusty seersucker), Trooper Redhardt (in uniform), Web Allen (another seersucker) and Harold E. Hossman (in a good dark suit with a heavy cane in his fist). All sit. It's a bright sunny day, 10 a.m. June 15, the outside temperature 90 F. Rain fell in the night and Klamatty's basement courtroom is somewhat damp.

"We have three matters before the court," Klamatty says. "So let's get started. Are you ready for trial, Mister Allen, Mister Doodle?"

Web Allen rises and so, slowly, leaning on his cane, does Hoss. "Please the court," Web Allen says. "Mister Hossman requests a continuance. He is in great pain at this time. He has a loose cartilage in his right knee. A partially torn anterior cruciate ligament. The knee he hurt playing football for Land Grant U. He is scheduled for surgery early next week and the strain of a trial at this time would be deleterious to his health. And he'll need some time to recover. At least a month, his doctor feels. I have a letter from his doctor, should the court wish to see it. Doctor Lewis Lewinski. Doctor Lewinski is a highly respected orthopedic surgeon in Minneapolis."

Elmer Hooter pops up. "Please the court," he squeaks. "My client Mister Strudel objects to a continuance."

"Objection noted," Klamatty says. "Sit down, Elmer. Let me see the letter." Web Allen hands it over. What is says is Mister Harold E. Hossman has "a long-standing condition produced by earlier trauma, the prognosis of which, if the surgical procedure recommended is not performed promptly, is likely to result in a severe loss of articulation." A stiff knee, then, which Hossman has been living with with no apparent difficulty for twenty-five years. But the court is sympathetic. "Objection overruled. The court extends its sympathy to Mister Hossman and is inclined to grant him a continuance in view of his medical condition. Mister Doodle and Trooper Redhardt, however, may be ready for trial?"

No, J.J. Doodle says, the County Attorney's office has no objection to a continuance and neither, much to everyone's surprise, does Trooper Redhardt. "One thing I want though," Trooper Redhardt says, while J.J. Doodle groans. "Is a subpoena. Subpoena a witness by the name William Hennessey."

J.J. Doodle and his boss, Winatchee County Attorney Sheldon Ravitz, spent half a day trying to talk Redhardt out of this foolishness, but got nowhere. Or so Doodle told Web Allen when they discussed the case and Web passed that along to Klamatty. They gave up when Redhardt threatened to refer the matter to the Patrol Commander, "Colonel" Dedrick (Ded) Wood, the holdover Democrat-Farmer-Labor in the Diptill Administration with a year to serve on his appointment and a man quick to alert the goddamn media to what he takes to be Republican shenanigans.

"Defense moves." Web Allen says. "To quash that subpoena. If granted. William Hennessey is twelve years old."

"Your boy Billy is it, Jerry?" Klamatty says.

"Yeah, I guess," Hennessey, shifting his chaw, says. "Trooper here come out our place and talk to Billy. Trooper says it was Billy seen this guy here go by the school bus. Seen his car go by, I mean. And damn near hit Strudel's kid. So Billy got to be a good citizen, Trooper says. Do his duty. Be a widness. But Billy don't want a be a widness. Billy's scairt you put him in jail, Jedge."

"Put him in jail!" Klamatty says. "Where'd he get that crazy idea?"

"Well, me, prolly," Hennessey, shifting his chaw, says. "I allas tell him, he done some thing he should'na, I tell you and you put him in jail."

Klamatty sighs. "Don't tell him that anymore, Jerry. All right, court will subpoena William Hennessey. Motion to quash is denied. Constable Poole will serve the subpoena. Let's set a new date for Mister Hossman's trial." She studies the calendar on her desk. It features full-color photos of Minnesota's four seasons, though many say there are only two: Winter and Road Construction. "July twenty-one suit everybody? That's a Saturday." Some big city offices are closed Saturdays now but this step on the Road to Perdition has not yet reached the hinterlands. July twenty-one suits everybody but Strudel, who grumbles, but, a minority of one, is largely ignored. By then, five weeks hence, Klamatty hopes, Harold E. Hossman's fate still technically in doubt, she'll be the new Village Court judge. August Schott, this an earlier report from Web Allen, is supposed to be getting in touch with two Twin Cities lawyers with access to Governor Diptill, both willing to "draw Diptill a picture." Web, Klamatty assumes, will update her later on the progress of these shenanigans and bangs her gavel. "July twenty-one then, ten a.m. Present bail continued."

J.J. Doodle and Trooper Redhardt depart through the basement's walkout door, Redhardt pawing at Doodle's elbow. Redhardt's patrol car, Doodle's Chevy, Hossman's big brown Buick and Web Allen's Merc are parked in the alley behind Hooter's Drugs.

Klamatty bangs her gave. "Next case, previously continued at Mister Strudel's request, Mister Strudel's response to Mister Hossman's action to replevy. Are you prepared to return the flute and the case, Mister Strudel?"

Elmer Hooter pops up. "Please the court. Mister Strudel requests the court grant a continuance in this matter."

"Oh f'chrissake! I object to that!" Hoss says, but Web Allen shushes him.

"What seems to be the problem?" Klamatty says.

Elmer opens his mouth but Strudel responds. "We ain't found that gotdamn flute yet. It's around the house somewhere but we ain't found it. I ain't got no bum knee. I don't need no operation. But I'm pretty busy, start my campaign get re-elected the Legislature and all. My wife and Apple, Imogene. They lookin' for the flute. They just need some more time is all. And you give Hossman here nearly kilt my Apple one them continwances."

"Plaintiff," Web Allen, making it easy for Klamatty, says. "Withdraws his objection."

"Fair enough," Klamatty says. "Mister Strudel's response to the action to replevy is continued. Why don't we do this all at once? July twenty-one, ten a.m. You understand, Mister Strudel, you will have to produce the flute and its case at that time. Or be prepared to write the Diptill Music Company a check for, what is it? Well, whatever. Or I'll find you in contempt of court."

"Thank you, Your Honor," Elmer squeaks. "Defendant thanks you too." Strudel grunts.

Hoss mutters something that sounds like "Fuckin pig farmer. I'm out a here then?" Klamatty nods and Hoss, following some brief words with Web Allen, departs, limping, leaning on his cane, and Klamatty observes through the window in the walk-out door a miracle. A miraculous cure. Hoss' limp disappears, he strides through her garden, whacking at her tomato plants with his cane and jumps into his big brown Buick.

But Klamatty is not competent to judge knee injuries. She bangs her gavel. "Next case. Also continued at Mister Strudel's request, Mister Hennessey's objection to that overruled. The adjudication regarding the boar. Or have you something else for the court, Mister Allen?"

"No," Web Allen says. "But I have some free time. I'd like to observe. If the court has no objection. I find this an interesting case."

"Court has no objection," Klamatty says. "Are you, Mister Strudel, and you, Mister Hennessey, prepared at this time to offer proof of ownership of the boar in question?"

"Yah," Strudel says. He pulls from a pocket several three-by-five black-and-white snapshots and hands them over. "These the pitchers my wife took, my boar, we had him up the State Fair."

"Please the court," Elmer says. "Exhibits one through five."

"Never mind that, Elmer," Klamatty says. She studies the photos while Hennessey sneers and chomps on his chaw. They depict a large white or dirty gray Spotted Poland China flopped down on its right side in a pen full of straw beneath a sign SWINE JUDGING. "Frankly, Mister Strudel, the court does not find these photos conclusive. The animal is a pig. The court can see that. A boar, in fact. But I do not see a black spot like a football on its shoulder. Which Mister Hennessey cited at our previous hearing."

"He layin' on it," Strudel says. "It's there awright but his right side his other side and he layin' on it. I got a pitcher shows it but I ain't found it yet. My wife lookin' for it. She finds it, I bring it right in and show it you."

Hennessey has had enough of this "The hell you got a pitcher like that, Strudel! You're a goddamn liar! You're a politician, lying comes natural you! It's my boar got a big black spot like a football on his right shoulder. We go down the Stockyard and look him, you see, Judge. And my boar, old Chubby, he come when I call him. We go see him, I show you. I call Chubby and he come. I guess that prolly prove he's my boar and we get this goddamn bidness over with."

"I call him too then!" Strudel says. "Anybody call a pig, he prolly come. But I never give my boar no name. Give a pig a name, that's a dumb thing."

Klamatty bangs her gavel, producing a semblance of order in the court, and rules. "The court will consider Mister Hennessey's offer of proof. We'll take a ten-minute recess, the court has to change, and reconvene at the Stockyard. Everybody have transportation?" Everybody has. "Would you, Mister Allen, drive the court?"

Klamatty goes upstairs and gets out of her judicial robe and into a sensible dress and returns and off they all go to the abandoned stockyard in two pickup trucks and Web Allen's Merc, a bumpy five-minute drive on the Hayfield's pot-holed streets.

"Any peep," Web Allen says. "Or other sign of sentient life from the governor's office?"

"No," Klamatty says. "Is anything happening anywhere else? Did August ever get in touch with those attorneys he mentioned? Have you any news for me?"

"I have some good news and some bad news. The good news is August remembered who those attorneys were and Mabel Murphy tracked them down. The bad news is one is dead and the other one is in a home and thinks he's Oliver Wendell Holmes."

"Oh hell!"

"But there's more good news. August remembered another St. Paul lawyer. Jack Sperling. He's a divorce lawyer and August is pretty sure he represented my client Mister Hossman's wife Louella when she was divorced. Years ago. August thinks Sperling still sees Louella socially. They both raise money for the Chamber Orchestra up there or something. August met Louella once or twice at some Republican shindigs. He says she's bigger and older and smarter than her brother, our governor. August thinks the best way to get to Diptill is through Louella via Sperling. He's going to call Sperling."

"If he doesn't forget."

"I'll remind him. Incidentally, the St. Paul Monitor-Union picked up on my client Mister Hossman's trouble. Finally. Yesterday. He had a clipping. Story says he's a former Land Grant U football star and Governor Marcus Diptill's brother-in-law. Makes a big thing out of their relationship, fact he's charged with passing a school bus and so on. Says trial is pending in a local court. Names you too or I guess it's you. Justice-of-the-Peace Jean Klemmety. Quotes Governor Diptill as saying he is not familiar with the case but feels strongly justice must be served. I wonder who."

"Horace Greeley Trudd, probably. Editor and Publisher. He puts out the weekly newspaper here. The Hayfield Star & Shopper. Strings for the Monitor-Union. Maybe three stories a year that see print. Nobody at the Monitor-Union talked to me."

"My client didn't say much. Just showed me the clipping. But the impression I got, his wife and his brother-in-law the governor were not pleased with that story."

"I'll tell you this, Web, this situation is wearing me down. There are times I think let's got to trial, find you client guilty, sock it to him, stiff fine, ten days in the slammer, make everybody in the Consolidated School District happy and the hell with it! I'll find another line of work."

They've reached the old stockyard beside the MSP&P's Main Line, a sprawl of pens inside high wooden fences weathered gray built fifty years ago and a busy place full of livestock awaiting shipment on a MSP&P freights until after The War when the railroads' livestock business pretty much lost out to the trucking industry and the MSP&P, though still holding title to the land and pens, abandoned the stockyard. The local lore is the stockyard is insured and the MSP&P hopes the small boys who try to set it on fire will succeed one of these days.

Hennessey and Strudel park their pickups and Web Allen parks his Merc close to the weathered fence enclosing a small pen with a rough wooden trough close to the fence and everybody climbs out and peers through the fence. The boar, a huge dirty gray Spotted Poland China flopped down in the pen, appears to be asleep. Hennessey removes two pails full of slops and a short length of broomstick from his pickup.

"No! No!" Strudel squeals. "That ain't fair! He's a gotdamn cheat! He got slops! Any pig come, you call it and you got slops! It ain't fair! Got damn you, Hennessey!"

"Objection!" Elmer Hooter squeaks. "My client."

Klamatty came prepared. She bangs the fence with her gavel. "Objection noted. But we'll proceed with the demonstration. Go ahead, Mister Hennessey."

Hennessey pours a pail of slops through the fence into the trough, bangs the empty pail with his broomstick and yodels the hog call he's perfected over thirty years. "Sooo-eeee! Sooo-eeee! Sooo-eeee, Chubby! Chubby Chubby Chubby! Sooo-eeee! Sooo-eeee!"

Chubby (if it is Chubby) pricks up his left ear, the one he has, opens his mean little eyes, observes the several humans observing him, gets slowly to his feet, grunts, waddles across the pen and buries his snout in the slops.

"So there!" Hennessey, triumphant, says. "I guess that prove he's my boar."

"No! No! It don't!" Strudel squeals. "Hell it does! It ain't fair! You cheat! I object!"

"Objection," Elmer squeaks.

Klamatty bangs the fence with her gavel. "Shut up, Elmer. Objection noted. Shut up, Mister Strudel. The court has a question. Where is the black spot like a football on the animal's right shoulder we've heard so much about?"

"It's there," Hennessey says. "It's cover with mud he been layin' in is all. I hose him off, we had a hose. Or wipe him off and show you. But Chubby kind a mean sometimes. He don't like and be touched. But spot's there awright. You got my word for it, Judge."

"Bullshit!" Strudel says. "It ain't your boar and you know it, Hennessey! It's my boar! Who you think you foolin' anyway? You bang on a pail slops and holler, any pig come!"

Klamatty bangs the fence with her gavel. "Mister Strudel's objection is sustained. The court finds the demonstration as conducted inconclusive. Likewise the animal's appearance in view of previous testimony. Would you two like to flip a coin and settle this?"

But neither Strudel nor Hennessey, after giving this suggestion brief thought, consider it an acceptable solution. "Hell, no," Hennessey says. "I be dammed I'm gonna give Strudel a chance he swipe my boar!" And Strudel repeats his favorite mantra: It ain't your boar, it's my boar!

Klamatty sighs. "Very well. The court will continue this adjudication. We'll take it up again on." Why not make it a big day? "July twenty-one, ten o'clock. At which time the court will consider further offers of proof of ownership. Meanwhile, the present feeding arrangements remain in effect." She bangs the fence again with her gavel. "Court is adjourned."

Strudel and Elmer climb into Strudel's pickup and depart. Hennessey dumps the other pail of slops into the trough, Chubby (though it may not be Chubby) gobbles them up, and Klamatty and Web Allen depart in his Merc.

"Well," Klamatty says. "What's the observer think?"

"I wouldn't wish this case on the worst judge I know," Web Allen says. "Crazy Kelly even. And I await with great curiosity the court's eventual decision."

"Decisions, decisions. They're both as stubborn as a goat, Strudel and Hennessey, and there's more to this than that damn pig. They don't like each other and they've tangled before. Twice over fence lines. Years ago. Fact, I think August represented one of them. Can't remember which. I found for Hennessey. Then two years ago Strudel stuck some of his campaign posters on Hennessey's fence posts. Hennessey tore them off and charged Strudel with defacing property. Law's clear on that, posting without permission. I fined Strudel ten dollars. I suppose Strudel figures it's his turn to win one. Strudel's got it in for one of Hennessey's kids too. Billy the witness."

"The one you subpoenaed?" Web Allen says. "Despite my objection. Why?"

"Defamation of character. Strudel says Billy, every day they're on the school bus, calls his darling daughter Apple a fat pig. Or fat sow. Apple is the kid your client almost killed. All right, allegedly almost killed. Strudel was all set to sue Billy for defamation but then Elmer Hooter failed his bar exam. I don't know the status of that potential case now."

"This Billy. The witness. He sounds like a charmer. I'm glad my client waived his right to a jury. Kid is a witness, juries are always sympathetic."

"Maybe not this kid. Reports are he's a brat. Steals, sets cats on fire. I granted that subpoena on the assumption you'll take this kid apart, he testifies. That's if I don't get the good word from Governor Diptill. I get the good word and I'm the Village Court judge, I'll dismiss the charge names your client. I'd rather not though. That would set off an awful uproar around here and I have to think about my reputation. Judicial reputation."

"Perish the thought, Jane," Web Allen says. "I'll take the kid apart. My client will get a fair trial and a not guilty verdict, lack of evidence. If Strudel and Hennessey can't stand each other, what were they doing sharing that rig the train hit?"

"It was cheaper that way," Klamatty says. They've reached her house. "Neither of them had a full load but Rahilly Trucking charges by the mile for the rig. You know, I'm beginning to think that damn pig is Hennessey's pig. But I'm not sure and, your client Mister Hossman aside, I prefer to see justice done. I think I'll call the Land Grant U Ag School. There might be somebody there with some expertise. Have to call my friend Eddie Devlin too. He can have some more fun with the damn pig."

"Six o'clock suit you?" Web Allen, lightly squeezing Klamatty's knee, says. They're booked for dinner at the Fish House. Six is fine with Klamatty and she gets out of the Merc.

* * *

The banner headline in the Bugle Call is IKE ALERT FOLLOWING STOMACH SURGERY, the subhed Surgeons Say Condition Encouraging, but the story Eddie Devlin turns to in his copy fresh off the press is on the Regional News page.

Who Owns Pig? Decision Still Pending

By Edward T. Devlin, Bugle Call Reporter

A bitter dispute as to the ownership of a prize boar that survived a collision between a livestock rig and an MSP&P passenger train a month ago in Hayfield remains under advisement in Justice-of-the-Peace Jane Klamatty's Justice Court in Hayfield.

Two Hayfield area farmers, District 33B State Rep. Wolfe Strudel and Gerald Hennessey, contend they own the boar, which Hennessey captured after it escaped following the collision. Justice-of-the-Peace Klamatty is attempting to adjudicate the matter, so far without success.

Both Strudel and Hennessey appeared before Justice-of-the-Peace Klamatty earlier today. Strudel, Justice-of-the-Peace Klamatty told the Bugle Call, presented a number of photographs taken at a recent State Fair, which he said matched the appearance of the boar.

Justice-of-the-Peace Klamatty, however, did not find these photos conclusive. She then took her court to the Hayfield Stockyard, which no longer is in use. The boar has been in residence there since its capture.

Hennessey poured slops for the boar and called it with the "hog call" for which he is well known in the area. The boar responded, but Justice-of-the-Peace Klamatty did not find that conclusive in view of the fact the boar was being fed. Strudel also objected to this procedure.

Justice-of-the-Peace Klamatty continued the case with a subsequent adjudication hearing set for July 21 in her court. She instructed Strudel and Hennessey to be prepared to offer further proof of ownership at that time.

Eddie rather likes "The boar has been in residence there" but feels the story, otherwise, is not his best work. Well, he has things on his mind. One thing is another trip to Connor's Men's Clothing. Evylee did not like the suit he bought On Sale at $39.95. She said it looked like a "cheap suit" (which it was) with a coat collar that rolled up his neck when he sat down, made him "look like the Hunchback of Notre Dame." And the pants, though Eddie had them taken in, were "baggy." Eddie can't return this suit, not with the pants taken in, and he's resigned to spending $50 for another suit. At which time he'll have four suits counting his corduroy. Enough for the rest of his life, Eddie figures, though Evylee may have other ideas. She's also said something about a summer suit.

Eddie sighs, folds his Bugle Call, says so long to Ralph Haney, struggling with the spelling in a Pearl Mulch epic detailing the qualifications of the four nominees for president of the local Business & Professional Women's Club, goes down the newsroom stairs, through the Ad Department and out onto Broadway, where he encounters District 33B State Rep. Wolfe Strudel, all dressed up in clean bib overalls and a grubby white shirt.

They know each other, these two, but they are not friends. Years ago in a softball game at a joint rural schools spring picnic, Strudel fanned Eddie four times and Eddie has not forgotten that. Or ever will. Still, he's civil. "Mister Strudel. You started your campaign yet?"

"No," Strudel says. "After the Fort, I start. I talk the Kiwanis Club. You put my name in the newspaper then?"

"Sure. Remind me. Give me a ring. I put your name in the paper today. That case you got going with a fellow name Hennessey. Which you own a pig."

"My boar! That gotdamn Hennessey! Who told you that?"

"Sorry. Can't reveal my source."

"I know who! That gotdamn Klamatty woman! She allas shootin' off her gotdamn mouth. She ain't much a judge neither. She givin' Hennessey all the breaks. Him and his gotdamn hog call! I give you that story straight sometime. Not now. I got a see a fellow."

Strudel hurries on along Broadway and goes into Yale Yeager's Photo Studio. Yeager, Eddie surmises, who also does the photo work for the Bugle Call, is producing a new campaign poster photo for Strudel. High time too. Strudel looked like the popular conception of a serial sex slayer on the posters he plastered all over District 33B two years ago.

* * *

Eddie is wrong. Yale Yeager, a middle-aged middle-sized man with fingers stained with developer, comes out of his darkroom and Strudel flattens on the counter in the studio a three-by-five snapshot of his beloved boar in its State Fair pen.

"I'm Wolfe Strudel," he says. "I'm a member the State Legislature."

"I know who you are," Yeager says. "You ought a let me shoot a new photo you, you can put on your campaign posters. The one you got."

"Not now," Strudel says. "I got another little job for you now. I want this pitcher made bigger and I want the pig in it turn the other way. Like he was layin' on his other side. And I want you put a black spot is like a football on his shoulder. You can do that?"

"You got the negative?" Strudel looks puzzled. Yeager explains what a negative is. Strudel does not have the negative. "Well, yes, I can do that. Be better I had the neg. But I can shoot this snap. Reverse the neg and enlarge it. Touch it up like you said. It might be kind of grainy." That won't matter, Strudel says, and at Yeager's request draws a football-shaped spot on scratch paper. "Not my business, I guess, but why do you want to reverse this photo?"

"This my prize boar. But his other side his best side. That black mark is what extinguish him. How long it take you, do this? How much it cost me?"

They settle on $5.95 for an 8 x 10 Strudel will pick up first thing July 21. This is the wedding season, weddings are Yeager's specialty and he's busy, eight weddings to shoot, develop, print and so on before he gets to Strudel's job. Strudel departs and Yeager puts the snapshot and sketch in his Work to Be Done basket under the counter. He's never previously encountered a hog farmer so besotted with a swine he wants an 8 x 10 displaying its best side, but it's not his place to wonder why.

* * *

Web Allen and Jane Klamatty pull into the crushed rock parking area behind the Fish House in Web's Merc at 6:45, get out of the Merc and go inside.

The Fish House is on a high steep bank overlooking Lake Winatchee ten miles north of Winatchee Falls. The lake is long and winding, forty feet deep in places. It was formed when the hydroelectric plant and the dam that provides it with a head of water were built beside and in the Winatchee River, a mile downstream, in 1919. An old iron bridge on County Road G crosses the lake beside the Fish House. Originally, this was the site of Walt's Bait & Tackle shack. Who Walt was no longer is known but there were rickety wooden steps down the bank to a floating dock then. Local anglers tied up at the dock or fished from it for sunnies, croppies, smallmouth bass and a rare walleye. Once Prohibition set in, these sportsmen if Walt's friends or recommended by one of Walt's friends could buy illegal beer and whiskey at the shack. A record spring flood took the steps and the dock out in 1923. Walt did not replace them but built an addition to the shack, the speakeasy business by then more profitable than the bait and tackle business. He also bought a secondhand gasoline generator, installed dim electric lights and built a second outhouse with "Setters" on its door. This establishment was raided now and then by Prohibition agents, closed for a time thereafter, but soon back in business. It burned to the ground shortly after Prohibition was repealed. This fire was considered suspicious by some including the St. Paul Fire & Casualty Insurance Co., but nothing was ever proved. Walt eventually collected his insurance, sold the land and ruins to a Winatchee Falls carpenter and former customer named Bud Benjamin and vanished.

Benjamin built a new building on the site with cramped quarters for his wife and several children: nothing fancy, just a rough bar and booths, all the studs and wiring and some of the primitive plumbing connected to the single indoor restroom exposed. This establishment was known as Benny's. It had a beer license and sold set-ups and when the REA (Rural Electrification Administration) lines reached the bridge in the late 1930s, Benjamin retired the generator, by then a very cranky machine. Benny's was popular with aging adolescents. Benny did not require any proof of age (twenty-one the legal drinking age) and did not close until dawn if any customers wished to watch the sun rise over Lake Winatchee. A number of local maidens were deflowered over the years in various automobiles parked outside Benny's while waiting for the sunrise. This dawn closing was highly illegal but Benjamin was distantly related to Winatchee County Sheriff Ham Canker and blood proved more significant than Minnesota's one a.m. closing law. Benny's trade fell off during The War, when gas rationing and aging tires discouraged travel, but had five more good years after The War and in 1950, his kids grown and gone and he was sixty-three and sick to death of watching the sun rise, Bud Benjamin retired. He sold the place to Nick Shepka, a Winatchee Falls liquor store owner and bar manager, moved to Arizona and, this a subsequent report, went bad. Dumped his wife, developed a taste for tequila, found a Mexican girlfriend and took up golf.

Nick Shepka, a Croatian immigrant with a firm grip on the American dream, assuming the growing American inclination to eat out would continue, put some money into the place: enlarged it, hid the studs etc. with paneling, installed a new bar, new booths, a kitchen, modern restrooms, built new steps down to a new floating dock and renamed it the Fish House. It's a popular place now through three seasons (Nick was right about the eating out trend) and open weekends in the winter, when fishing shacks dot Lake Winatchee.

The Fish House seats about sixty in booths along its two long walls and tables in between and it's close to full when Klamatty and Web Allen slide into the booth with a lake view they reserved. Two water skiers showing off on the lake are taking splashy tumbles. Clyde Dobermann is with a short busty blonde woman in a booth without a lake view. He sees Allen and Klamatty, beams, waves to them, corrals a fat waitress and sends her to their booth.

"Mister Dobermann," the waitress says. "Wants to buy you folks a drink."

"Why not?" Web Allen says. He orders gin-and-tonics and waves thank-you but Clyde is deep in conversation with his date. Date? Current mistress? Somebody else's wife? But he wouldn't bring somebody else's wife to the Fish House. Or would he? Clyde sometimes lives dangerously. No, the woman with Clyde is named Bremer. She's in real estate. Web doesn't know her but knows who she is.

"How," Klamatty says, resuming a conversation launched earlier. "Is August taking it?" Taking his wife Elaine's quiet death at 4 a.m. in the Schott home on West College Street. "Following a long illness," her obit in the Bugle Call said. That's a euphemism for cancer.

"He seems to be holding up pretty well," Web Allen says. "He was prepared for it, of course. As much as anyone ever is. No one ever is, quite. Well, you know that. Birdshot is pretty broken up. In fact, August called that lawyer I mentioned,

Sperling, yesterday. The one in St. Paul who knows my client Mister Hossman's wife. Sperling is out of town but he'll be back Monday. Will you be at the funeral?"

"No. I never really knew Elaine. Just August, some. You told me he bought a plot for her. Him too. In Dobermann's cemetery?"

"It's not Dobermann's cemetery. It's Everlasting Rest Gardens. Yes, a double plot at the top of the slope. Don't worry, Jane. I'll remind August, call Sperling again. When this is all over."

"Who's worried? Still, look at this." Klamatty digs a Hayfield Star & Shopper from her purse and Web Allen reads the banner story:

Local Man Likely to be New Judge
By Horace G. Trudd, Editor & Publisher

A Hayfield man most likely will be the new Hayfield Village Court Judge that Gov. Diptill will be appointing one of these days pretty soon. He is Elmer Hooter, 26, the son of our beloved druggist Win Hooter. Elmer is a lawyer now since he passed the Bar Exam and our well-known District 33B State Rep. Wolf Strudle is going to recommend Elmer for the new Village Court judge job.

"Elmer Hooter is well versed in the law," State Rep. Strudle told the Star & Shopper, "and that is something the governor will think about when it comes to appointing a new Village Court Judge." The Legislature passed a law in April getting rid of justice-of-the-peaces and replacing them instead with Village Court Judges on August 1.

State Rep. Strudle said he is going to write Gov. Driptill and recommend Elmer Hooter for the judge job. The Village Council is looking for a place for the new Village Court and most likely will rent the space upstairs over Bonnie Poole's cafe on Main Street if they can get together with Bonnie on a price.

Elmer Hooter was a Hayfield High School graduate in 1949 and was voted Most Likely To Go Into The Drug Business by his classmates. Elmer did not choose to go into his dad's drug business however. He went to Winona State University and Law School up to the University.

Far as the Star & Shopper knows, Elmer Hooter is the only candidate for the new judge job and The Star hopes he gets it. There has been some talk around town that Justice-of-the-Peace J. Klametty might want the judge job. But Klametty is getting on in years and a good many Hayfield citizens who have been in her court do not think she is well versed in the law. The Star & Shopper supports Elmer Hooter.

"Chatty style," Web Allen says. "Fair amount of editorial opinion though. I didn't realize you were getting on in years. What'd you ever do to Trudd?"

"He used to run Birth Reports in the Star & Shopper. Around five years ago he ran one, eight-pound baby boy born to the Essie Pembertons. Essie Pemberton was, still is, has been forever, she's a local girl, the eighth grade teacher in Hayfield. She's at the Consolidated now. A maiden lady then in her fifties and a strict Baptist. Once she got over the shock, she was hell bent on suing the Star & Shopper. For libel, slander, something. I made Trudd run a correction and an apology or I'd hold him in contempt. Turned out the eight-pound boy was born to the Esau Penningtons. Esau runs the Standard station. Trudd's been after me ever since. Won't put my name in the Star & Shopper except I'm re-elected and he has to run the village election results. Then spells it wrong."

"I noticed that," Web Allen, says. "The Star & Shopper seems to have trouble with names. Spelling them, I mean. Yours, Strudel's."

"The Star & Shopper has a lot of trouble with names. Like most newspapers. Part of the trouble is Trudd handsets the type.

And he writes his stories in longhand. Says that's the way Mark Twain did it. You've heard the saying? A man and a half-witted boy and a crippled lady can put a newspaper out? That's the Star & Shopper. There's Trudd. Ralph Sackett, maybe sixteen. He writes the sports and delivers the paper. His dad's the Liberty Insurance agent in town. And Julie Nordstrom, the ad manager. She's in a wheelchair. Had polio when she was a kid. They put the Star & Shopper out."

"How old is Trudd? How'd he get into the newspaper business?"

"Close to seventy. He inherited the Star & Shopper. How else? His dad, Trace, started it. Trace rolled into town in a buggy around 1890, just before the railroad came through, with a flatbed press tied to the back and numerous angry creditors somewhere behind him. Trace died around twenty years ago and left the Star & Shopper to Horace G. I don't know what'll happen to it when he goes. His wife is dead. They had no kids. But enough about the Star & Shopper. If Strudel recommends Elmer, what will Diptill do?"

"Dammed if I know, Jane. Is Elmer a Republican?"

"Probably. He'd vote the Republican ticket, I think, we still had those ballots with pictures. An elephant, a donkey. That's if Elmer could tell them apart. What I hear from some JPs who were passed over for the judgeships in their villages, Diptill is appointing Republicans if they're warm and breathing."

"Well, you're warm and breathing, Jane. You might be a Republican for all Diptill knows. You have his brother-in-law in your court. Awaiting trial on a serious charge. I'd say the situation looks promising. And old August will get hold of this Sperling."

The fat waitress turns up at their booth wondering, "What'll you folks have tonight?" They order salads, the broiled walleye and two more gin-and-tonics. It's Friday, Catholics still eat fish on Friday and they are Catholics, more or less.

"Speaking of trial," Web Allen says. "I suppose the subpoena for that kid, the one Trooper Redhardt considers a witness, was served?"

"I assume it was served. I sent Constable Poole off with it anyway."

"Constable Poole. Quite the bailiff, he is. A local character is my guess."

"One of many. But don't sell him short. Constable Poole, as they say, used to be a war hero. He grew up in Stiles. You know Stiles? A wide place in the road."

"Yes . August owns a farm near Stiles. I was out there with him once."

"Marlin, that's Constable Poole, left Stiles though when he was nineteen. To look for work when The Depression started. Hear him tell it, he went back and forth across the country thirty times, riding freights, working here and there, all kind of jobs, before he joined the Navy. He was a Navy cook. His ship, I think it was a destroyer, was torpedoed late in The War. Sank. Somewhere in the Philippines. Marlin saved one of the officers and another sailor. Got them on some kind of raft and swam for six hours, pushing the raft and kicking at sharks. They fetched up on a little island. Uninhabited. Marlin kept them alive for two weeks. He caught crabs and frogs they ate raw and laid out a sign on the beach, SOS, with seaweed. A Navy plane saw it finally and the Navy sent a boat and picked them up. The officer put Marlin in for a medal. Bronze Star, I think. He wears it on state occasions. But he'd had enough of the Navy. War was over, he came back to Winatchee Falls and married Bonnie Peterson, she's a Hayfield girl, and worked construction. Haber Construction in Winatchee Falls. Till he fell off a house Haber was building and hurt his back and went for the workmen's comp. That took a couple of years. Par for the course. But Marlin got some kind of settlement finally and Bonnie, she was a waitress here and there for years and they don't have any kids, doubt they ever will, used the settlement and started Bonnie's."

"All of which, actually," Web Allen says. "Is more than I wanted to know about Constable Poole. Except, I suppose, how he got to be constable."

"Well, you brought him up. He seemed to be the logical choice when the Village Council took a great leap forward and voted twenty-four-hundred a year for a constable. Before that, there was trouble in town, domestic strife or a teen beer bust, somebody had to phone the Winatchee County Sheriff and by the time the sheriff got a deputy out whatever it was was all over. By logical choice I mean Marlin was unemployed but his back was okay and he was driving Bonnie crazy, hanging around the café. The Christian thing to do was get him out of Bonnie's hair. And he was, is, big. He has a certain presence. That's why I hired him, be my bailiff. Dollar-fifty an hour, fifty-cents he serves a legal document. Fact is, Marlin's a pretty good constable. He's good with drunks, differences of opinion at the Muny Liquor. He knows all our juvenile delinquents by name and modus operandi. Most of the kids in town are afraid of him."

Their salads arrive but Web, toying with his, has more to say. "Constable Poole will soon have numerous legal documents to serve. That collision a month ago, the train and the truck, is having a ripple effect. Celestial Vanderhoeven and several Custer Women aim to sue the owner of the pig they contend attacked them, inflicting personal injuries and pain and suffering. Schott and Schott has that case. It's on hold since we don't yet know whose pig it was and who to sue. When we do know, Vanderhoeven wants it tried in your court. Grounds you're a jurist the equal of Oliver Wendell Holmes and play bridge and golf with her. But Vanderhoeven and the Custer Women are but one ripple. Schott and Schott also is representing a dozen passengers who were on the train and aim to sue the MSP&P and J. P Rahilly Trucking. For personal injuries and pain and suffering. We'll file those in Winatchee County District Court and settle out of court, I expect. I guess you know, you can sue a railroad in any county in which it operates."

"Yes, I knew that. You know J.P. Rahilly? Whip Rahilly? He's a hard case."

"Yes, I know Whip. The Teamsters Local's business agent. In fact, we negotiated for a while when the Hotel and Restaurant Employees Union tangled with the Dobermann Hotel and he was advising their local. Then Dobermann got a hired gun. A professional negotiator. They're still negotiating. Might strike even. But don't tell me about hard cases. I ever tell you I was an MSP&P lawyer once? Right out of Law School. My job was to settle out of court with farmers who'd had livestock, always prize livestock, killed by MSP&P trains. I rode the MSP&P on a pass. Gagged on the coal smoke. I knew every whistle-stop between Milwaukee and Omaha and some of those farmers were hard cases. We had to go to court, we avoided Winatchee County like the plague. Sought change of venue. Winatchee County juries, mainly retired farmers who still figured the railroads had gouged them on freight rates, which they had, were famous for sticking to it any railroad. Hope that's still the case."

"This ripple effect," Klamatty says. "You're looking at a busy summer then."

"Yes, and there's more. The MSP&P is suing Rahilly Trucking and he's suing the MSP&P. We had to pass on those. Conflict of interest, we've got the passengers. Mergenthaler Swan & Hoops is representing the MSP&P. Slick Riordan's representing Rahilly. And finally there's your fire chief, Wyncoop. He'd like to sue Vanderhoeven, assault with a deadly weapon he says 'was like one them mace things them Knights used to bash each other skulls in with.' But Wyncoop thinks the Village Council should pay his legal fees, grounds he was on duty at the time, and he's run afoul of Vanderhoeven again on the Village Council. Wyncoop pursues this, that'll be another case for you, Jane."

"It's an ill disaster," Klamatty says. "Blows numerous law firms no good. Or so they say. Another thing they say, or I say, is your client Mister Hossman and his confounded replevy are blowing no good. Strudel, now he's acquainted with that legal weapon, phoned me this afternoon. He wants to replevy the hams and pork chops and sausage in half the refrigerators in town purchased at Steckle's Fresh Pork Sale, grounds they came from pigs that were his. He has a point. Fair's fair. So I phoned Steckle and he said, without quoting any price, he'll pay Strudel and Hennessey for the pigs he butchered and sold. But he thinks the Village Council should pay him first for removing all those carcasses, grounds they were a health menace. Steckle, he's a local boy, was in the Navy too. Like Constable Poole."

Their dinners arrive and so does Nick Shepka, a heavyset man in his mid-fifties proud to be an American, wearing dress slacks and a Shepka's Liquor bowling shirt. He expresses pleasure at finding them in his Fish House again, hopes they enjoy their walleye ("Fresh," he says, "from Canada, not froze, just pack on ice.") and moves on to tell the couple in the adjoining booth the same thing.

"I know you were in the Service too, Web," Klamatty says. "The War. But I don't know where or what exactly."

"The Army,' Web Allen says. "Southwest Pacific. Australia, New Guinea. But no war stories now. I'm hungry. Let's eat."

Web Allen seldom dwells at this late date on his (1941-45) war. His service therein was not valorous. Relieved of duty twice, sent home before it was over and put to pushing paper, numerous boys (he considered them boys) and young men in his National Guard rifle company KIA or DOW, one in particular the Japs chopped up and beheaded, whose life might he have saved, for awhile anyway. He scarcely remembers the Red Cross girl, Jill Tucker, or their brief steamy affair. Well, thirteen years have passed. And Jill Tucker is dead. He thinks. He saw a name anyway (Jillene Tucker, 43, Boston) among the 128 listed killed when those airliners collided high above the Grand Canyon. Web Allen starts on his walleye.

* * *

At just about this same time in the basement rec room he remodeled himself in his three-bedroom rambler on Winatchee Falls' eastside (the furnace etc. walled off with plywood, the concrete block walls painted green, brown plastic tile on the floor), State Trooper Lionel Redhardt, hunched over the secondhand desk he calls his office, is hard at work preparing the case against Harold E. Hossman. This is not exactly his job. That goddamn Doodle and County Attorney Sheldon Ravitz, they're the one should be preparing this case. But they clearly are reluctant to prosecute the governor's goddamn brother-in-law.

No matter. Trooper Redhardt the minute he left Klamatty's damp courtroom, Hossman's trial postponed, discussed this by phone with his leader, Patrol Commander "Colonel" Ded Wood, and what "Colonel" Wood said was, "You keep on it, Trooper. I back you ever inch the way. Take some time off, your patrols, you have to. We are going to convict this guy! Embarrass the hell out of Diptill. Those jokers you mention stall, you ever hear they might move and dismiss you let me know. Pronto! I'll call the TV and the newspapers. Alert them we got like a terrible miscarriage justice! I might call them anyway and stir up some trouble. You keep me informed, Trooper."

Trooper Redhardt studies the case he's preparing, all laid out on a yellow legal pad like a lawyer would do it. Upstairs, his wife, the former Tootie Wilson, six months pregnant, is doing the supper dishes (some Winatchee Falls aristocrats call this meal dinner but not the Redhardts: dinner is what you eat at noon and lunch is sandwiches and some fruit you take to work or school in a lunch bucket) and their sons, six and four, are watching television. Hopalong Cassidy by the sound of it, six-guns booming. They had meat loaf for supper and Tootie as usual riddled it with onions and green peppers. Trooper Redhardt belches and yells, "Turn that damn TV down!" The gunfire susbsides, somewhat, and he studies his case. It looks to him to be a pretty solid case.

Witness: William (Billy) Hennessey. A snotty little kid in Trooper Redhardt's professional opinion, another year he'll be a juvenile delinquent, when he tracked Billy down with help from the Consolidated School principal and found Billy shooting baby robins with a BB gun in the tree behind the Hennessey's dilapidated farm house. Billy was scared momentarily when he thought Trooper Redhardt was after him (What for, Trooper Redhardt wonders?) but hauled into the house and in the presence of his mother, a heavyset woman exhausted by life or whatever, soon recovered his aplomb.

Queried by Trooper Redhardt, he whined, "Yeah, I seen it good. I got pretty good eye sight. You seen me hittin' them robins, dint you? Car went by the school bus, almost kilt Fatso Strudel, was a Fifty-Four Buick Roadmaster, color they call Desert Dawn. I dint see all the license figgers then but I seen they was eight-eight-eight and I seen that Buick again, the school, they was eight-eight-eight-seven-oh-two. Guy drivin' it was a big guy used to be a football player."

"But you didn't know then, Billy," Trooper Redhardt said. "He used to be a football player."

"Well uh no. Not right then. But I seen he was a big galoot. He look like he might been a football player once and Gruber's kid, Alky, that Gruber runs the liquor joint, he told me his old man knew him, he was a football player."

"Are you sure about the car, Billy? What kind it was, I mean, what color? It must went by the school bus pretty fast. You sure it almost struck the Strudel girl?"

"Would a prolly, Fatso dint jump in the ditch. Yeah, I'm sure. I'm sure! I'm sure! Chrissake! That's all everbody been ask me for a month."

"Watch you mouth!" his mother said. "You take the Lord's name in vain again and I'll wash it out with soap!"

"And you won't be scared, Billy," Trooper Redhardt said. "Go into court, Missus Klamatty's court there in Hayfield, and testify? Testify means tell her what you just told me. Under oath. That means you got to tell the truth."

"No," Billy said. "I ain't scairt. But I ain't gonna go in no court there either! I ain't gonna tell old Klamatty nuthin'. Old bat, she prolly put me in jail!"

Nor could Trooper Redhardt talk Billy out of that misconception. But that's all settled now with Billy under subpoena and, snotty little kid though he be, Trooper Redhardt reckons Billy will be a good witness. That lawyer Allen challenges his veracity, Billy no doubt will give him the "I'm sure I'm sure" treatment.

Witness: Wade Cummins, the school bus driver. Trooper Redhardt got Wade's name from the Director of Transportation (also the Phy Ed teacher) at the Consolidated School and tracked Wade down at his parents' home in Winatchee Falls. Wade said he didn't want to get involved and miss work at the canning factory and all he saw anyway was "a glimpse like" of the suspect vehicle in his rear view mirror, but changed his mind when Trooper Redhardt threatened to subpoena him. Trooper Redhardt doubts Cummins will prove a great witness but his testimony such as it is will corroborate Billy Hennessey's and it's just about the only corroboration Trooper Redhardt has managed to dig up.

Witness: Imogene Strudel. Trooper Redhardt also spoke with Imogene and her parents, but Imogene struck him as not very bright and all she seems to know or remembers is "I just seen it was a car comin' and it went right by the school bus and almost like hit me so I close my eyes and jump in the ditch and lose my flute and I like look and look but never find it and my Pa he's still mad at me 'cause I lost my flute." Imogene will testify, however, evoke a little sympathy perhaps, though Justice-of-the-Peace Klamatty's sympathy quotient in Trooper Redhardt's experience is just about invisible. But she's tough on traffic offenders. Socks it to them and Trooper Redhardt is banking on that.

Imogene's old man, that Strudel who is a member the State Legislature, denied he was still angry with Imogene in regards to the lost flute and offered to testify. He also went on at great length, goddamning Hossman and his driving habits, some kind of legal action brought by Hossman in regards to the flute, which Trooper Redhardt did not understand, and the high costs run up by the Consolidated School's bus fleet, but conceded finally he'd not actually seen Imogene escape death by inches. Strudel is not on the witness list.

Neither is Elroy Simmons, the kid sitting next to Billy on the bus, sneaking a smoke. Trooper Redhardt tracked him down at his father's farm but all Elroy knew, he finally admitted, was what Hennessey told him. Hearsay. Inadmissible.

Trooper Redhardt tracked down some other kids who were on the bus but they all proved as useless as Elroy. Either they did not want to get involved or were, they said, "Sittin' the other side the bus and dint see nuthin'." They are not on the Witness List and Trooper Redhardt turns to the Crime Scene drawing he's prepared on a large sheet of wrapping paper. It depicts County Road K, the end of the Strudels' long driveway, the school bus parked with STOP arm extended and warning lights flashing, the path taken by Hossman's Buick (a dotted line) when it went by the school bus and the spot (a red X) at which Imogene was almost killed and jumped (or fell) in the ditch. A damn good Crime Scene drawing, Trooper Redhardt thinks. He should have been a lawyer.

In fact, Lionel Redhardt, fresh out of the Army in '45 with four years of college under the GI Bill in hand, thought briefly about going back to college and Law School. But he never was real big on school. Finished the eighth grade in Stiles, Winatchee Falls High and a year at Winatchee Falls Junior College, but dropped out when, very lucky in the middle of The Great Depression, he got a night job wrestling milk cans at the Co-op Dairy. Lucky in the Army too, enlisting the day after Pearl Harbor, transferred to the Military Police following basic. He was small for an MP but rock solid at 195 pounds and soon discovered he liked police work, bracing drunken GIs with their pockets unbuttoned etc. He had a pretty good time, in fact, through half The War with the 301st MP Co. in Townsville, Australia, bracing drunken GIs and popping a few sheilas. Eddie Devlin, a former Stiles kid who's a reporter now for the Bugle Call, was in Tville too, once or twice. They did not meet in Tville but had, they discovered one night at the Legion Club, a mutual acquaintance (Sgt. Harry Parker) in the 301st. Eddie sometimes puts Trooper Redhardt's name in the newspaper now, when he apprehends somebody. Hollandia, New Guinea, the next stop for the 301st, wasn't all that bad either except for the everlasting steamy weather and the goddamn mosquitoes. Pfc. Redhardt spent most of his six months there guarding a Quartermaster beer dump surrounded by razor-wire, apprehending a few GIs trying to tunnel into it. Neither was Manila, thought also very steamy, where the 301st finished The War and he popped a few tiny Flips.

The War over, Lionel Redhardt got out of the Army and came home and thought about going back to college. But he met Tootie Wilson, they fell in love and got married and he took the State Highway Patrol exam instead. His grade was only fair but he had four years in the MPs and his Veterans Preference going for him. He soon was a State Trooper. He did his probation in the Winatchee Falls Patrol District, once apprehending Clyde Dobermann but that didn't go anywhere, then was assigned to the Hibbing Patrol District, where he drove endless miles in his squad car at a steady 58 mph on narrow blacktop roads slicing through second-growth jackpine, alert to the threat posed by bull moose crossing those roads, apprehending occasional speeders, usually dumb fucking tourists, and (in season) deer hunters operating motor vehicles while under the influence. But Tootie didn't like Hibbing, so far from her folks. He put in for the Winatchee Falls District when a trooper there retired and, lucky again, got it.

Six years they've been in the Falls, both boys born there and another something on the way. The last one, Tootie says: she hopes it is a girl. Almost ten years, he's been a trooper. Ten more, he can retire on a half-pension. But he'll probably go for thirty, Trooper Redhardt thinks, retire with a full-pension. He still likes the work, apprehending lawbreakers. Especially it's a lawbreaker like that big galoot, Harold E. Hossman.

Tootie, done with the supper dishes, the television blessedly silent, comes down the basement stairs preceded by her big belly and flops down on the old couch. "I finally got them to bed," she says. "What a you doing?"

"Preparing my case. That asshole Hossman's related the governor I told you about. Patrol chief, Colonel Wood, he told me put it together. He said he wants this Hossman nailed good. But the goddamn county attorney's office, they dragging their feet. Prolly on account of Hossman is related the governor. So I better do it, Colonel Wood said. I tell you, Tootie, how I apprehend the big galoot?"

"Three four times." Tootie says. But Trooper Redhardt, half-launched on his current favorite law-and-order story, tells her again.

"I stop the big asshole in his big-ass Buick, County O outside Hayfield, and give him a mail-in speeding ticket and he takes off. Then I hear on the sheriff's radio he is wanted on suspicion passing a school bus with Stop arm extended and almost kill a kid and I set out in hot pursuit him. I got held up where they fixin' the bridge there but I drive on in a town and dammed I dint see his big-ass Buick park outside that Moon Beam Motel. I know his name is on my copy the speeding ticket. Harold E. Hossman. So I go in the motel but the goddamn kid's the desk clerk won't give me Hossman's room number. Not I ain't got a warrant, he says. Says the Moon Beam got a policy, protect guests' privacy. I ought a charge him, the goddamn kid. Obstruction justice. He says Hossman ain't in his room anyway. He just left with some puss. So I go get some lunch and patrol a while out north town and come back and Hossman's Buick still outside the motel. I figure the goddamn kid clerk prolly lied and Hossman is there all the time. So I screw the valve-stems out the tires on his big-ass Buick. Hossman ain't goin' anywhere then and I stick around a while. Stake him out like. I seen that woman, Bremer, sold us our house, come out the motel and get in that big blue Caddy hers and leave. Then be dammed Hossman don't come out the motel and seen he got four flat tires and start cussin' a blue streak and I apprehend him. Told him what for, the school bus thing, and cuff him, he dint like that, and took him down the City Jail and call Klamatty, that JP out to Hayfield, schedule his arraignment. The sonofabitch give me a hard time, all the way the Jail. Call me a asshole and said I better back off him, him and the governor is related, they brother-in-laws. That dint scare me. Don't scare me now. Colonel Wood, he says he back me ever inch the way on this case. Y'know, Tootie, I nail that sonofabitch Hossman I might be up for corporal."

"That'd be nice," Tootie says. "We sure could use the money, another baby coming. I think I go watch TV a while." She heaves herself off the couch and goes upstairs and Trooper Redhardt turns to his case again.

* * *

At just about which time, Harold E. Hossman, slumped in a leather lounger beside the fireplace in the vast gloomy vaulted living room full of heavy furniture in the stone monstrosity the late Marcus Diptill Sr. had built on Summit Avenue in St. Paul, is listening or half-listening to his wife Louella, president and CEO of the Diptill Music Co., berate him in her loud strident voice. Louella has been at this for twenty minutes though it seems longer, working up a head of steam, and Hoss is pretty much letting it all roll over him: let the bad times roll. He swallows a yawn and closes his eyes.

"Open your eyes!" Louella screeches. "You look at me, I'm talking to you, you big baboon!" Hoss opens his eyes and studies the naked nymphs or whatever they are carved on the beams on the vaulted ceiling. "I told you, you big baboon!" And now tells him again. "We wanted that stupid school bus thing settled! Over and done with! So the damn newspapers would forget about it and get off Marky's back. We wanted you to plead guilty, pay a fine. Get it over with! I told you that! That's what Marky wanted. Marky is terribly upset now. But no! You had to fake a bad knee! And surgery! And go running to your old college buddy, Lewinski! How he ever got through Medical School is beyond me! I wouldn't let him treat a cat! Orthopedic surgeon! If he's an orthopedic surgeon, I'm Madame Curie!"

"Who?"

"The woman who discovered radium. Oh shut up! Whose bright idea was that anyway? That knee business. Yours? Or that hick lawyer's you hooked up with? What's his name. Allen."

"I dint hook up with him. It was you phoned where he works, Lou. They just sent him me was all. Anyway, he's pretty smart."

"Shut up! I've half a mind to call Jack Sperling. Jack'd take a criminal case if I asked him. Well, a traffic case. Answer me! Whose dumb idea was it? That stupid knee business."

"Well, mine, I guess. But Allen thinks, we stall awhile, county attorney or whoever it is might just forget the whole thing. Besides, christ, I got a bad knee. You know that. And I got, it got, the damn trial postponed. Now Allen got some time, prepare my defense."

"Shut up! What are you talking about, you big baboon, your defense! You practically admitted the day you were arrested and phoned me, you went by a school bus and almost hit a kid!"

"I dint almost hit a kid! I dint even nick her. Dumb kid should looked both ways anyway before she cross the road. I thought I supposed and be innocent too, I ain't prove guilty. That's the Constitution the United States."

"Shut up!"

Hoss sighs. Louella's tirades he's learned to his sorrow may run for an hour if she's in good form. He gazes for a time at the numerous photos of Marcus Diptill Sr. scattered about the room.

He looks, Hoss thinks, like Atilla the Hun in a suit and high stiff collar. Louella resembles him. There also are two photos of the late Mrs. Diptill Sr., a thin pale woman with a puzzled expression. Marky got her genes. Give my left nut, Hoss also thinks, for a drink. But Louella when she said "I want to talk to you, bozo!" and this tirade began, dropped the key to the liquor cabinet down the front of her dress.

"Not just any kid either" Louella snarls. "Oh no! It had to be a kid her father's a member of the Legislature. Wolfe Strudel. House District Thirty-three B. He's crazy. Probably certifiable. He never yet has voted an appropriation. He has no conception of party loyalty. Bur Marky may need his vote. For the highway program Marky will be proposing."

"Highway program? What program is that? Where is Marky anyway? Marky's so upset like you say, why ain't he here."

"Shut up! Do you ever read anything in the damn newspapers? Besides the damn sports? Marky is in Willmar at the Kandiyohi County Convention. Lining up delegates. I'd be there too but somebody has to watch the store. I'm going up there tomorrow. Marky will get the nomination for another term. He's not worried about that or the election. Not for himself. But he's worried about the Legislature. Especially the House. Will he have enough votes in the House for his highway program. He may need every vote he can get. Including Strudel's."

"Marky wants a build some roads or what?"

"Shut up! Marky is sure Congress will approve that nationwide interstate highway system President Eisenhower wants and fund most of it. Ninety percent. But the state will have to come up with ten percent. Else we won't have any interstate highways. But why am I telling you this, you big baboon? You don't know what I'm talking about! You don't give a damn for Marky's program!"

"Yes I do. I like Marky."

"Then do him a favor, for gods' sake! Plead guilty to that damn school bus thing and get it over with! The Company will pay your fine."

"Yeah, but my lawyer, Mister Allen, he don't think I be found guilty, we have a trial. That seem to me to be the best idea. The thing is, I say I'm guilty it might not just be a fine is the problem. What Allen says, I might wind up in jail."

"Jail! For a traffic offense! Good god! Is the judge there crazy! What's her name? Judge Klemetty, the newspaper said."

"Newspaper got it wrong. Klamatty, her name is. She ain't exactly a judge. She's one them justices-the-peace. But she's a bitch on wheels, traffic offenders, Allen says. That asshole state trooper arrest me kind enough and tell me that too. Which is something I want a talk to Marky about. I want that asshole transferred the hell-and-gone up the north woods! Koochiching County."

"Shut up!" Louella ponders, chewing her lip. "I wish to god you'd told me, this first came up, this Klemetty is a justice-of-the-peace."

"Klamatty. I did. Soon's I knew."

"Shut up! You did not! You said judge."

"Well, she's like a judge."

"Shut up! You did not say anything about Jail either. But never mind that now. When Marky gets back, he'll be back Monday, we are going to have a talk. You and I and Marky. And whatever we decide, Marky and I decide, in regards your damn traffic case, you are going to do it! Is that clear?" Hoss grunts. "You work in the store Monday. We'll talk Monday night. My god! My poor father must be spinning in his grave! A Diptill Music field representative facing possible incarceration!"

"In what?"

"Shut up. This discussion regarding your stupid traffic case is closed. What's the status of that Winatchee Falls High order for forty band uniforms you were supposed to get?"

"Signed and sealed like I told you," Hoss, lying, says. "Or just about." Band Director Ludwig Bock is still waffling. "Just depends the School Board puts the money in the goddamn budget. I'm supposed see the chairman the School Board, or I guess she's the chairwoman, next week, convince her."

"You better convince her! I'm going to bed. Are you coming?"

"Pretty soon. Watch The News first."

Louella stomps from the room, the key to the liquor cabinet still down her dress. Hoss sighs. There'll be no nookie tonight but there seldom is now. They have separate bedrooms and Louella rarely "feels like it." Running the company wears her out, she says. She also is busy with the Marcus Diptill for Governor Campaign Committee and, though this one is still in its infancy, the Marcus Diptill for U.S. Senator Campaign Committee. Marky by law can serve but two terms as governor.

Hoss sighs, gets off the lounger, skips The News and goes into the kitchen, where he has stashed under the sink with the maid's cleaning stuff a half bottle of Jim Beam. Had stashed. It's not there now. The goddamn maid no doubt found it and snitched and Louella locked it in the liquor cabinet. Or poured it down the sink. Born rich, Louella will do that, committing what Hoss' Irish friend Sean Healy calls the Eighth Cardinal Sin.

* * *

Jane Klamatty and Web Allen, side by side on the sofa in her living room, enjoying a nightcap, watch The News on the new Philco TV set Klamatty bought a month ago for $695, antennae not included. The antennae rising from her roof cost another $125. The Philco, big as a refrigerator, has a 12-inch "super" screen and sometimes more or less "gets" one or the other of the three Twin Cities stations ninety miles away as crows and electrons or whatever they are fly. It's not getting any of them clearly tonight, however. The WCCO newscaster appears to be at work in the middle of a howling blizzard. But The News doesn't amount to much anyway. A minor fire (Live from The Scene!) in an abandoned factory in Hopkins. A dump truck rolled over at a construction site. Several pushy preschoolers (the obligatory Feel Good segment) mugging for the camera at a Doll Parade in one of the suburbs. A routine homicide by gun in the Negro section on Minneapolis' north side, the victim "a Negro male not yet identified," no known suspects. And a report by phone from the Kandiyohi County Republican Convention in Willmar, at which "Governor Marcus Diptill, who will be seeking the nomination for a second term at the State Convention in July, appears to be the choice of a solid majority of the delegates here."

Klamatty rises and snaps off The News. "I've had enough of Diptill for one day. You want another nightcap?" No, Web Allen says, he's ready for bed, and that is where they go.

* * *

And in Willmar, Governor Marcus Diptill is working the convention floor in the grand ballroom of the Willmar Hotel, shaking hands with delegates, slapping backs, pecking female cheeks and telling those who ask, "Louella will be here tomorrow. Somebody has to watch the store, you know. Ha-ha."

A youthful aide, Micky Seibens, pushing through the crowd, clutches Diptill's elbow and whispers in his ear. "Louella is on the phone. She says she wants to talk to you tomorrow. Alone. Soon as she gets here. Around ten o'clock prolly. She says it's important."

"Sure. My suite, tell her," Diptill says. "Well! If it isn't my dear friend Freida Hohenzollern on whom I lay eyes! So good to see you, Freida!" Freida, a small town banker's hefty wife and longtime Kandiyohi County delegate to the State Convention, beams and giggles and Diptill gives her fat powdery cheek a little peck and her pillowy left love handle a little squeeze.

5.

It's a hot muggy Saturday, July 21, afternoon thunderstorms forecast, good corn weather, and at 8:30 a.m., a big day in court upcoming, Justice-of-the-Peace Jane Klamatty is in her kitchen, in pajamas and a robe, drinking coffee and consulting her Bible, when somebody bangs on her front door.

It's Web Allen and he bursts through the door full of news when Klamatty opens it. "Did you get the good word, Jane? No, I guess not. You'd be dancing a jig. I then am the bearer of glad tidings! It worked, Jane! Our strategy! Justice delayed is a wonderful thing."

"What are you talking about? You want some coffee?"

"Yes." They go into the kitchen and Klamatty closes her Bible and pours coffee. "What I'm talking about is Governor Diptill finally woke up! Your appointment is as good as in the mail! Elmer Hooter is history!"

"Slow down," Klamatty, pouring coffee, joining Web at the kitchen table, says. "I don't know what you're talking about."

"What I'm talking about is a Micky Siebens, he's one of Diptill's aides, called old Dollar Dobermann with a message. Just before the Fourth. And Dobermann called old August. But that conversation, unfortunately, slipped old August's mind. Temporarily. He remembered it this morning and told me, I was leaving the office."

"Skip the details! What was the message?"

"Right. Now this is third-hand, Jane, but I think it's the straight goods. What Siebens told Dobermann, I gather he was pretty cagy, was it was his 'understanding that a member of the governor's family so to speak' was awaiting trial on a 'traffic charge' in a Winatchee County Justice Court and that, while the governor naturally 'wishes to see justice done,' the governor also was hopeful that the jurist presiding in the matter would 'find in her heart' in view of the defendant's exemplary driving record except for a few speeding tickets to 'temper justice with mercy.' In which case the governor would be grateful and would not forget that and would deeply appreciate it too if his old friend Mister Dobermann would find time to 'apprise those persons interested in this matter' of the governor's feelings."

"Which means what exactly?" Klamatty says. "Something? Nothing? Diptill, whose name I notice did not actually come up in your report, will promise anything. He often does. His batting average though, it comes to keeping a promise, is about a hundred."

"I think," Web Allen says. "It means the next move is up to you, Jane. Dismiss the charge. Set my client Mister Hossman free! Or at least find him not guilty. Next move then will be up to Diptill and he'll appoint you the Village Court judge. It sounds like a firm offer to me. Or as firm as you'll ever get from a politician anyway."

"And all this happened two weeks ago. But old August forgot it! They better put old August out to pasture!"

"Well, he was still getting over Elaine's death and all. Anyway, better late than never."

"Did August ever talk to that lawyer in St. Paul he thought he remembered? Sperling. The one supposed to know your client's wife?"

"I don't know but it doesn't matter, Jane. Somebody snapped a light on in the dim corridors in Diptill's brain."

"And all this came from old Dobermann? Why him? He hates me. Ever since I nailed his worthless son Clyde. Tried to nail him. That snowmobile DWI."

"Well, my understanding, old Dobermann is Mister Republican emeritus in Winatchee County. County Chairman for umpteen years. Big contributor. Who better to do a little favor for the governor? And preserve deniability. Seibens, it ever comes up, can truthfully say he did not speak with any of the persons interested in this matter. Likewise Diptill. Diptill in fact is miles away. In Washington, for the Governor's Conference. Tell you the truth, according to August, Dobermann was not keen on apprising the interested persons. He said he was only doing it because he'd been asked to, a personal favor for the governor. He had a lot to say about you persecuted his son. But he's a loyal party member. So he did apprise in a roundabout way the persons interested in this matter. Or one of them anyway. Me. And I've apprised you. We get into court, I'll move for a dismissal."

"No. I can't dismiss, Web. Not now. Not with the uproar the case has roused around here. Passing a school bus with STOP arm extended! Many parents think your client should be tarred-and-feathered. Then lynched. We'll have to go to trial. Make it look good. There's Rep. Strudel too. He'd like to see your client drawn-and-quartered."

"Maybe not. Old Dobermann, he was talking to August, said he had to get hold of Strudel and draw him a picture. August thinks he said that. Whatever that mean."

"Hard to say. Dobermann pretty much runs Strudel. Whatever, we will take your client Mister Hossman to trial. Before I find the evidence insufficient. That will raise a god awful rumpus too on the local scene, but I can live with it. Then we'll see what Diptill does. If anything. Find out, was this Seibens really making an offer. Or talking through his hat. Diptill's hat. Speaking of the local scene, you and I are what they call an item now in Hayfield."

"Oh? How's that?"

"Last time you were here you parked on the street and old Missus Gabble lives across the street, she's a light sleeper, saw you leaving at three in the morning. By eight o'clock the identity of the mysterious gentleman with whom I am assumed to be sleeping was the subject of much conjecture at Bonnie's Cafe. You were not positively identified. But Constable Poole, he roams around sometimes in the middle of the night, line of duty or he can't sleep, saw your car in front of my house and named you the chief suspect and that was good enough, juicy enough, for the breakfast bunch at Bonnie's. All of which, I let your damn client off the hook, will really set tongues to wagging."

"Oh hell, Jane. I'm sorry."

Klamatty shrugs. "Don't worry about it. All the wagging tongues were sure I was screwing somebody. Now they think they know who is all. Fact is, you are a big disappointment. Be a much better scandal, you were somebody's husband."

"Well, whatever you say. Now on though, I'll park in the alley. Go out your back door. Or park in front of Missus Gabble's house."

"And I'll run the gantlet at Bonnie's and the Muny until a better scandal comes along. Mainly Bonnie's. The Village Council finally got together with Bonnie on a price and the new Village Court will be upstairs over her cafe. But you have to go through the cafe to get to there. The upstairs is just one big room but the Council grit their collective teeth and appropriated five-hundred dollars for an honest-to-goodness bench and a partition. So I'll have chambers. I'll have chambers? That's if Diptill appoints me. Still a big if, I think."

"I don't think so, Jane. Relax. Do your part, you know what I mean, and you'll get your appointment. What are you doing with the Bible? I didn't know you."

"I was looking something up. More coffee?"

"No. I have to meet my client Mister Hossman. At Bonnie's. Prepare him for trial."

"Expect some knowing looks then. Sly smirks, anybody there knows who you are. You'll have plenty of time, prepare your client. I've got a heavy calendar today. Two local cases. Strudel and your client's replevy. And that damn boar! Before we get to your client. I should warn you too. There'll be a story about your client in the newspaper. The Bugle Call. My friend Eddie Devlin, he's back from his honeymoon, called me, wants my decision and I owe him one. Matter of public record anyway. A reporter from the Monitor-Union called me too. Yesterday. From St. Paul. He said he'll call again today for my decision. Meanwhile hold the press, I guess."

"My client Mister Hossman is found not guilty," Web Allen says. "I'll call the Monitor-Union myself. Time he goes to trial doesn't matter. We're billing the Diptill Music Company for Mister Hossman's legal fees. You think I should go out the back way?"

"Hell, no. Go out the front. Make Gabble's day. She'll think you were here all night."

Web Allen goes out the front and waves to a dim face peering through the curtains in the house across the street and Klamatty opens her Bible.

* * *

"All rise!" Constable Poole bellows and all rise: Strudel in clean bib overalls with a large manila envelope in his fist, his daughter Imogene in a frilly pink dress, Elmer Hooter with his bowtie, Hennessey in smelly bib overalls, Len Steckle the butcher in blood-stained white coveralls, Ev Geisel in levis and a dirty tee-shirt, and two sullen teenage miscreants, Pat (Pud) Cassidy and Karl (Koot) Doerfer, likewise in levis and dirty tee-shirts, all of these litigants hot and sweaty, Justice-of-the-Peace Klamatty's basement courtroom damp and muggy.

Klamatty, nothing under her black judicial robe but a bra and panties and pumps but nobody knows that, her Bible on her desk, bangs her gavel. "First case. That's you, Ev." Ev Geisel, a part-time employee mounting tires at Ford Deal's Ford garage these days, slouches forward. "What is it this time. Constable Poole?"

From left, Trooper Redhardt, Old Jerry Hennessey and his son Billy, Elmer Hooter, Wolfe Strudel and his daughter Imogene, J.J. Doodle.

"Indecent exposure," Constable Poole says. "Ev here was sittin' in his truck park on Main Street in front the hardware noon yesterday, eatin' his lunch, potato chips, and uh well playin' with hisself. With his dingus. In public like. Old Missus Bjork, she seen him out her apartment window. She watch him about twenty minutes, she says, then she call me."

Twenty minutes, Klamatty thinks: I should charge the old biddy with voyeurism. If that's a crime. Window-peeking is. And life is hard for Ev Geisel. Orphaned at six in 1942 when an MSP&P troop train demolished his parents Model A coupe, he wasn't in it, he was taken in by his Uncle Herman Geisel, a carpenter, who regularly beat Ev until they were same size. But the statutes are clear enough on indecent exposure and a man's truck, there are precedents, is not his castle. "Were you, Ev, doing what the Constable says you were doing? On Main Street?"

"No," Ev says. "I got a itch there and I was scratchin' it was all. A rash like. Old biddy think she seen my dingus she must got eyes like one them eagles."

Klamatty considers this defense. It lacks a ring of truth but Uncle Herman will get help and beat Ev again if he's convicted of indecent exposure. "Did you yourself, Constable, see Ev engaging in this alleged act?"

"Not exactly," Constable Poole says. "He was back at work at Deal's, I seen him. I dint exactly apprehend him. I just told him what Missus Bjork said and he give me this story he's got a rash like there and I told him be here this morning."

"Missus Bjork then," Klamatty says. "Is the complainant. And the witness. Where is she?"

"She ain't comin'," Constable Poole says. "She dint want a get involved."

Klamatty bangs her gavel. "Case dismissed. Lack of evidence. Don't do it again, Ev. Get out of here." Ev treats Constable Poole to a sneer and gets out of there. "Next case. That's you, Pat and Karl." Pud and Koot rise from an old pew and slouch forward, sullen but also somewhat scared. "I see you're the arresting officer, Constable. What's the story?"

"I catch these two down the Stockyard," Constable Poole says. "Ten oclock last night. Drinkin' beer. Six-pack Hamns. They ain't either them old enough. I know them. I had my eye on them all summer. Pud here, he ain't but thirteen. Koot, he ain't but twelve. Pud supposed to be in traning too, he's gonna fight in the Golden Gloves over the Falls like he says."

Klamatty turns a fierce judicial scowl on Pud and Koot. "Were you two drinking beer? Both with great reluctance nod. "You know that's against the law, you're not twenty-one?" Two more reluctant nods. "How'd you get a six-pack?"

"We found it," Pud, a practiced liar, says. "Out behind the Muny. I guess somebody must dropped it there. We was owny tastin' it was all. See what beer taste like."

An unlikely story, Klamatty thinks, or two unlikely stories, then ponders. What to do with juvenile delinquents is always a problem. There are two schools of thought. (1) Treat the little bastards with mercy, a little scolding and some good advice, or (2) scare the bejesus out of them.

"You found this six-pack?" Klamatty says. "You're sure somebody didn't buy it for you? I'd like to know who if somebody did." But Pud and Koot, sullen, protecting their source, stick to their story. "Very well. You want to plead guilty then? Guilty to possession of a non-intoxicating malt beverage though not of legal age, a misdemeanor in the State of Minnesota. Say so if you do."

"Well, yah, I guess, gilly then," Pud and Koot mumble.

Klamatty, choosing option (2), bangs her gavel. "Court fines you ten dollars each!" Poor Pud and poor Koot gasp, neither has ever seen $10 in one piece, and Pud whines, "Jeepers, I ain't got ten bucks! Koot neither. I got about a dollar, change."

Klamatty bangs her gavel. "All right. You can't pay your fines, the court is going to sentence you to hard labor. What's the Park look like, Constable?"

"Pretty bad," Constable Poole says. "Volunteer Fire Department had one their training sessions there last night. There's beer cans and crap all over it."

Klamatty bangs her gavel. "Patrick Cassidy. Karl Doerfer. The court sentences you to go clean up the Park. Clean it up good. Constable Poole will be checking on you. And if I ever see either of you in here again, Constable Poole catches you drinking beer or anything else, I will really lower the boom on you! Now get out of here."

Pud and Koot get out as fast as they can through the walkout door. No doubt, Klamatty surmises, they soon will have nasty things to say about her. But they just might, if in fact she scared the living bejesus out of them, wait a week or a month even before, though not yet of legal age, sampling any more non-intoxicating malt liquor. Just to see what it tastes like.

She would not bet on that, however, and Assistant County Attorney J.J. Doodle and Trooper Redhardt are pushing through the walkout door. Doodle in his seersucker is lugging a lawyer's fat briefcase. Trooper Redhardt, in uniform, has a large roll of wrapping paper under his arm.

"Where's the defendant at?" Trooper Redhardt says. "Hossman. We're ready for trial. He's supposed to be here."

"He'll be here," Klamatty says. "He's conferring with counsel. Big calendar today. Court has two more cases before we get to him."

"Oh hell," Doodle says. But he's used to the eternal delays indigenous to courts. "We might as well go have some coffee, Trooper. Okay I leave my briefcase?" Klamatty nods, Doodle leaves his briefcase, Trooper Redhardt clings to his roll of wrapping paper and they go for coffee.

Klamatty bangs her gavel. "Mister Strudel. We come now to the action to replevy brought by Harold E. Hossman, plaintiff, on behalf of the Diptill Music Company, in which you are the named defendant. Are you prepared at this time to surrender the flute and case described in the said action?"

"No, Your Honor," Strudel, rising, says. "We look all over the house but we never find that gotdamn flute. Or case either. Imogene here, she think she might dropped them when that big bast. I mean Hossman, he almost kilt her with his car. Come close anyway. So we look in the ditch. Where she jump so she don't get kilt. But we ain't find the gotdamn flute there neither. Or the case. I don't know where the hell they are, Your Honor."

"That being the situation," Klamatty says. "The court has no choice, Mister Strudel. You bring your checkbook?" Strudel nods. "You write a check then, eighty-nine-dollars-and-ninety-five-cents, payable to the Diptill Music Company. I'll put it in the mail to the Diptill Music Company and that will conclude this action to replevy."

Strudel, voicing no protest, that a considerable surprise, produces a checkbook, spreads in on Klamatty's desk and, though clearly in great distress, slowly writes the aforesaid check and hands it over. There is, Klamatty realizes, something wrong with

Strudel. He looks sort of crestfallen. He's not his usual screaming belligerent aggressive self. Some problem perhaps with his re-election campaign?

Whatever, that is Strudel's problem, not Klamatty's, and she bangs her gavel. "Next case. The dispute regarding ownership of the Spotted Poland China boar that survived the collision. The court is going to decide that today. One way or another. Are either of you, Mister Strudel, come forward, Mister Hennessey, prepared to offer further proof of ownership at this time?"

"I am!" Strudel, perking up, more like his usual truculent self, says. "What I got here." He digs into the manila envelope: what is this, the Academy Awards? "Is that pitcher I mention before. A pitcher my boar up the State Fair, time he should of won a blue ribbon. I find it finally and had it enlarge and finally got that. This morning. Court look it, court is gonna seen it's a pitcher my boar is down the Stockyard." A grainy 8 x 10 photo slides out of the envelope onto Klamatty's desk. "Look that black spot like a football is on his shoulder! Right shoulder. Aint that my boar is down the Stockyard!"

Klamatty and Hennessey study this photo. It depicts a large dirty gray Spotted Poland China boar at rest on its left side in a pen full of trampled straw. And there is a black spot like a football on its visible shoulder.

"What the devil is this?" Klamatty, her finger on a sign at the rear of the pen, says. A sign that says GNIGDUJ ENIWS

"That's a sign," Strudel says. "Says Swine Judg! Oh shit! That goddamn dumb Yeager!"

Hennessey, smarter than he looks, slams the photo with a calloused fist. "You goddamn cheat, Strudel! He got that goddamn pitcher he show us before fixed, Judge! Make it look like my boar! Boar in that pitcher he show us before was point the other way! You ought a trun the goddamn cheat right out a your court!"

Klamatty bangs her gavel "Watch your language. Both of you. But I think you have a point, Mister Hennessey. What's the story here, Mister Strudel?" She picks up her Bible. "Maybe I should swear you in, Mister Strudel. Put you under oath and get the truth."

"No! It's the troot. What I said," Strudel stutters. "I just had it enlarge. That Yeager photo place in Winatchee Falls. That dumb Yeager! He must done it backwards or something. Switch it around. I never notice that goddamn sign when I pick it up this morning. But it's my boar!"

"You switch that pitcher around," Hennessey, triumphant, sensing victory, says. "You think me and the judge here is dumb? You the one is dumb, Strudel! You goddamn dumb cheat."

Klamatty bangs her gavel. "Shut up, Jerry. If I were sure you were trying to pull a fast one on the court, Mister Strudel, I'd hold you in contempt."

"Hold him contempt!" Hennessey says. "He ought a be lock up! Goddamn cheat!"

Klamatty, she is growing extremely tired of these two, bangs her gavel. "The court does not find this photo conclusive, Mister Strudel. Put it in your photo album. Now the court has a suggestion. Mister Steckle our beloved butcher is here as a friend of the court and he is willing to buy the damn pig at whatever price the B&P is paying today. Why don't you two just calm down. Sell Mister Steckle the pig and split the proceeds."

But neither Strudel nor Hennessey finds this solution acceptable. "It's my boar!" Strudel squeals. I ain't gonna give Hennessey half!"

"In a pig's ass it is!" Hennessey, not watching his language, says. "It's my boar! And Steckle here, he awready owe me for them carcasses he swipe was my pigs."

Klamatty bangs her gavel. "Mister Steckle will pay for those carcasses. He's discussed that with the court. But that matter is not before the court at this time. We'll adjudicate that, God help us all, at some later date. The court will now rule in the matter of the boar confined at the Stockyard. This is not a suggestion. This is a ruling. Mister Steckle is going to cut that boar in half and you'll each get a half."

"You can't do that!" Hennessey howls. "It's my boar!"

"My boar!" Strudel howls.

Klamatty bangs her gavel. "The court darn well can do that! It just did. And I'll cite you a precedent. From the Bible. Pilgrim Edition, Oxford University Press. First Kings, Chapter Two, Verses Sixteen through Twenty-Eight. King Solomon, confronted by two women claiming the same baby, said cut the baby in half. And what's good enough for King Solomon is good enough for this court."

"I get the back half then," Strudel says. "Half with the hams. It's my boar!"

Hennessey opens his mouth but Klamatty bangs her gavel. "If I hear 'my boar' one more time I'll hold you both in contempt. The court is not informed as to the manner in which King Solomon proposed to cut the infant in half but Mister Steckle is going to cut the damn pig in half lengthwise."

Imogene Strudel, she's been fidgeting on the old pew for five minutes, interrupts these proceedings. "Pa?" she whines, stands and whispers in Strudel's ear.

"Judge," Strudel says. "Imogene got to go the bathroom. She has trouble, hold her water."

"Go upstairs, Imogene," Klamatty says. "Use mine." Imogene plods up the basement stairs and Klamatty bangs her gavel. "The matter regarding the boar confined at the Stockyard is concluded. Mister Steckle is going to go get it now. Tranquilize it or something and remove it to his butcher shop. You two can go with him if you want to. But don't give him any trouble."

"I got to stick around," Strudel says. "Wait for that trial. That fella almost kilt my Imogene. She's gonna be a witness at it. Let Steckle and Hennessey do it." Strudel's previous truculence has evaporated. He again looks somewhat crestfallen. He stuffs his doctored photo back in its envelope. He's conceded defeat, apparently, or half a defeat, in the matter of the boar.

Billy Hennessey, he's been fidgeting through all of the above, says he wants to go with his Pa and watch Steckle cut the pig in half. He can't, his Pa says, he's got to stay and be a witness, like Imogene, and Steckle and Hennessey depart. Hennessey is still muttering but who cares. Billy, disappointed, sulks and fidgets and Klamatty bangs her gavel. "Court will take a ten minute recess." She has to go to the bathroom and Imogene is plodding down the basement stairs.

"All rise!" Constable Poole bellows when Klamatty returns. All rise: Strudel, Imogene, Billy Hennessey, Web Allen in a dark three-piece lawyer's suit, Hoss Hossman in slacks and a gaudy sports coat, J.J. Doodle in his seersucker, Trooper Redhardt in uniform with his roll of wrapping paper, Horace G. Trudd in ink-stained pants and a baggy white shirt, and a skinny young fellow with thick glasses wearing a wrinkled brown suit and stringy tie.

"Who are you?" Klamatty, aiming her gavel at this young fellow, says.

"Peter P. Hohn," Peter P. Hohn says. "I'm a reporter, the Monitor-Union. I spoke with you yesterday, Your Honor. On the telephone. But then our Outstate Editor decided we should cover Mister Hossman's trial. I guess I'm the right place? Lady over the cafe direct me."

"This is the right place." Klamatty says. She is not thrilled with this scrutiny by the Twin Cities press but can't prevent it. Hohn's story, no doubt, Hossman found not guilty, will hint at a fearful miscarriage of justice. The Monitor-Union, a morning-afternoon combination, is not impressed with Governor Marcus Diptill, Republican though he be. Considers him soft on Welfare, for one thing. It endorsed the former corporate executive plunging into politics Diptill defeated in the '52 primary and that still rankles. Its competition, the Standard & Herald, a dying morning-afternoon, endorsed Diptill. The Monitor-Union often raises questions as to Diptill's leadership qualities on its Editorial page and this muted vendetta often leaks into its news pages. Trudd will roast her too, of course, in the Star & Shopper's garbled version of the events about to unfold. But so it goes, you have a free press. "Are we all ready for trial?" Everybody is ready. "How is your knee, Mister Hossman? How did your surgery go?"

"Mister Hossman," Web Allen, speaking for his client, says. "Got a second opinion. Surgery was not indicated. He still has some pain. But he's ready for trial."

Klamatty bangs her gavel. "Call your first witness, Mister Doodle."

Doodle's first witness is Trooper Redhardt. Sworn in, his hand on Klamatty's Bible and so on, he takes the witness stand, the folding metal chair set up beside Klamatty's desk, and unrolls his wrapping paper and holds it up, revealing a drawing he calls "an accurate depiction the scene of the crime." Proposed County Exhibit One.

"Objection!" Web Allen says. "We are here to determine if in fact there was a crime. There has been no evidence or testimony placing Trooper Redhardt at the alleged scene. His alleged depiction therefore, particularly the path allegedly taken by defendant's motor vehicle, is pure fiction. And highly prejudicial."

Doodle argues, thought not very forcefully. "Please the court, there is no question as to the location of County Road K and Mister Strudel's driveway as depicted. This drawing will assist the court and subsequent witnesses will testify as to the path taken by defendant's motor vehicle."

"Objection!" Web Allen says. "Alleged path."

"Overruled," Klamatty says. Peter P. Hohn and Trudd are busy taking notes. "County Exhibit One is admitted for the purpose of assisting the court. Let's display it."

Constable Poole mounts the drawing on the wall behind Klamatty with thumbtacks and Doodle takes Trooper Redhardt through a laundered version of the way in which Trooper Redhardt learned who the defendant was, that he was wanted for passing a school bus with STOP arm extended and so on and subsequently apprehended the defendant outside the Moon Beam Motel.

"Subsequent to I apprehend the defendant," Trooper Redhardt also testifies. "I locate and I question two witnesses. Colonel Wood, State Patrol Commander, told me I should do that. They both them witnesses tell me the defendant here, his motor vehicle, rip right by the school bus."

"Objection!" Web Allen says. "Hearsay!"

"Sustained," Klamatty says and that, Doodle says, concludes Trooper Redhardt's testimony. "Cross-examine, Mister Allen?"

"Just a question or two," Web Allen, fixing Trooper Redhardt with a fierce disdainful lawyer's look, says. "It's come to my attention, Trooper, you have a nickname. A number of motorists in this Patrol District, I'm told, call you Dog Food. Is that correct?"

"Objection!" Doodle says. "Irrelevant and immaterial!"

"Sustained," Klamatty says, while Trooper Redhardt scowls and grinds his teeth.

"Withdrawn," Web Allen says. "Now let's go back for just a minute, Trooper. When as you testified you were waiting for the defendant at the Moon Beam Hotel, did you at any time in any way tamper with the defendant's motor vehicle?"

"I pull the valve-stems on his tires," Trooper Redhardt, though reluctant, mumbles. "So they went flat and I got a call and had a leave he couldn't of start a flight avoid prosecution."

"Pulled the valve-stems on his tires!" Web Allen, evincing shock, says. "Is that a procedure regularly practiced or recommended or condoned by the State Highway Patrol?"

Trooper Redhardt thinks about that then mumbles, "Might be unner the circumstances. I figure this defendant, crime he commit and all, he prolly be a flight avoid prosecution."

"Whoa! Just a minute!" Web Allen, evincing more shock and dismay, says. "Our purpose here today is to determine whether the defendant committed a crime. The defendant was innocent, presumed to be innocent, when you removed the valve-stems from his tires. I think you are the one, Trooper, who should be facing a charge here today! Malicious mischief."

"Objection!" Doodle says. "Argumentative."

"Sustained."

"And then the big bab. The defendant," Trooper Redhardt says. "He threaten me. He tell me him and the governor, they is brother-in-laws and I better back off or he'll get me transferred the hell-and-gone up the boonies."

"Move to strike," Web Allen says, no court reporter present but a phrase with a nice ring to it. "Irrelevant and immaterial."

"Sustained," Klamatty says. "The court will ignore those remarks."

"Defense moves to dismiss," Web Allen says. "Grounds defendant's Constitutional rights were infringed prior to his arrest." Denied. "No further questions."

Trooper Redhardt steps down (as the saying has it) and glares at Web Allen. Hossman, Klamatty observes, slumped in one the former Lutheran pew, is not so far as she can tell taking much interest in these proceedings. He may of course be bored, awaiting what he takes to be a foregone conclusion. He looks to her though to be vaguely worried.

Whatever, Doodle calls Wade Cummins. Wade's testimony is not very exciting. He only got "a glimpse like" of the suspect motor vehicle in his rear vision mirror. But he corroborates the fact that this vehicle went by the school bus at high speed and says County Road K, the end of the Strudels' long driveway, the location at which he halted the bus "with the STOP arm stuck out" and Imogene jumped (or fell) in the ditch are all "pretty close to like it shows on that picture there."

"Defense has no questions for this witness," Web Allen says: a lawyer's way of saying he finds Wade's testimony beneath contempt. Wade wonders can he go now, the court says he can and he goes, off to his job at the canning factory (where the pea pack is winding down) on his motorcycle.

Doodle calls Imogene Strudel. Strudel propels her out of the old pew and, sworn in, Imogene tells her story. Which, Klamatty surmises, is with a little coaching probably the whole truth and nothing but the truth or as close as they will get to any of that. But it doesn't amount to much. Imogene is extremely nervous, tying her fingers in knots when she's not picking her nose. She's never been a witness before.

"I was jist goin' a cross the road and git on the bus," Imogene, a true daughter of the Midwest fluent in its lingua franca, says. "And this car come and go by the bus goin' like sixty and almost hit me. Would of kilt me prolly. It owny miss me about an inch like. But I jump in the ditch there and I think it was I jump in the ditch I lose my flute and we look and look, me and Wade drives the bus, but we never."

"We won't talk about the flute right now," Doodle says. "Were you frightened, Imogene? When this car almost hit you?"

"Yah," Imogene testifies. "I so scairt I almost pee in my pants and after supper, we had stuff pork chop, I ate six, I frowed up." Whether this elicits the court's sympathy is unclear but it concludes Imogene's direct testimony.

Her cross-examination is brief: Can you tell us what kind of car it was, Imogene? "Pa says it was one them Buick Roadrunners." But that's hearsay, promptly struck. All Imogene actually saw "was it was one them cars with a lot of silver like, that chrome stuff, in the front."

"So, then, Imogene," Web Allen says. "You did not actually see who was driving the car. Not if it went by you going like sixty and you were jumping in the ditch. You don't know who the driver—"

"Yah I do," Imogene says, and aims at Hoss as if it were a six-gun a grubby forefinger. "Him! Pa and the policemen told me it was him." More hearsay, struck. Web Allen has no further questions and Imogene steps down. She has to go to the bathroom again and plods up the basement stairs and Doodle calls Mister William Hennessey.

Klamatty bangs her gavel. "It's getting onto noon. Is Mister Hennessey's testimony likely to be lengthy?" Somewhat, Doodle says, Mister Hennessey is a key witness. "Then the court will take a recess. Everybody go get some lunch. I recommend Bonnie's Café. We will resume at one o'clock."

"I ain't got no money get no lunch," the key witness wails. Doodle says the County will buy Mister Hennessey's lunch. And Imogene's. And Trooper Redhardt's. Imogene's eyes light up. Constable Poole, counting eight lunch customers (nine with Trudd but he's regular at Bonnie's), beams and everybody departs.

* * *

Be a big day at Bonnie's, Klamatty thinks, while dialing the Winatchee Falls Bugle Call on her kitchen phone. Be nice to have lunch with Web Allen but that's not fitting under the circumstances. She gets the Bugle Call and Eddie Devlin, brings him up to date on her decision in the boar case (in time for today's edition) and says she'll call him with her verdict in the Hossman case.

She's preparing her lunch, a tuna salad sandwich and ice tea, when the phone rings. The party calling is Mabel Murphy, old August Schott's secretary since the dawn of time. "Mister Schott," Mabel says, "wants to get in touch with Mister Allen. He has an urgent message for Mister Allen."

Try Bonnie's Café, Klamatty says, gives Mabel the number and is sitting at her kitchen table with her sandwich and tea when Mims McNeely (her cleaning day switched because she had to babysit the new baby while her son Elton took his wife Beth to Winatchee Falls, see her doctor, Beth's having some kind of postpartum trouble) knocks and bangs through the kitchen door accompanied by, surprise! her daughter Little Nell.

"Little Nell," Klamatty says. "What are you doing here? I thought you."

"My Little Nell got fired!" Mims says. "That damn guvner! First thing this morning! No notice or nuthin' hardly. He just up and."

"Let me tell her, Ma," Little Nell says. It's her story. "It really wern't him so much, the guvner. It his goddamn sister! Louella. She's a bitch on wheels, what I mean! The guvner, he give me a hunnert bucks! For a cab and my bus ticket. But let me tell you, Missus Klamatty, that goddamn Louella."

"Nell!" Mims says. "I dint bring you up, swear like that! But you lissen, Missus Klamatty. What Louella done my Little Nell!"

Klamatty sighs. She finds Little Nell's frequent problems with employment of minimal interest. But there's no stopping Little Nell or Mims once they're wound up.

"What happen," Little Nell says. "There was a party last night, the mansion. Or not a party exactly. But around a dozen big wheels, guys give the guvner money so's he can elected again, come over for drinks and dinner and give him money, I guess. Just them. They dint bring their wife or whatever. Only woman there was that bitch Louella. She's allas there times the guvner has people over. She's like a hostess 'cept she don't seat people. Her husband too. Louella's husband. He was there. I think Louella make him come because she don't let him loose much. And some the big wheels was old like him and remember he was a football player once. Harold, his name is. Harold Hossman."

"Harold Hossman!" Klamatty, now that's a familiar name, says.

"Yah. So they was done with dinner, I help serve it, and was sittin' around smokin' cigars and there's a little room next the dining room before you get the kitchen is like a bar. The guvner eats there he's home alone. And I was in there washin' glasses and Louella's husband comes in. He ain't so bad lookin' but he's awful big. He make himself a drink and ask me I want one. I say no on account a I'm on duty and he says well have sip his then. So what the hell. I come out from behind the bar and have a sip his drink and jeezuzz! He start in comin' on a me! Grab me. Grab my butt. Give me a slobbery kiss. Stick his tongue in my mouth. Take it out and say, When a we gonna get it on, baby? Which is when that bitch Louella walk in. All she says me is 'Get your butt back in the kitchen, you little slut.' Which I do but cook was in the pantry so I listen the kitchen door and Louella, she really give it her husband. Harold. Call him a over sex pschopad and a goddamn philanthroper. I d'know what that is. And say when they get home they are gonna have a long talk she been thinkin' about quite a while. Then pretty soon everbody leave and I help cook clean up and go up my room is in the attic and go to bed."

"When were you fired then?" Klamatty, curious now, says.

"Lissen Part Two," Little Nell says. "I jist bring the guvner his breakfast this morning, poach egg, slice toast, coffee, eight o'clock, when that bitch Louella come stormin' in the Mansion. All she says me is 'Get your butt back in the kitchen.' Which I do and I don't listen the kitchen door but I hear her yell anyway. Louella yell. She yell she is fed up and she finally had it with Harold. Her husband. Yell she caught him neckin' with the help. Yell she got reports he is screwin' anything moves down in his territory. Yell his sales last six months been dismal. Yell he lied her. Yell he said he got a order for some high school band uniforms in Winatchee Falls which he dint. Yell he blew that order. Yell she just call the band director down there, got him out from bed. Yell the damn Bailey Company got that order. Yell she a fired Harold awready but he took off early, that trial his. Yell she is gonna divorce from Harold and throw him out the house. Yell she call a lawyer already, Jack Somebody, got him out from bed."

"Jack Sperling, I think," Klamatty says, but Little Nell is not finished.

"Guvner try and talk some sense in her. Don't do nothin' hasty like. Wait'll Harold's trial is over anyway, he says. Harold's not guilty, no smear on his Ministration, the music company. Louella yell she don't give a damn, that trial. You tell Micky, she yell, Get hold the interested parties down there and I hope they hang the big bastard! Micky Seibens, he's a young fella run errands like for the guvner. And one more thing, Louella yell, Fire that little slut was in here with your eggs! That bitch Louella, she's older'n the guvner and I guess she allas boss him around. Or else she think she still in the goddamn Army she was in, givin' orders. Anyway, Louella storm out the Mansion then and I go ask the guvner he wants more coffee and he says he is awful sorry but something come up and he got to let me go and I better go pack. Then he give me a hundred bucks! Because I dint get no notice, he says, and cab fare. So what the hell. I pack my stuff, I dint have that much, and took a bus the bus station and caught the nine-thirty Jefferson and here I am! Surprise Ma and I still got eighty-eight bucks and change. I'm goin' go work at Bonnie's next week. Harriet is there got to get her gallstones out."

"All of which," Klamatty, slowly digesting this sorry tale, says. "Sounds like a clear case of hell hath no fury like." But that rings no bell with Little Nell and Mims says it's time they got busy cleaning Missus Klamatty's house.

* * *

Meanwhile, at Bonnie's Cafe, which smells of burned grease and feels like a sauna, the busy lunch hour is underway. Bonnie's is not air-conditioned. Bonnie runs her old oil furnace in the winter but thinks people should simply endure the weather the Lord sends in the summer. Soaked with sweat, she's bent over the grill behind the counter, shovelling out the food and serving the customers at the counter while her waitress, old Mrs. Bjork's other daughter Harriet, a harried fifty-plus divorcee easily confused, confuses other orders. Constable Poole, at the counter, his lunch on the house, is plowing through the Special, stuffed pork chop with mashed-potatoes-and-gravy, string beans and a side of sauerkraut. Beside him four farmers in town for one reason or another and Clarence Vanderhoeven, the Bank & Trust president, are having pie and coffee and happily goddamning the goddamn federal government's goddamn agricultural policies.

Beside them, Peter P. Hohn, the Monitor-Union reporter, and Horace G. Trudd are munching Bonnie's greasy cheeseburgers served with a pickle and greasy french fries.

J.J. Doodle, Trooper Redhardt, Strudel, Imogene and Billy Hennessey share a table. Web Allen and Hoss grabbed a booth. Doodle, a light eater, has a grilled cheese sandwich and ice tea. Trooper Redhardt and Strudel opted for the hot-roast-beef-sandwich-with-mashed-potatoes-and-gravy. Billy Hennessey, the county paying for it, chose the hot-turkey sandwich and a double chocolate malt and plans to top off with apple pie ala mode. Imogene is halfway through three cheeseburgers with fries and a strawberry malt and is studying the dessert menu.

"That goddamn lawyer, Allen," Trooper Redhardt, gravy dripping down his chin, says. "He got no business, that Dog Food business. What the hell them valve-stems, defendant's Constitutional rights got to do with it anyway? I like and catch Allen, he fail and stop a stop sign or somethin' some day."

"Allen is just doing his job," Doodle says. "He was just trying to upset you, that Dog Food business. Confuse the issue. You know the way lawyers are. I thought your testimony was effective." I also think, (J.J. Doodle does not say) you are a royal pain in the ass, Trooper. You and "Colonel" Ded Wood, darling of the media, and your Crime Scene depiction and the witnesses you dug up. This case is a royal pain in the ass. J.J. Doodle would like to win it of course, get a conviction, his lawyer's pride at stake. But there are rumors: powerful political forces are at work on Hossman's behalf. County Attorney Sheldon Ravitz as much as said win, lose, don't worry about it, let's just get this damn case over with. Still, Doodle will rally his troops: that's the ethical thing to do. "I thought Imogene's testimony was effective too. Considering she's never been in court before. Didn't you think she was a good witness, Mister Strudel?"

Strudel, plowing through his hot-roast-beef, grunts. He seems to be down in the dumps, evincing little interest in the case. He's not once suggested they burn Hossman at the stake.

"And Billy here," Doodle says. "I'm sure you'll be a good witness. You won't let that other lawyer scare you, will you, Billy?"

"Nuh," Billie, slurping up the last of his malt, says. "C'n I have a piece apple pie with ice cream and you pay for it?"

"Absolutely," J.J. Doodle, a big spender with public funds, says. He catches harried Harriet's attention and she says, One blueberry ala mode coming right up.

There's not been much conversation between Web Allen and his client in their booth, both busy sawing at the tough steaks in their steak-sandwiches-on-toast with fries, but Web Allen starts one. "You've been pretty quiet today, Hoss. You're not worried about the case, are you? You understand we have to go through the motions."

"No. Ain't that," Hoss says. "It's more I had a big fight with my wife last night. Not the first one. She been on my case ever since this goddamn school bus thing started. She even wanted I should plead guilty. Get it over with. I told you that. She back off when I told her this Klamatty, way she's in cahoots with that asshole Redhardt, socks it to traffic offenders. Might send me to jail. Not that Louella give a shit about that prolly. Except it give the goddamn music company a bad name. We had a talk then with Marky and she tell him put some clout in. It wasn't that we fight about."

"What? Well, that's not my concern. This school bus thing will soon be over. That will please your wife, I'm sure. She won't have that to worry about or the company's reputation. You can both relax."

"Yeah. Maybe. Oh what the hell. You're my lawyer. I guess I can tell you. What we fight about was there was a dinner the mansion last night, Marky got back form the Governor's Conference. Bunch of big mucky-mucks give him campaign money. Presidents corporations and like that. Guys build roads mostly. Louella always goes those. She's Marky's official hostess like and she makes me go too. Dinner was okay. But then they sit around yapping about Marky's highway program. One he's got in his head. Hunnert-fifty million bucks. Some figger like that. For that interstate thing. I stand it awhile but then I need a drink. There's bar like next the dining room. Nuthin' but the best there. So I went this bar and make myself a drink and there's one the maids there. Washin' glasses. She ain't been the Mansion long. I don't know her name. Thinks it's Belle. Whatever, she's a piece of work! Maybe twenty-five. Built like that brick shithouse guys alIas saying. She ask me she can have a sip my drink? Well, what the hell. I give her a sip and chrissake she start comin on a me! Grab my ass. Gimme a big kiss. Then, goddamn! Don't Louella walk in! She send this Belle or whatever packin'. Back the kitchen. Then call me some unsavory names and says, we get home, me and her are gonna have a long talk. Which we do. Or she talk and I listen. I get a earful this Belle and all them other women she says I'm screwin' I'm on the road and why I ain't sellin' more fuckin high school band uniforms, specially some in Winatchee Falls I guess I told her I sold but dint actually get a order for yet. She finally run down around two a.m. and we go to bed. But we dont sleep together much anymore, me and Louella. Hell, we each got our own bedroom. Why not? That fuckin' house her old man built got eight bedrooms."

"Well, I guess," Web Allen says. "Every marriage has its ups and downs."

"Yeah, I guess. Anyway, I got up five-thirty, Louella still snorin', and got out the house. I had a drive down here, the trial. And Louella, she got a real head a steam going, she like and start right in on me again, she wakes up. I don't need that! Fact is, I am gettin' pretty tired of Louella. And her me, maybe. This about the worse fight we had. But maybe it all blow over, we get this goddamn trial over with. Hell with this alleged steak." Hoss shoves his plate aside and lights a Lucky "Y'know, I could use a drink. We got time for a drink? Up that Muny place."

"No, not now. After the verdict, you're not guilty, we'll have a drink. Celebrate."

Harriet heaves to at their booth. "Somebody says you is Mister Allen. You got a phone call, phone up by the counter there."

Web Allen goes to the phone. Hoss puffs his Lucky. He's grinding the butt into what's left of his steak sandwich when Web returns. "What was that all about?"

"I don't know. It was my boss' secretary. She said he wants to talk to me but he went somewhere for lunch and she doesn't know where. I expect he just wants to check on the progress of the trial. He's been in touch with other parties interested in it. It's time we got back to court."

"It's time we got back to court," Horace Greeley Trudd says. "Keep an eye on the old bitch or she might pull a fast one. Dismiss the case."

"Right," Peter P. Hohn, scooping up the last of his coconut cream pie, says, and makes some rapid calculations: $1.10 for the cheeseburger, 35 cents for the pie, dime for coffee and a dime tip. Comes to $1.65. He'll put "Lunch with news source $4" on his expense account and pocket the difference. Four bucks, he calculates, is the max the old nitpicker in Accounting at the Monitor-Union who approves reporters' expense account will approve. Plus the 8 cents a-mile times 190 miles he'll get for using his own car, a spavined '48 Ford, that figure in the Monitor-Union's Newspaper Guild contract, he'll clear close to a day's pay on this assignment! And the $4 was money well spent (or not spent). Trudd, a prime though perhaps not entirely reliable news source, gave him the lowdown, some deep background.

"The old bitch is the JP," Trudd said. "She'd give her left tit she gets appointed the Village Court judge the governor's supposed and appoint. I bet you a buck, young feller, she finds this Hossman, governor's goddamn brother-in-law, not guilty. Grease the skids. She does, I'll roast her, my Star & Shopper! Bitch made me run one a those goddamn Clarifications once, my Star & Shopper. While ago, but I got a memory like a elephant."

"There's an old guy on our Sports copydesk, him too," Peter P. Hohn says. "He says this Hossman used to be a hell of a football player, the U, way back when."

Trudd evinces no interest in that. He is not a sports fan. His hobby is The History of Hayfield Township, a major work not yet published in which the Trudds are prominently featured he's been writing and rewriting for fifteen years.

J.J. Doodle and Web Allen leave Harriet $1 tips, making her day. All bound for court pay their checks, Bonnie ringing them up on her ancient cash register, wait while Imogene goes to the bathroom, then troop out onto Main Street, Constable Poole leading the way, observed by many with great curiosity. They are after all the principal current attraction Hayfield.

Trailing along behind the others, Peter P. Hohn (six years out of J-School, a year with the Monitor-Union, an ace reporter in his own estimation though he frequently has trouble with names) composes the story he now assumes he'll phone in for the Outstate Edition. It might, he thinks, barring a three-fatality car crash somewhere, lead the Outstate Section, and he pictures it in print:

> By Peter P. Hohn, Monitor Union Reporter
>
> HAYFIELD—Despite overwhelming testimony to the contrary, Harold G. Hossman of St. Paul, Gov. Marcus Diptill's brother-in-law, was found not guilty in Justice Court here today on a charge of passing a school bus with stop arm extended and warning lights flashing.
>
> The charge, a gross misdemeanor, was filed two months ago by State Highway Patrolman Lyman Redhard. He and other witnesses testified that Hossman's vehicle when passing the school bus very nearly struck and injured Emiline Studel, 12, of near Hayfield, the daughter of House District 33B Rep. Rolf Studel.
>
> But veteran Hayfield Justice-of-the-Peace Jean Klementy, hearing the case without a jury and ruling

from the bench, found Hossman not guilty for lack of evidence. Local sources said Klementy has made no secret of the fact she hopes to be appointed judge of the new Village Court that will replace her Justice Court on Aug. 1. Gov. Diptill will make that appointment.

* * *

"All rise!" Constable Poole bellows and, stuffed with sauerkraut, belches. All rise etc. Klamatty would give just about anything for two minutes alone with Web Allen, but that's out of the question under the circumstances. She does ask if his office got in touch with him?

"Yes," Web Allen says. "At Bonnie's. It wasn't important."

Klamatty bangs her gavel. Doodle calls Billy Hennessey and Billy, sworn in, one grubby hand on the Bible, settled in the witness chair, asked by Doodle to "Just tell us what you saw, Billy," no lawyer fella is going to scare Billy, testifies, loud and clear, with a rolling syntax.

"I was sittin' in back the bus with Simmy and Wade drives the bus he stop the bus so's to pick up Fatso, the Strudel kid, and I look out the back window and I seen this car comin' like a bat out a and it come right up behind the bus but then it pull out and go by the bus like a bat out a like it show on that map there I help the cop draw and almost hit Fatso, the Strudel kid, owny she jump in the ditch there or else fall in it and I seen it was a Fifty-Four Buick Roadmaster color they call Desert Dawn and it keep right on goin' like a bat out a and we get the school I tell Wade and old Kammerpuss is the principal what kind car it was and you gonna ast me am I sure what I seen. Yah, I'm sure."

"And did you, Billy" Doodle says. "Subsequently see that Buick Roadmaster again? See it again that same day, I mean?"

"Yah. I seen it to school we went out for recess and it was pullin' out the parking lot and I told Miss Bauer I seen it and she took me old Kammerpuss' office and I told him and I seen the guy was drivin' it out the parking lot too." And, like Imogene, Billy aims a forefinger like a six-shooter at Hoss. "Him."

Hoss scowls at Billy but that doesn't scare Billy, Doodle has no further questions and Web Allen launches his cross.

"You must have pretty good eyesight, Billy. How long was it, do you think, you had that car you say went by the school bus in sight? Two or three seconds? You said it was going like a bat out of. I guess that means it was going pretty fast?"

Billy turns stubborn, sticks his lower lip out. "Yah. Sixty prolly it was goin' but yah I got pretty good eye sight I see with. I know cars pretty good too. I seen a hubcap or else a taillight, Mister, I tell you what kind car it is. Them Fifty-Four Buicks got a backup light built-in like the middle their taillights."

"But did you, Billy, at some later time, discuss all this with Trooper Redhardt here? Talk to the Trooper about it, I mean? Think now. Did Trooper Redhardt ever tell you the car that, it is alleged, went by the school bus was a Fifty-Four Buick Roadmaster?"

"No. Well, yah. The State Cop, he come out our place and we talk about it. But he never tell me what kind car it was. I tell him and you gonna ast me I'm sure. Yah, I'm sure!"

"No more questions." Web Allen has had enough of Billy, why go on with what is essentially a farce anyway and he is growing somewhat weary of the whole business.

In fact, everybody looks to be wearing down. Klamatty's court is marginally cooler than Bonnie's Cafe but nevertheless very hot and muggy. Her black judicial robe is sticking to her back. Doodle's seersucker has lost its faint press. Strudel is sweating like, what else, a pig. Hossman is mopping his brow with a handkerchief. Dark half-moons of underarm sweat stain Trooper Redhart's uniform shirt and Constable Poole's. Imogene's tresses are damp and sticky. Billy Hennessey wipes the sweat from his little face with the tail of his yellow sports shirt, briefly displaying his belly button, and gets out of the witness chair, looking triumphant.

"County rests," Doodle says.

"Defense moves for dismissal," Web Allen says. "Grounds the evidence and testimony before the court, there is in fact virtually no evidence that I can discern, is insufficient to sustain a conviction." And along with everybody else waits, expectantly.

A dramatic moment, Klamatty thinks, and prolongs it, pretending to weigh this and that, then bangs her gavel. "Motion denied. Will the defendant please rise." Hoss stands, slouching, beside Web Allen. "The court finds you guilty as charged, Mister Hossman. Fines you one-hundred dollars and sentences you to ninety days in the County Jail."

The maximum whack for a gross misdemeanor and a brief stunned silence ensues, promptly followed by various reactions. "What the fuck!" Hoss, evincing disbelief, says. Web Allen, evincing shock, shushes Hoss. Trooper Redhardt expresses glee and emits a laugh that sounds like a large dog barking. J.J. Doodle and Wolfe Strudel evince surprise. Peter P. Hohn and Horace G. Trudd, likewise surprised, evince dismay and disappointment. Billy Hennessey though somewhat puzzled grins. And Imogene has to pee again and plods up the basement stairs.

Constable Poole says, "I guess you're done with this pitcher then, Judge," and removes Trooper Redhardt's Crime Scene from the wall.

Web Allen recovers, if not his aplomb, his voice. "Please the court. Defense moves for a stay of sentence pending appeal."

"Denied." Justice-of-the-Peace Klamatty bangs her gavel. "The court will grant Mister Hossman five days in which to pay his fine. But he's going to jail. Trooper, I take it you'll deliver Mister Hossman to the County Jail?" Bang with the gavel. "Court stands adjourned."

"You bet!" Trooper Redhardt chortles. He grabs the handcuffs on his belt, cuffs Hoss, using just the necessary force, and hustles Hoss, despite some profane protests, out the walkout door. Billy Hennessey, Peter P. Hohn and Trudd tag along. Billy never saw anybody in handcuffs in real life, just in some movies, and can't wait to tell his pals what it really looks like.

Peter P. Hohn seeks a quote and gets one but it won't appear in print. "Fuck you!" Hoss says. "Goddamn reporter!"

At which point old Jerry Hennessey arrives in his beat-up pickup in, for him, reasonably high spirits, the boar (Chubby or one without a name as the case may be) cut in half lengthwise and Strudel got half of it, but he has Steckle's check for $291.30 in his pocket. He lets Billy watch Trooper Redhardt, using some unnecessary force, shove Hoss into the backseat of a State Patrol Ford, Hoss the while saying several words Billy knows but if he says his Ma washes his mouth out with soap.

Trudd, disgusted, no story in hand as he sees it, heads for the Star & Shopper. Peter P. Hohn, still seeking quotes, returns to the courtroom but draws a blank. All the comment he gets from the old biddy is the JP and the two lawyers is they have no comment, and Hohn, likewise disgusted, heads for Bonnie's Cafe to phone in his story. Such as it is.

J.J. Doodle, now evincing puzzlement, shakes hands with Web Allen, commiserates briefly with him, the usual post-trial baloney, and departs. But Doodle is not entirely happy. Sure, he got a conviction but County Attorney Ravitz may be less than estatic about that. Good god, the governor's brother-in-law, jailed! What the devil possessed Klamatty? Judges are always hard to read, of course, and there's no way, Doodle decides, you can read Klamatty, The Law West of the Winatchee.

Imogene returns from the bathroom. "Well, I guess, Judge," Wolfe Strudel, likewise puzzled, says. "I guess you surprise me. I mean I thought for sure you. Well, you know. What I heard, I mean." But what Strudel thought or heard or thought he heard remains a mystery and he and Imogene depart, leaving the courtroom to Klamatty and Web Allen.

"I guess I surprised everybody," Klamatty says. "Especially your client Mister Hossman. I suppose you're wondering why."

"I am indeed," Web Allen says. "Unless it's you suddenly developed some kind of death wish? Or momentarily lost all your marbles? Or do you plan to take up some other line of work?"

"Come upstairs, you have a minute," Klamatty says. "We'll have a drink and I'll tell you all about it. Maybe I'm crazy and maybe I'm not. I'd like your opinion anyway, once you have all facts. Assuming they are facts."

They go up into Klamatty's kitchen. She phones Eddie Devlin at the Bugle Call with her verdict in the Hossman case and goes to change, get out of her judicial robe, while Web calls his shop to find out what it was old August wanted. He's just off the phone when Klamatty returns wearing a mumu and asks, "What did old August want?"

"I don't know. Dollar Dobermann called August but August can't remember what Dobermann said. He thinks it was something to do with Hossman but I told him that's moot, our client is on his way to jail. Following a surprising verdict. August said we'll appeal. He also said you must be crazy."

"The jury is still out on that," Klamatty, busy building gin-and-tonics, says. It's early in the day for those but under the circumstances. "Now hear me out. I was having lunch when my cleaning lady, I let her change her day, came. Mims McNeeley. You met her. Her daughter Little Nell was with her. Little Nell used to be a maid at the Governor's Mansion. Now she's unemployed. Abruptly so. You don't know Little Nell but she's what's known locally as hot stuff. A piece of work."

"No, I don't know Little Nell," Web Allen says. "But that's the second time today I've heard her so described. A piece of work. My client Mister Hossman."

"I know all about your client Mister Hossman," Klamatty says. "Shush now and I'll tell you Little Nell's story. Once upon a time in the Governor's Mansion up in St. Paul."

"Essentially," Web Allen, digesting Klamatty's report, says. "Some of that is the story my client Mister Hossman told me, we had lunch. Except it was Little Nell came on to him in his version. But that's irrelevant and immaterial. What you're telling me is, based on some secondhand information from a source I would not consider unimpeachable, you decided to find my client guilty. And socked it to him! You yourself did not speak with Micky Seibens?"

"No. But Little Nell's story had as they say the ring of truth. So I took a chance. A calculated risk. Pleased Louella, I hope. The power behind the throne. Besides, your client, you say, corroborated these events."

"Only Part One, more or less. I expect he'll find Part Two if true another nasty surprise. Like your verdict. I'm beginning to feel sorry for Mister Hossman."

"I'm not. For the record, I found Billy Hennessey's testimony impressive. Just about conclusive. Whatever else comes out of this damn case, if anything, I think justice was served. West of the Winatchee."

"Pending appeal. But forget Mister Hossman. What is Mister Marky the governor going to do now, Jane? Assuming you pleased him. Or pleased Louella."

"Who knows? Whatever, I'll soon know. Ten days, there'll be a Village Court here. With a Village Court judge, whomsoever that may be. You want another drink?"

"No," Web Allen says. He has to get going and he won't be around for a while. He'll be in Wyville, Wisconsin, and elsewhere, deposing the crew aboard the Omaha Flyer the day it hit Rahilly's truck and some of the passengers aboard that Schott & Schott is representing in personal injury suits against the MSP&P, which, a further complication, is seeking a change of venue to Worthington in far southwestern Minnesota, a city in which juries historically have been soft on railroads. Then he's going to Montana for two weeks to visit his daughter and her husband the National Park Service Ranger, now stationed in Glacier Park, this arranged with old August before he joined Schott & Schott.

"I'll miss you," Klamatty says.

"I'll miss you too," Web Allen. "You hear from the governor, you let Mabel Murphy know. She'll know where I am and let me know."

* * *

Eddie Devlin at just after 2:30 p.m. in the Bugle Call newsroom, leaving to others the daily check for gross errors etc., is reading a portion of his contribution to the day's news, which happens to be the lede story on the Regional News page:

> **Solomon-Like Decision Settles Pig Case**
> By Edward T. Devlin, Bugle Call Reporter
> Hayfield Justice-of-the-Peace Jane Klamatty, handing down a decision worthy of King Solomon himself, brought to a conclusion today a case involving the ownership of a prize 800-pound Spotted Poland China boar that had been before her court for more than two months.
> Ruling from the bench in her Hayfield courtroom, Justice-of-the-Peace Klamatty ordered the boar cut in half lengthwise by Hayfield butcher Lem Steckel, who then paid the two men both claiming ownership for each of their halves.
> The two are Gerald Hennessey, a Hayfield area farmer, and District 33B State Rep. Wolfe Strudel, who also farms in the area.
> Justice-of-the-Peace Klamatty also cited a precedent for her unusual ruling. It was the story of wise King Solomon when he was confronted by two slave women both of whom contended a baby boy was their infant. King Solomon ruled the baby should be cut in half and the two women then agreed to joint custody.
> The boar in the case before Justice-of-the-Peace Klamatty survived the collision between the MSP&P's

Omaha Flyer passenger train and a livestock truck in Hayfield in mid-May. It was captured after the collision and confined in the Hayfield Stockyard pending Justice-of-the-Peace Klamatty's ruling regarding its ownership.

Justice-of-the-Peace Klamatty told the Bugle Call both Hennessey and Strudel subsequently offered some proof of ownership, but she did not find those proofs to be conclusive. The price paid for the boar's two halves was based on the price the B&P Meat Packing Co. in Fairbow was paying today for similar swine.

In another case dating to mid-May, Justice-of-the-Peace Klamatty found Harold E. Hossman of St. Paul guilty on a charge of passing a school bus with stop arm extended, fined him $100 and sentenced him to 90 days in the Winatchee County Jail.

That last graph barely made the paper. The July 21 edition was on the press, in fact, when Eddie took Klamatty's phone call and told Cadence Snorkel, "Holy smoke! The JP there in Hayfield, Jane Klamatty, found that guy is the governor's brother-in-law guilty on that school bus thing and gave him ninety days!"

Snorkel, exhibiting some Fearless Journalism, promptly issued a rare Stop the Press order and told Eddie, "Tack that on the end that pig story, don't make a big thing out of it." But no one can ever say now the Bugle Call ducked that story because Harold E. Hossman, though not so identified, was Governor Diptill's brother-in-law. Harold E. Hossman's name was right there in the newspaper for all to see.

His reading completed, Eddie heads for home, a new "ranch" house in Haber's First Subdivision across the Winatchee River from the Municipal Gold Course, and a probable matinee with Evylee. Now she's a married woman, committing no sin when fornicating, Evylee is proving to be a tiger in bed when the time is ripe. Or not ripe. That is determined by the Rhythm Method reluctantly approved by the True Church. Evylee discreetly keeps track of her menstrual periods, noting her "safe days" with an X on her desk calendar and today is one of those days. Evylee's not interested in motherhood, though both the potential grandmothers and her old man, T.J. (Slippery) Hanrahan, if Eddie reads the signs correctly, are hoping.

Evylee's and Eddie's wedding went off well. They exchanged thin gold rings and both made the usual promises. The post-nuptial reception at the Winatchee Falls Golf & Country Club also was a big a success, several people pushed or tossed into the club swimming pool. It was followed by a dinner, just for the immediate families. Eddie's parents did not embarrass him and he feels a little guilty now for thinking they might. They don't have much money but Ceil after all is a past-president of The Friends of the Public Library and still active in that organization, and Hack Devlin and T.J. Hanrahan found common ground in their contempt for the funny little cars, the Volkswagen Beetle one of them, those nations the U.S.A. soundly defeated in World War II are trying to sell in the U.S.A. now. T.J. Hanrahan's take on that is "the goddamn krauts are pretty good engineers but the Japs don't know shit about building cars and even if they did Americans, they like big cars, they'll will never buy those goddamn kiddy cars!" Then Evylee and Eddie drove off in their new (used) Pontiac with a "Just Married" sign and tin cans tied to the rear bumper, bound for historic Mackinac Island and a week-long honeymoon. Which, it turned out, Evylee planning ahead, was a "safe time."

Eddie is rather enjoying married life, smokes a cigar now with Slippery and listens to Slippery goddamn the goddamn government following their Friday night command performance dinners with the Hanrahans. And it's all but certain now, Snorkel's as much as said so, Eddie will be the Bugle Call Sports Editor when Art Kealey retires August 31.

* * *

Meanwhile, at the Monitor-Union up in St. Paul, Peter P. Hohn's collect phone call from Bonnie's Café ("Shit! The old bag's the JP found Hossman guilty and gave him ninety days!") is producing consternation and dismay and the Outstate Editor is conferring with the Managing Editor, the Executive Editor and the Publisher.

All four naturally are disappointed with this guilty verdict and, worse, confronted with this verdict, unable to think of a way in which to include in the story a line or two suggesting "Gov. Marcus Diptill's possible use of undue influence in the case." One solution to this dilemma offered by the Outstate Editor is "let's just forget the whole thing." The Hossman business after all is or was just another outstate traffic case, a minor blip in the day's news, and there's a pretty good pipeline spill in Goodhue County much higher on the outstate disaster scale.

But the Monitor-Union, the Publisher notes with some agony, has "fifteen goddamn dollars!" invested in the Hossman story: Hohn's likely expenses what with the way reporters eat when they're sticking the paper with the tab and his goddamn mileage and all. This is a considerable sum in the Publisher's opinion and it'll be $15 down the tube if they don't do something with the goddamn story.

The Executive Editor, paid to make major news decisions, finally makes a major news decision. The Monitor will run the goddamn Hossman story in both its morning editions, Outstate and City, and run it by god on page one! That at any rate will embarrass Soft on Welfare Diptill. The notes the Oustate Editor took when talking to Peter P. Hohn are turned over (copy to kum) to the Monitor's ace copy editor, Tiger Peterson, who presently comes up with a pretty good hed: **Gov's Kin Guilty in Near-Fatal School Bus Case**

So all is not lost. But the Outstate Editor, a weary old-timer counting the days to his retirement, will think twice before sending another reporter somewhere for a maybe story at a cost of $15!

* * *

Late this same afternoon, old August Schott, bent over his desk in his big corner office in the First National Bank building, shuffling legal documents having to do with an estate, pauses in his work. "Mabel? Was I supposed to call Dobermann?"

"No, Mister Schott," Mabel Murphy, busy typing seventy words a minute with no errors in her tiny adjoining office, says. "He called you."

"Oh? What did he want?"

"I don't know, Mister Schott. I did not listen."

"Mmmm. Well, I guess it was important, he'll call again." Old August goes back to shuffling his documents and Mabel sadly goes on with her typing.

How much longer, Mabel wonders, before poor dear Augie forgets his name and they take him away and put him in a home somewhere? Not much longer, she fears. When they do, she'll retire. She is after all sixty-four and she'll not work for young Mister Birdshot Schott, nine years her junior. Birdshot Schott is nowhere near the man his father is or was. And she'll be all right for money. She'll have her Social Security and a miniscule pension and the older North Broadway house already cut up into four apartments with parking space behind it dear Augie advised her to buy thirty-two years ago with a 30-year mortgage, her first Christmas bonus the down payment. It cost $4400 but it had, dear Augie said, "location." It's worth four times that now and it's paid for, free and clear. She lives in one unit, never has trouble renting the other three. She'll go on living there with her old cat for company. But oh god, she'll miss the old goat! Poor dear Augie!

Mabel Murphy, then twenty-five and a virgin, fell hopelessly in love with August Wendell Schott, head-over-heels as the saying goes, the day he hired her and she became his legal secretary. August was forty-five, just back from his war. Nothing came of that for three years. Then August took Mabel with him to Winona, where he was deposing witnesses in a personal injury suit triggered when a steam threshing engine exploded. They were there three days and Mabel, afterwards, no longer a virgin, was beset by her Irish Catholic conscience. Sleeping with a married man! Committing adultery! Confess that to Father O'Herlihy, the Holy Redeemer pastor! Not on your tintype! Poor Mabel skipped her next regular confession and the next one and two months later dear Augie took her to Mankato, where he was trying a case she no longer remembers except it lasted a glorious week. Thereafter, Mabel no longer went to confession or took communion, though going to Mass every Sunday and the Holy Day of Obligation, always dropping 50 cents and later $1 and in recent years $5 in the collection plate. Buying her way into heaven perhaps.

Dear Augie's wife, Elaine, no fool, soon put a stop to these pleasant legal junkets and, this pretty clear in retrospect, evidently flayed dear Augie to a fare-the-well. Dear Augie at any rate subsequently said Mabel and he must keep their "friendship" very discreet.

No matter. Poor Mabel was smitten, a hopeless case, prepared to out wait, outlast, Elaine. Which she did, as of mid-June, Elaine at everlasting rest now at the top of the slope in Dobermann Enterprises' new Everlasting Rest Gardens. Over the years Mabel also discreetly blew dear Augie now and then in the privacy of his office, the door locked and the blinds pulled, dear Augie for office consumption said to be concentrating on a difficult case. But dear Augie is long past that now and, unfortunately, often forgets Elaine is dead. His and Mabel's "friendship" remains discreet. He won't visit her four-plex. They sometimes share in his office a strange bring-in lunch from Wong's Chinese Dragon, dear Augie's developed a taste for Chinese, but that's about it.

There has been no sound from dear Augie's office for some minutes. Mabel investigates and finds August Wendell asleep in his chair. Breathing though, with a faint pulse. Mabel gently removes his spectacles. She'll wake him at 5 o'clock and Birdshot will drive him home to the big empty house on West College Street he insists on living in still. The live-in housekeeper will fix him a TV dinner and, Mabel's had reports from the housekepeer, he'll drop off to sleep again in his lounger in the early innings of a baseball game on the TV or whatever is on the TV. But wake up eventually and go to bed. While Mabel communes with her cat.

Her life's been a Gothic tale, Mabel Murphy, back at her typewriter, thinks. Grotesque. Many no doubt would think her incredibly stupid, some no doubt do, devoting her life to August Wendell Schott, taking other men into her bed at rare intervals when her libido threatened to explode but rejecting all the serious suitors and there were a few. But all those Christmas bonuses put her nephew Jerome Kennedy through the Pretzell Brothers' Midwest Chiropractic College in Winatchee Falls. Jerome is a muscle doctor with minor administrative duties now at the Pretzell Chiropractic Clinic that runs the College, married, seems grateful, always has Mabel over for Thanksgiving and Christmas, etc. And it's the life she chose and would choose again and she sometimes hopes she won't be among the living when at last poor dear Augie is laid to rest beside Elaine in Everlasting Rest Gardens. Be too much for her, Mabel fears.

* * *

No such fear assails Harold E. (Hoss) Hossman. There are several people he'd plant with great pleasure. Slumped on the thin stained mattress on the bottom half of an iron bunkbed in his 6 x 6 foot cell in the ancient stone Winatchee County Jail, sweating like a pig (the old stone walls soak up the heat and the cell feels like a clammy oven), Hoss ticks them off: Louella, Trooper Redhardt that asshole, the old bitch who put him in the slammer, the smartass kid with the 20/20 vision. He's not worked out the details yet, but some day by god he'll get even with all of them! And he has, at any rate, look at the bright side, a "private room wit a bat and a view."

That was the lousy joke offered by the old duffer in a baggy uniform, not armed, Hoss takes to be the jailor, when he led Hoss into the cellblock and up a spiral iron staircase to the second level. "Gonna give yer a private room wit a bat and a view, har-har!"

The bat is a stained smelly toilet with no seat and a small rusty sink with a cold water tap. The bunkbeds have thin salvaged Army blankets and hard gray pillows. The view through the narrow barred window high on the stone wall consists of the cupola on the old red brick Winatchee County Courthouse adjacent to the slammer. And all the clowns in the slammer have private rooms wit bats. There are about a dozen clowns, near as Hoss can figure, in the twenty cells on the two levels connected by the spiral staircase, five either side of a narrow passageway. They are like the cages in a goddamn zoo: inch-thick floor-to-ceiling steel bars four inches apart on three sides with a door with a big iron lock opening to the passageway. They have concrete floors and a forty-watt bulb protected by heavy-gauge wire in the ceiling. "Lights out is nine o'clock," the jailor said. One additional lower level cell enclosed in concrete has a solid iron door with a judas flap. "We puts the troublemakers in that one," the jailor said. 'Yer knows yer gits time off yer ninety yer good behavior? Yer gits to go sit on the Courthouse lawn and smoke too, hour a day the weather's good, yer good behavior." There's a shower stall beside the solitary cell. "Yer gits a cold shower ever week," the jailor said.

The lower-level cells are behind the Sheriff's Department, two offices in one of which Hoss was "processed in" when delivered by Trooper Redhardt, relieved of his personal possessions and clothes except his shoes, socks and underwear and issued grimy white coveralls too short and tight in the crotch wth JAIL in big black leters between his shoulder blades. The upper-level cells are behind the apartment the jailor said "goes with the sheriff job, he's my cousin."

The jailor appears with a scrawny guy in his twenties in tow, locks him in the cell next to Hoss and disappears down the spiral staircase.

"Hi ya, fella," this guy says. "You just come in? I been out sittin' on the goddamn grass on account I been on good behavior. What yawl name? Mine Sam Hutch. Or yawl can call me the Ding Dong Man. That's everbody the carnival call me. What yawl in foh?"

"Hoss Hossman," Hoss says. The Ding Dong Man evinces no flicker of recognition. "Ninety fuckin days. Old bitch she's the JP in a one-horse burg they call Hayfield found me guilty, passing a school bus with its goddamn STOP arm stickin' out."

"Hey, me too! That old bitch, I mean. Ninety days. All I done was give a little gal I figgered was old enough a little treat. Turn out she was jail bait, this part the country. We prolly lucky that old bitch cain't give nobody life. Widout parole."

Hoss and the Ding Dong Man shake hands through the bars between their cells and Hoss wonders, "What's the food like here?"

"Shee-it!" the Ding Dong Man says. "Sheriff's wife, she fix the food wit dough the county give her. But the bitch owny spend about half it, feed us. One thing yawl gonna do here, pal, yawl gonna lost a few pounds."

Hoss soon finds this to be true. The meal on a beat-up metal tray the jailor pushes through the cell door at 5 p.m. (which Hoss eats with a spoon, knives and forks considered risky) consists of a thin slice of meat he can not identify, a miniscule blob of soggy gray mashed potatoes, a spatter of gravy out of a can, slice of Wonder Bread, not fresh, no butter, a watery dab of pudding he can not identify and half a tin cup of coffee, black, brewed in the distant pass.

"What I tell yawl?" the Ding Dong Man says. "Yawl got any dough though, yawl personal possessions, yawl give the old grifter's the jailor a buck, he keeps two-bits but he git you some candy bars. Say, pal, there's a magazine unner the mattress there, yawl bunk. Guy before you left it. There's pitchers naked wimmin in it. Yawl don't want it, lemme have it." Hoss finds this literature and hands it through the bars. "I look the pitchers, lights go out, I beat off."

The Ding Dong Man retires to his bunk with the magazine and Hoss, pulling at the tight crotch on his coveralls, flops on his. Ninety days, or eighty-nine if they count this one, is beginning to look like a very long time.

Hoss and the Ding Dong Man, rewarded for Good Beahavior, get to sit on the Courthouse lawn.

Escape then, when with good behavior he gets to sit on the Courthouse lawn? The idea flickers briefly in Hoss' brain. But he'd have no shoes, no money, no ID. He'd get about a block in his goddamn dirty white coveralls with JAIL on the back. The Winatchee County Jail despite its antiquity is a high security penal institution. And the lawyer, Allen, said he'd appeal. But a fat lot of good that will do! Hoss though no legal scholar knows appeals wander around for months in the legal jungle.

Stretched on his bunk, soaked with sweat, Hoss watches two bedbugs crawl out from under his mattress and up the bunk's frame. So that's where they hide in the daytime.

6.

Eddie Devlin is not a Biblical scholar. The reference in his pig story to wise King Solomon and the two women both claiming the same infant was not entirely accurate. Half a dozen local Bible-thumpers promptly latch onto that and write Letters to the Editor. The two women, they all note, were not slaves, they were "harlots." Several judge Eddie to be "a hedonist who would do well to study his Scriptures" and the Bugle Call with great reluctance eventually (today, Saturday, July 28) runs buried deep amid the Church News on the page preceding the Classifiedes a goddamn:

> **Clarification**
> A recent reference in these pages to the story of King Solomon and the two women both claiming the same infant was not entirely accurate. When Solomon ordered the infant cut in half, one of the women said the other might have it and Solomon judged her to be the true mother. The women did not agree to joint custody. The Bugle Call regrets this error.

This of course upsets Cadence Snorkel II, who likes to think despite overwhelming evidence to the contrary that the Bugle Call is infallible, and once the papers hot off the press are checked for other gross errors etc., he speaks harshly to Eddie. Eddie's defense is he was writing on deadline, had no time to check it out in the Bible and there is no Bible anyway in the Bugle Call library. In fact, this library consists of an out-of-date Winatchee Falls City Directory, a 1950 Rand-McNally Road Atlas, a 1954 Legislative Manual listing state officers and elected officials (District 33B State Rep. Wolfe Strudel among them), a year-old Winatchee Falls High School yearbook and a couple of drawers in a tall green metal filing cabinet full of Bugle Call clippings stuffed in manila folders. Pearl Mulch the Society Editor is the librarian in her spare time and only Pearl can find anything among the clippings. Her filing system is one she devised herself. Aviation news, for example, is in a folder labeled "Dangerous Occupations."

Snorkel grudgingly accepts Eddie's explanation, tells Pearl go buy a Bible after work and issues an edict. Bugle Call reporters from now on if moved to include Biblical reference in their stories better "look it up in the Bible first and by god get it right!"

Eddie feels bad about the King Solomon business. Not a lot but some. He also likes to think despite evidence to the contrary that his reporting is infallible. And he still is in line to become the Sports Editor (a field with scant need for Biblical references) when Art Kealey after thirty-five years on the local sports scene retires August 31 to devote full time to Kealey's Soft Water Service. Snorkel once the Bible business was out of the way confirmed that and told Eddie he should (on his own time) get acquainted with the coaches in the circulation area in the weeks ahead. By phone. Just give them a ring so they will know who he is and that Art is retiring. Eddie already knows some of these coaches, more or less, the ones at Winatchee Falls High, Holy Redeemer High and Winatchee Falls Junior College. But there are forty or fifty other coaches in the twenty-odd small towns in the circulation area he doesn't know. Yet. Art knows them. Art in thirty-five years followed some of those coaches from the time they were playing Pee Wee football through high school and college and into teaching and the coaching profession.

There will be a party for Art, drinks and snacks in the composing room after the paper comes out on the 31st. The big question is will Snorkel in view of Art's long years of faithful upbeat service (when the Winatchee Falls football Tigers took a 42-3 pasting at the hands of the Fairbow Packers, Art found a silver lining in the 22-yard field goal) give Art a check at this party, a retirement present? The betting in the newsroom and the composing room is 2 to 1 Snorkel will not.

Whatever, Eddie thinks, they and Art will soon know and he might as well (Evylee is spending the afternoon with two former high school girlfriends back in town) start phoning a few coaches. But where to start? School is out. He'll have to phone them at home. Get their numbers from Information. Art has all those numbers somewhere but Eddie doesn't know where and Art left an hour ago. But there is another way. He'll call Jane Klamatty. Time he spoke with the old girl again anyway. She'll tell him who the Hayfield football and basketball coaches are or it might be the same guy and give him their or his home phone numbers or number. Be a start anyway on this project.

Eddie phones J. Klamatty, a 15-cent call because Hayfield has an independent telephone company, Gopher Telephone Inc., but no one answers.

* * *

No one answers because J. Klamatty is making her daily visit to the Hayfield Post Office, a small red brick federal building behind the old MSP&P Depot with parking behind it for the Rural Route carriers, of whom there are two. Cedric Klamatty when alive was one of them.

"Quite a storm we had last night," Merlie Burdick the Postmistress, forty-something, speaking through the barred hole in the racked mailboxes that divide the Post Office, nobody else present, says. "Heard it blew a shed down at Jerry Hennesseys." Merlie's got a finger on the local news, gets it from people visiting the Post Office. Her husband Stanton is paralyzed, the waist down, he fell from a windmill he was wiring, but Merlie is always pretty cheerful, considering.

"Hope Jerry has insurance," Klamatty says, and rather envies Millie her cheerful take on life, despite. In less than seventy-two-hours, Klamatty's Justice Court will cease to exist and there's been no word of any sort, not a peep, from Governor Diptill. She half suspects Elmer Hooter got the appointment and is sitting on it, waiting for August 1 while Horace G. Trudd prepares a major announcement in the Star & Shopper. She opens her mailbox and empties it: a seed catalog, a plea from an insurance firm offering Big Savings, her Gopher Telephone bill and a legal size envelope, the return address the Great Seal of the Great State of Minnesota and Office of the Governor. Klamatty rips it open.

Office of the Governor
July 25, 1956

My Dear Mrs. J. Klamatty:

It is with great pleasure that I herewith under the authority granted me in Senate Bill 808/56 appoint you effective this date the Presiding Judge of the Village Court in and for the Village of Hayfield, said appointment to remain in effect pending the November 6 Village Election in the Village of Hayfield.

Sincerely
Marcus B. Diptill, Governor

7.

At breakfast this bright sunny morning (Tuesday, September 4, the day after Labor Day, the day school starts) Imogene (Apple) Strudel, slumped at the Strudel's kitchen table in a new pink school dress and pink bobbie socks and new penny loafers, slowly but steadily, while her mother Annie packs her a good substantial lunch, plows through a large glass of orange juice (from concentrate), two tall glasses of 100% fat milk, four big pancakes slathered with butter and Aunt Jemima syrup, six little link sausages, four more pancakes afloat in cream and brown sugar and three Twinkies.

"Hurry up, Apple!" Annie says, while Apple hunts down some Twinkie crumbs. "Or you'll miss the bus! You don't want to miss the bus, first day of school and you're in the Eighth Grade! Your Pa can't take you today. He left awready for his campaign. See Mister Dobermann and talk the Four-H leaders, their Leadership Conference. You got all your stuff together?"

"Mmmm," Apple says. There is a new notebook, pencils, ruler, protractor etc. in a new school bag under her chair. Apple's summer school proved a success. She got a D in Remedial Math and on the strength of that and because Miss Ardis Melrose did not want her for another year was promoted or propelled into the Eighth Grade, where Essie Pemberton will have her.

All the Twinkie crumbs caught and consumed and pushed along by Annie, who tells her "Do good in school now," Apple reluctantly leaves the table, collects her school bag, a new red plastic jacket and her lunchbucket, slouches out of the kitchen and plods down the Strudels' long driveway.

The driveway is full of puddles. A late summer thunderstorm, thunder and lightening and four inches of rain accompanied by scattered hail the size of golf balls and damaging winds, thundered through the Hayfield area in the night. The school bus is rolling down Hennessey Hill. It halts opposite the driveway with STOP arm extended and warning lights flashing and the driver honks the horn. Apple speeds up, marginally, halts at the end of the driveway and looks both ways along County Road K, the time that car went by the bus and almost killed her still a fairly fresh memory. The ditch the driveway crosses is full of swift-running muddy water. The horn honks again. Apple crosses K and gets into the bus, where she finds Billy Hennessey and Elroy Simmons in a front seat. "H'ya, Fatso," Billy says. Apple whacks him with her lunchbucket.

"Cut that out!" Wade Cummins says. "Both you! Billy, shut up!" And thinks: Jeezuzz, nine more months of this! Wade thought he had a part-time job racking balls at the Empress poolhall in Winatchee Falls but a jerk related to the Empress' manager got that job. So Wade, he'll be a sophomore starring in Creative Writing II at Winatchee Falls Junior College when it opens next week, is back driving the goddamn school bus and enforcing a new rule laid down by the Consolidated School's Director of Transportation. Billy Hennessey, Elroy Simmons and other troublemakers have to sit in the front seats now, where they can't smoke and burn more holes in the rear seats.

Wade sighs, retracts the STOP arm and starts the bus. At least, though, he'll soon be back at work on his novel with 200 pages to go, which he may now offer publishers as non-fiction. The working title is "Why I Hate Kids: The Memoirs of a School Bus Driver."

"Yah, that thunnerstorm last night," Billy Hennessey says. "It blow down our old machine shed and a big tree behind our house and hail beat the shit out some our corn." Billy has been describing the damage the thunderstorm wrought at the Hennessey farm since he got on the bus. Elroy finds this boring but a welcome change. He is sick and tired of Billy's "I seen the state cop handcuff the guy almost kilt Fatso" story.

* * *

District 33B State Rep. Wolfe Strudel, wearing the new $37.95 green pinstripe suit and bright green tie he bought a week ago off the rack at Sears' big End of Summer Suit Sale with a portion of the $591.30 Len Steckle finally paid him for half the boar Hennessey swiped and half the carcasses Steckle salvaged following the great collision, is sitting in old Dollar Dobermann's big office off the Dobermann Hotel mezzanine while old Dobermann, scrunched over his big desk, studies some kind of document.

"Storm last night hit your place?" old Dobermann, scrawling his signature on this document, leaning back in his big leather chair and lighting a big cigar, says.

"Not much," Strudel says. "Tree limbs down is all. Some hail damage but I got hail insurance. Blew Jerry Hennessey's machine shed all to hell though. Serve the bastard right, he swipe my prize boar."

"How's your campaign going?" Dobermann does not now, nor ever did, give a damn about the famous boar case. "How are you fixed for campaign funds?"

"Pretty good. I got about six-hunnert in my war chest." Strudel, old Dobermann notes, in his years up at the Legislature has picked up some political jargon and a thin, very thin, veneer of sophistication. "I'm gonna talk the Four-H leaders, their Leadership Conference over the Armory, eleven o'clock."

"Don't spend that money now," old Dobermann says. "Save it for the general election. Doubt you'll have any trouble though, get re-elected. Not with Starbuck's the goddamn DFL candidate."

The primary election will be September 10, but Strudel has no primary opposition and it's Winatchee Falls insurance man

Wilbur Starbuck's turn again to be the DFL's sacrificial lamb in the November general election.

"I won't," Strudel says. "I might not even spend it then. I just figger on put some posters up. Talk some places. Outline my program I'm back the Legislature. Hold the line, spending. Cut taxes. Cut the state gas tax. For farmers anyway. Farmers got gasoline tractors."

"Matter fact," old Dobermann, getting down to business, says. "The state gasoline tax is one of the things I want to talk to you about. Reason I asked you come and see me. Are you familiar with this nationwide interstate highway program Eisenhower got through Congress?

'Well, yah," Strudel says. "I mean I read about it some in the newspaper."

"That is a program that is going to change the nation," old Dobermann says. "And Governor Diptill is behind it one-hundred percent. My information, he is going to ask the Legislature for an appropriation, next session, with which to match the federal funding Eisenhower got out of Congress. So we, Minnesota, can build some interstate highways. That probably will be a billion dollar program, time it's finished. Initially though, my information, Diptill is going to ask for two-hundred million. When he does, Strudel, you vote for that. Vote Aye. You understand what I'm saying?"

"Yah. But jeezuzz, Mister Dobermann! Billion bucks! Two-hunnert million even! State ain't got that kind of money, Mister Dobermann. How?"

"My information, Diptill is going to ask the Legislature for a three-cents-a-gallon bump in the state gasoline tax. When he does, Strudel, you vote for that too. Vote Aye. Do our great state and the governor a favor. Two favors. You understand what I'm saying?"

"Yah. Well, sure, Mister Dobermann, you say so. But I awready done the governor a favor. I mean I was ready do him a favor. Not make no fuss like you ask me, that goddamn Klamatty woman went and find his goddamn brother-in-law almost kilt my Imogene not guilty, that school bus thing. But she dint."

"That plan changed," old Dobermann says. "I don't know the particulars. All Micky Seibens, he's one of Diptill's aides, said when he phoned me was let justice be done and the brother-in-law deserved anything he got. I don't know how Klamatty got wind of that. Unless old August Schott, rest his soul, got word to her. I spoke with him after Seibens called me. But that's all over and done with. Ancient history. Those interstate highways, Strudel, are going to be the Transportation System of the Future. So you vote Aye like I just told you. Do not stand in the way of progress. Good luck with the Four-H leaders."

That's a dismissal and Strudel, dismissed, departs and on his way to the Armory revises the talk he'll give the 4H leaders and later on other groups. He won't mention the state gas tax but he'll praise the proposed nationwide interstate highway program, the Transportation System of the Future. Might as well (more political jargon) jump on that bandwagon.

Old Dobermann, at rest for the moment in his big leather chair, puffing his big cigar, pictures the Transportation System of the Future. Broad ribbons of concrete, four lanes divided with no grade level intersections, rolling across the nation, up hill and down dale, leaping rivers on long concrete bridges, tunneling through mountains, slashing through the nation's cities, connecting the forty-eight state capitals, one big semi rig after another pounding over them, the concrete soon bumpy as a washboard. Eisenhower, bless him, sat up in his bed at Walter Reed Army Hospital following abdominal surgery and signed into law the bill launching this system, funded at $25 billion a year for twelve years.

The future, old Dobermann reckons, lies with trucking and the ready-mix concrete industries and he's just about ready to make on behalf of Dobermann Enterprises a low offer for the J.P. Rahilly Trucking Co.

It's not much of a trucking company at the moment, one beat-up tractor, the one trailer it had smashed when hit by that train and never replaced, and it's involved in litigation with the MSP&P and he detests J.P. (Whip) Rahilly, a goddamn union business agent besides he is (or was) in the trucking business. But personal animosities fade in the face of what Dollar Dobermann considers a sound investment. He gets his hands on Rahilly's just about defunct trucking firm and its ICC permits, but nothing to do with the pending litigation included, Dobermann Enterprises will be in the trucking business. And out of the railroad business. The railroads are dying, in old Dobermann's considered opinion, and he's slowly divesting Dobermann Enterprises' MSP&P stock. And once those interstates are built and Dobermann Enterprises has a fleet of Peterbilts and Freightliners, well, the sky will be the limit.

Old Dollar Dobermann, though not much given to dreaming, dreams.

There might even be a place in the trucking business for the boy. The boy does not seem to be making a real go of the Everlasting Rest Gardens subsidiary. Scarcely thirty plots sold. But people, old Dobermann surmises, are reluctant to buy burial plots for themselves, admitting to a future possibility or certainty they'd rather not think about. A marketing campaign targeting children with aging parents may be the way to go.

Be years of course before all the interstate highways are built. But old Dobermann does not plan on dying either. Some day perhaps but not yet. He finds among his papers the lowest offer he believes he can make for Rahilly Trucking likely to arouse Rahilly's interest and glances at his desk calendar. It says "A. Schott, First Episcopal, 2 p.m." Damn! That will break up his working day. But he'll duck out when the eulogy starts.

* * *

Old Jerry Hennessey, wearing his smelly bib overalls and red rubber overshoes ankle deep in the mud and manure in his barnyard, surveys what used to be his machine shed, mostly weathered kindling now scattered across the barnyard, half the tin roof in the pasture behind the barn, the other half collapsed on his old John Deere tractor and manure spreader.

Old Jerry swears a little. Goddamn storm. What he ought to be doing is pulling the wreckage off the John Deere. He can't function without it and what he planned to do today was plow the forty acres he had in oats, threshed two weeks ago, get it ready for some spring wheat. But the goddamn insurance man, Starbuck over in Winatchee Falls, said, "Leave everthing the way it is so my claims adjuster can assess the damage. Might not be today though. There's a lot of damage out your way."

Hennessey inserts a fresh chaw in his cheek and observes his oldest son, Young Jerry, twenty-four, whacking away with a dull axe at the old elm in the yard the storm blew down. Young Jerry's efforts are slowing, Hennessey notes. Any minute now, Young Jerry will abandon this chore, borrow the truck and head for Hayfield. He outlined this plan while they were milking their thirty head. "I'll chop up the tree blew down then there ain't nuthin' else do prolly go see what's goin' on the Muny." And that will be the end of Young Jerry for the day. Lord willing, he'll come home eventually, himself and the truck intact. He's a good worker, though, still lives at home, saves Hennessey half the cost of a hired hand. Hits the sauce, he gets a chance. But old Hennessey's resigned to that Irish failing.

He could, Hennessey thinks, dig his scythe out of the machine shed wreckage, go up the hill where the hail hit his cornfield, knock down and slash more cornstalks, fool the claims adjustor and screw the goddamn insurance company out of some additional hail insurance. Not worth the effort, he decides, and goes into the old farmhouse his grandfather built, leaving his overshoes on the sagging backporch.

His wife Bridget pours him coffee and Hennessey inflicts on Bridget for perhaps the ten-thousandth time in the thirty years they've been wed his usual monologue. He accepts with resignation the storm. The weather, he's learned in a lifetime of farming, is either too wet or dry or too hot or too cold or all of those and if it is not sundry rusts, molds and insects will ravage his crops, then the ADM elevator will screw him. But he has other complaints. The goddamn government. Goddamn insurance companies. Goddamn claims adjustors. Goddamn Strudel (this a recent addition) got half his boar.

Bridget at intervals murmurs, "Mmmm." Her mind is on her forty White Leghorn hens. They and the old rooster survived the storm in their chicken-coop but the hens are restless, thunder scares them, they may not lay their full quota of eggs today and her "egg money" looms large in Bridget's household budget. An occasional "Mmmm" is all the fuel Hennessey's monologue requires.

* * *

The fuel Trooper Lionel Redhardt's SHP Ford requires, unfortunately, is gasoline, the needle on the goddamn gas gauge is riding the E and Trooper Redhardt is confronting a totally embarrassing possibility. He may run out of gas before he reaches

Ely, twenty miles to the north on Minnesota Hwy. 1 and the last outpost of civilization in this particular portion of the vast North Woods.

Out of gas! Stranded on Hwy.1, mostly bumps and gravel flanked by endless acres of second-growth jackpine and a few birch. He might wait half an hour before a logging truck or a dumb tourist comes along and takes him into Ely. Then have to cage a lift back to his stalled Ford with five gallon of gas, like a dumb fucking tourist. While the gas pump jockey in Ely spreads the hilarious news: new State Cop run out a gas first week he was up here!

Trooper Redhardt, slowing to 35 mph to conserve gas, crests a low hill, puts the Ford in neutral, rolls down the far slope and curses. Curses his own stupidity. He should have remembered gas stations in the goddamn Hibbing Patrol District are few and far between. But he got used to the gas stations everywhere in the Winatchee Falls Patrol District.

Trooper Redhardt also curses, not for the first time, several individuals. That goddamn Hossman, first and foremost, who though guilty and jailed evidently went through with his threat to get Trooper Redhardt transferred the hell-and-gone up the boonies. Governor Diptill, another asshole. And the new State Patrol commander, Eustis Overholt, a friend of Diptill's who as Trooper Redhardt understands it used to run a Security company, renting rent-a-cops. It was Overholt actually transferred Trooper Redhardt and several other Troopers. It was going to be his policy, the mealy-mouthed bastard said on TV, to rotate troopers between districts "So they may become familiar with the conditions throughout our Great State."

Bullshit! It was Hossman and the goddamn governor got him transferred effective August 31, just in time for the Labor Day weekend. There'd been no fucking transfer if "Colonel" Ded Wood was the Patrol commander. But "Colonel" Wood resigned unexpectedly a month ago, citing a desire "to spend more time with my family and pursue other interests," that following a big hullabaloo in the goddamn newspapers and on the TV having to do with Patrol fuel contracts awarded service stations allegedly owned and/or operated by persons allegedly related to "Colonel" Wood. Trooper Redhardt does not fully understand all that but he knows one thing. The way "Colonel" Wood's former friends at the goddamn newspapers and TV turned on the "Colonel" proves, if any further proof were needed, all those goddamn reporters are a bunch of hyenas, never to be trusted. Trooper Redhardt's inherent peace officer's distrust and suspicion when dealing with reporters, print or TV, is now set in concrete.

Trooper Redhardt drops the Ford into gear for the climb up another low hill and considers another problem: finding a house. He's bunking at the moment in an empty office in the Highway Department building in Hibbing, using the shower the mechanics use. Tootie and the boys are still in Winatchee Falls, the Redhardts' house there on the market. Trooper Redhardt is looking at the Houses For Sale ads in the Hibbing Daily News and there are a couple he'll call the listing realtors about when he goes off duty at four p.m. But he can't actually buy a house in Hibbing until somebody buys his house in the Winatchee Falls, listed with Bremer Realty. And Tootie doesn't want to move anyway. Not until after the baby she hopes is a girl comes. Maybe not then. She can always live with her folks awhile, she says.

The Ford tops the low hill and Trooper Redhardt puts it in neutral and coasts. Tootie hates the North Woods, its long cold winters and summer mosquito swarms. And moose. A big bull moose wandered into the parking lot behind their apartment in Hibbing when first Trooper Redhardt was stationed there and scared poor Tootie half to death. Be fine with her, Tootie says, if she never sees another moose—

Moose! Jeezuzz! Thirty yards dead ahead a 1500-pound bull with a 12-point rack emerges from the jackpines onto Hwy. 1. Trooper Redhardt slams the Ford's brakes and skids it to a stop and the engine kills. The moose halts in the middle of Hwy. 1, surveys the Ford and Trooper Redhardt with what appears to be disdain, then ambles into the jackpine across the highway.

Trooper Redhardt swears and fumbles with the ignition. The starter grinds but the Ford will not start. Out of gas! Dead in the water, blocking half of Hwy.1. Trooper Redhardt swears, the gas gauge needle rests on the E, and gets out of the Ford. Five thousand mosquitoes promptly sail out of the jackpine and attack him. He'll have to push the damn Ford onto the shoulder and thumb a lift to Ely. But there is no shoulder, just a yard of soft earth and a soggy ditch before the jackpine starts. He'll have to set flares or a logging truck or a dumb fucking tourist will come over the hill and cream the Ford. The flares are in the trunk. Trooper Redhardt opens it while five thousand mosquitoes feast on his flesh. Getting their share before a big swarm arrives.

* * *

Eddie Devlin, humped over an old Remington with sticky keys in the Bugle Call newsroom at just past noon, sticky with the candy bars Art Kealey used to eat while typing, types, stickily:

> A violent thunderstorm accompanied by damaging winds and golf ball-size hail roared through the Hayfield area early today, damaging several farm buildings, destroying trees and snapping power lines and leaving more than a hundred Southern Minnesota Power Co. customers in and near Hayfield without electricity.
>
> A machine shed on the Gerald Hennessey farm eight miles south of Hayfield was virtually leveled, and a portion of Hennessey's corn crop suffered hail damage. A roof was blown off a silo at the Ernest Simmons farm. Rainfall in the area was measured at nearly four inches in some areas and Salem Creek south of Hayfield was reported to be over its banks throughout much of the forenoon.

> A spokesman for the Southern Minnesota Power Co. said electricity would be restored in the area by late today.

Eddie is the Bugle Call Sports Editor now, but Snorkel drafted him to write the storm story because the new reporter is not up to that and both the other reporters are missing today. Ken Crackers is out sick with one his asthma attacks and Stewie Popple is drying out at a detox place in Minneapolis. The new reporter, Miles Pender, ten weeks out of the LGU J-School, is proving incompetent. Miles has a problem with syntax. It was Miles wrote an obit last week (which weary Ralph Haney somehow missed) that read in part:

"Funeral plans [the preferred word is arrangements] have been finalized for Mr. Wermer Benner, 68, of the city, a former Winatchee Falls garage employee thought to be in good health who died yesterday following a sudden heart attack at Community Hospital. He will be buried Friday at Everlasting Rest Gardens."

Many who knew Werner (not Wermer) Bremer (not Benner) are wondering. What if so healthy was he doing at the Community Hospital? Or did he know in advance he was going to have a heart attack and go there?

Whatever, Mr. Werner Bremer, Eddie knows (but he won't speak badly of the dead), was also a former felon convicted of bootlegging early in The Great Depression. Did eight months in Leavenworth. He was Margie (Bremer Realty) Bremer's dad. Margie was the first and for some years the only girl to let Eddie see her Thing and vice versa. In an empty boxcar on the MSP&P spur track in Stiles one rainy Saturday. But that (they were nine years old) was a long time ago, when the Devlins and the Bremers lived in Stiles, an unincorporated dot on the prairie on the MSP&P's Main Line.

Eddie still sees Margie now and then, runs into her here and there, but that long ago Saturday has never come up in their brief conversations. Margie is reckoned to be doing very well these days in the real estate business she inherited (so to speak) when Wes Cooley, her longtime boyfriend, former boss and mentor and subsequent partner in the real estate business died three years ago. They really were partners, it turned out. There were papers to that effect. The Mrs. Cooley of record, though estranged, challenged this arrangement but the Probate Court found for Margie. She drives a big blue '56 Cadillac now with all the accessories and tail fins like a rocketship: prima facie evidence all across America of Success with a capital S. Her reputation since Wes died is she sleeps around but hardly anybody considers her a tramp. Tramps do not drive late model Caddies. Margie's upward mobility has exceeded Eddie's. Still, Eddie phoned her for old time's sake and offered his condolences in regards to her father. She seemed to be taking Werner's death, her mother dead for five years, in stride. Merely said, "Thanks." Eddie used to think he would like to screw Margie some day. He still thinks of that but of course he's a married man now.

Eddie bangs out the rest of the storm story, writing to a formula equally useful when blizzards howl across the prairie, only the names and the details change, drops this work on Ralph Haney's desk and goes to lunch.

Eddie usually lunches now as befits the Sports Editor in the Bar & Grill at Manny's Steakhouse on Broadway, Winatchee Falls' premier steak place, at just past noon. By then he's slapped his Sports Page together: a wirephoto, the Major League roundups and standings, some other wire stories and a few local stories, the night-before softball results, a rare hole-in-one perhaps at the Country Club or the Municipal Golf Course, the Winatchee Falls Tennis Club's annual under-12-boys tournament seeds, an advance promising mayhem at Winatchee Falls promoter Pinkie Stern's weekly Saturday night professional wrestling card at the Armory, etc. Eddie doubts any of the pro wrestling fans he's seen, they vanish between cards, though gullible are literate, but Pinkie sets great store by these stories and Eddie's subsequent reports on the promised mayhem and slips Eddie a $5 bill now and then. This may not be entirely ethical but Art Kealey before he retired confessed he'd been on Pinkie's pad for years.

Those $5 bills help. Cadence Snorkel reluctantly gave Eddie a $10 raise to $90 a week when officially naming him Sports Editor, but lunch at Manny's with a drink while talking sports with local aficionados may run as high as $1.50. If Pinkie doesn't pick up the tab. Worth it, though. Eddie, thought to be an instant expert now he's the Sports Editor, enjoys these lunches. His afternoons are largely free once he's touched base with a few coaches or dredged up a local feature story or some items for his Wednesday column, "The Sports Scene." Wednesdays historically are slow news days.

Eddie also got another welcome $5 when the AP Bureau in Minneapolis chose his "Solomon Like Decision in Pig Case" story the week's Best Outstate Feature Story.

Eddie thought Evylee with her predelection for steamy matinees would like his new schedule but that unhappily is not the case. Evylee's sexual enthusiasm has diminished, mainly because she thinks she may be pregnant. She blames Eddie for this, if in fact she is pregnant, though she's the one keeps the Rhythm Method calendar. She's going to see her doctor next week for some kind of test involving a rabbit and a sure Yes or No and she's actually ambivalent about the whole thing: no desire to be a mother part of the time but somewhat thrilled and excited by the prospect at other times. Eddie too is ambivalent. He'd not planned on fatherhood, not yet anyway. One thing, if in fact Evylee is pregnant she may in future give up on the damn Rhythm Method and agree to some artificial means. Eddie won't bring that up just now, however, and they've not said anything yet to any of the potential grandparents.

Eddie comes into Manny's, greets Manny Hohenfelder's son Hump, the lunch maitre'd, and goes into the Bar & Grill, pleased to find Pinkie Stern present.

* * *

The Bremer Realty office (actually two offices) is off the Dobermann Hotel lobby with a door to the lobby that bears a sign, Please Use Other Door. This Other Door is on West College Street. The office is somnolent in the early afternoon though back to business as usual. It was closed part of Friday with a sign on the West College door, Closed Until 2 p.m. for Funeral. Werner Bremer's funeral and burial. But the sales associates, there are three now, staffed two Open Houses over the Labor Day weekend and Monty Swallow, the Number One associate, got an offer on one of them, the Redhardt place (3B fin bsmt gd loc, the ad in the Bufle Call says).

Margie Bremer, a short busty woman with good legs and hair the color of honey, wearing a dark suit, sitting at her desk in the larger of the two offices, is reviewing that offer now: $10,200 from a young fellow starting out in the insurance business with the Wilbur Starbuck Agency. The Redhardts listed at $12,000 but they are anxious to sell or Redhardt is anyway, his wife seems somewhat confused. She'll let Monty wrangle with that one and considers another offer: $9,500 from a just married minor functionary at the First National Bank for an older two-bedroom with no garage, free and clear, no mortgage or other ecumbrances, on Winatchee Fall's far East Side, listed at $11,500. She can, Margie reckons, citing "location," close to Hawthorne School, get the potential buyer up to $10,500. So the trick will be to convince the seller $10,500 less Bremer Realty's five percent commission ($525) is a fair price. The seller is Mrs. Pauline Bennett, a fifty-something physical therapist at the Pretzell Chiropractic Clinic. She wants to sell the house, move into an apartment and invest the proceeds for her adopted grandson Slade's college education six years hence. Margie doubts this makes good financial sense, but that's Pauline's problem. She really doesn't know Pauline though she knew Pauline's late son, Chesty, Slade's father. Laid Chesty once or twice in fact. Years ago. Before the War. In which he was killed. But Margie seldom dwells on the distant past. Or the recent past, much.

One thing she'll tell Pauline Bennett is the buyer, working for the bank, won't have any trouble with his financing. Another thing is a bird (offer) in the hand etc. Last resort, Bremer Realty will cut its commission to $400, half of that or $62.50 (Margie does commissions in her head faster than an adding machine) coming out of the forty percent of the five percent due Wilma Hoff, the Number Two sales associate who got the offer. All the associates in theory are on straight commission.

This settled (in her head), Margie checks the Bremer Realty "Homes For Sale" ads in today's Bugle Call, which Monty composes subject to her approval. Alone in the smaller office, he's composing some now. Wilma is out showing a house. Monty is a sly old gent in his sixties with white hair and a red honest face, crooked as they come. Wilma is forty-something, long divorced. Both are veterans of the real estate wars. An ad catches Margie's eye.

> For Sale. Everlasting Rest Gardens burial plot. Excellent Location. Perpetual Care guaranteed. $995 or make offer. Call Bremer Realty 529-0755.

Does somebody, Margie wonders, not plan to die? Then dwells just for a moment on the recent past. Her father Werner Bremer lies at rest in Everlasting Rest Gardens. She did not know where else to put him when, suddenly, he died. Ma, who embraced or re-embraced her original faith while slowly dying with some kind of cancer, is in Holy Redeemer. But Holy Redeemer wouldn't touch Werner, born a Lutheran and a practicing agnostic. So she called Clyde Dobermann. Clyde may have his faults but he's a true friend. Former lover as well, a little fling they had four or five years ago. He did not bring up the fact he'd offered Bremer Realty (over dinner at the Fish House) an "exclusive" on Everlasting Rest plots and a 10 percent commission but she'd turned him down, too much time and effort for the sums involved.

"Don't worry about a thing, Marge," Clyde said. "I'll take care of it. I'll pick out a nice plot for your dad. High up the slope. Give you a discount too, that ten percent would been your commission, on account of you and me. Maybe again some time, huh? You get to use the chapel, you know, you want to. No charge."

So Margie bought a plot at Everlasting Rest. Nobody else in the family had $800. Werner Bremer is at rest high on the Gardens slope close to a huge red granite headstone with an inscription Margie did not bother to read. She'll have to pop for a headstone for Werner, she supposes, one of these days. There were other headstones here and there and an open grave at the foot of the slope beside the Sales Office when Werner was lowered into his. Buried.

It wasn't much of a burial though or much of a funeral either. Just a brief one-fits-all service in the Everlasting Rest chapel and a few words at the grave, the Unitarian clergyman drafted for the purpose anxious to get to his golf game, the only mourners three of Werner's old cronies and the family. Sister Sylvia, her worthless husband Bert and their youngest, the other four long gone. Brother Petey wearing his eye patch and his dumpy wife and their dumpy teenage daughters. Brother Larry was not present or expected. Larry is in the Minneapolis VA Hospital with a brain full of shrapnel collected in the Battle of the Bulge. While Margie was counting GI socks or something in a Stateside Women's Army Corps supply unit. She's not seen Larry in years but no matter. Larry no longer knows who she is. Or who he is. Petey missed The War, thanks to Larry, who destroyed Petey's right eye with a BB gun when they were kids playing William Tell.

Margie sighs. At any rate, it's over. Both her parents dead, at rest in different cemeteries. She's a thirty-six-year-old orphan. They'll meet again presumably in the Hereafter. If there is a Hereafter. She cried when Ma died, remembering Ma's hard life, but won't cry over Werner, who often whipped her, all his offspring, he liked to use his belt. And she'll have in hand now the hundred a month it cost to keep Werner in cigarettes, his room and a meal a day at Brinkley's Rooming House, after the emphysema got him and he had to quit his car wash job at T.J. Hanrahan Auto Sales & Service.

Margie wonders, did the Bull Durham cigarettes Werner rolled and smoked, thirty or forty a day for forty years, contribute to his death? The medical profession has never suggested that. Hell, the men in white coats in the glossy magazine ads presumably are some of the doctors said to "Prefer Camels 2 to 1!" Whatever, it's over, and Margie again reads the mysterious Everlasting Rest burial plot For Sale ad. "Monty, what's the story on this burial plot ad?"

"Lady called," Monty, communication between the two offices no problem, says. "Said she had one she wants to sell. Paid nine-ninety-five, she said, but consider any reasonable offer."

"Who, Monty?"

Monty paws through the mess on his desk. "Mabel Murphy. She's a legal secretary. Schott and Schott. She said."

"Hey!" Harold E. (Hoss) Hossman, the new Number Three sales associate, banging through the West College Street door, exultant, interrupting Monty, says. "I sold the Skooner place! Unloaded the sonofabitch! I mean I got a offer on it."

"Hip-hip-hoo-ray!" Monty says. "Harold bust his cherry."

"Let me see it," Margie says.

"Fuck you, Monty," Hoss says, and goes into Margie's office with the sacred earnest money contract signed by the potential buyer and the said potential buyer's earnest money check for $50.

The potential buyer is Lester Alcotte, twenty-two, single but engaged ("To get married," he told Hoss), in business with his father at Al's Appliance & Lawnmower Repair. He is offering $7,200 for the late William Skooner's derelict two-story three-bedroom on the city's far north near the State Mental Hospital, a "Handy Man Special" in Monty's ad, empty since old Bill Skooner died a year ago, on the market since, listed at $9,900, the title following probate held jointly by old Bill's six eternally squabbling offspring. Bremer Realty was reluctant to list this sad property. Margie only listed it as a favor to Bill Junior, with whom she went to bed once or twice when he was a rookie cop and stopped her for rolling through a stop sign.

"But I can get this kid jack his offer up some," Hoss says. "I'm pretty sure. Eight grand prolly. Place needs work."

"Family won't take seventy-two," Margie says. "I know that. But this kid goes eight I'll call Bill Junior and tell him they better take that. Or pay the property taxes until hell freezes over. Bill Junior's got a little sense. His sisters though, they'll be a bitch and convince. Be good experience for you, Harold, put this deal together."

"Right," Hoss says, and goes into the other office, where he shares a desk with Wilma Hoff, and gets on the phone to young Lester Alcotte, who thinks the Skooners want $11,000 for their dump because that is what Hoss told him. Lester is pretty shrewd though for twenty-two, quick to screw folks pricewise (Hoss surmises) when repairing their appliances or lawnmowers.

Margie reads the other For Sale ads Monty composed. She doubts Lester Alcotte and the fighting Skooners will ever get together on a price (but you never know) and the fact Harold even got an offer on the dump bodes well for his future in real estate. Well, he said he'd had "lots sales experience" when he came to see her (the day after he got out of jail, she learned later). He also said, "I resigned my position at that music company I was with, no future there, and I'd like and find a position in real estate." Which was not the whole truth either, she learned later. And he was, she remembered, very good in bed, but that had nothing to do with the real estate business. Despite his bravado, Hoss looked beat. Down on his luck. Perhaps, Margie thinks, she has a soft spot for Harold Hossman. She hired him at any rate though making no promises with the understanding they'd "see how things go," and when, embarrassed, he stuttered he was "a little bit short," put him on a draw, $50 a week against his commissions. This violates Bremer Realty policy, Monty and Wilma know nothing about it, Harold is into her for $250 and he has young Alcotte on the phone. Margie listens.

"Lester? Harold Hossman here. Bremer Realty. Lissen, I talk your offer on the Skooner place over with Miss Bremer. I guess you prolly know her. Know who she is anyway. Know she's knows about all there is and know it comes to property values here. Okay. She says the Skooner place be worth nine-five easy, the present market. What? Well, sure, it needs some work. But you got to think about location, Lester. That's a hell of a location there. Right near the State Hospital. You fix that place up some, Lester, some day you want a sell it, you'll take three four grand out of it easy. What? Well, yeah, I know you just plan on live in it. But you got a good bidness there, Lester, your repair bidness. Be yours some day, I guess. There come a day, Lester, not so long be my bet, you and Missus Alcotte be ready and move up in the housing market. Skooner place be like an investment then. What? Well, personally, Lester, I was in your shoes, I'd go another grand. I tell you why. I really ain't supposed and do this but I will. One the other sales associates here got another party interested in that property. They ain't made an offer yet but it looks like they prolly will. What? Well, sure. You talk it over with your dad, Lester, and get back to me. Or I call you. First thing tomorrow be fine. Like I said, Lester, you be makin' a damn good investment."

What a line of shit, Margie thinks, pleased with her acuity in recognizing in Harold a probable high-powered sales associate once he found his true calling. A line of shit is the nature of the business and Harold, it appears, is taking to the business like the well-known duck confronted by water.

"What a line of shit!" Monty, surveying Hoss with newfound respect, says. "You sell that Skooner dump, I'll buy you a drink!"

"Piece of cake," Hoss says, which may not be the case, but he's feeling better about himself (and things in general) than he's felt since, well, 7:45 a.m. May 17, when suddenly confronted by a goddamn school bus with STOP arm extended and warning lights flashing. It's good to be selling again, selling something other than those goddamn band uniforms. The twenty-four miserable days he spent in the Winatchee County Jail are a fading memory.

* * *

Twenty-four days because Allen, who must be a pretty good lawyer, moved for a reduction of sentence in Winatchee County District Court and District Judge Lamar Kelly, never too swift, under the misapprehension perhaps that Governor Diptill's brother-in-law still was on the diplomatic list, granted same. The Ding Dong Man by then with time off for good behavior was long gone, hitch-hiking to Rapid City, South Dakota to catch up with his carnival, and the old jailor had served Hoss with the legal document outlining Louella Diptill-Hossman's plan to divorce him, forthwith. Which Hoss, coming swiftly to the conclusion d-i-v-o-r-c-e spelled "relief," promptly decided he would not contest. By then too the Sheriff's Department was holding for Hoss a battered cardboard box full of socks, some underwear, two ratty shirts, wrinkled chino slacks and an old torn sport coat dispatched by Louella, accompanied by a brief note the gist of which was Louella sincerely hopes (a) she never sees Harold E. Hossman again and (b) he "rots in Hell!" Which Louella assumes he will. Assuming there is a Hell. But that's not something Hoss will dwell on.

Officially free at noon, Hoss traded his grimy coveralls for one of the ratty shirts, the wrinkled slacks and the sport coat. The suit he was wearing when processed in smelled like the jail. He was seventeen pounds lighter at 218 thanks to the Sheriff's Wife's Diet and had $42.20 after spending $10 for candy bars. Web Allen was there to see him get out of jail and offer some good news and some bad news and more bad news. The good news was Hoss' legal fees to date would be billed to the Diptill

Music Co., per August Schott's initial conversation with Louella. The bad news was the Diptill Music Co. sent somebody to get the Buick out of the WFPD Impound Lot, leaving Hoss a pedestrian. The other bad news was, should Hoss wish to appeal his conviction, the Diptill Music Co. would not cover those legal fees.

"Hell with an appeal," Hoss said. Allen agreed to handle the divorce business for $200 if Hoss did not contest it. "Hell, no," Hoss said. "I won't contest it. I just want a get rid a the bitch." An initial divorce hearing Hoss plans to miss is set for late October in St. Paul and a final decree, presumably, will be issued six months later.

Thanking Allen and parting from him, Hoss walked to the YMCA on North Broadway, got a room there for $2, took a long hot soapy shower, washing off the goddamn jail smell, spent $4.50 at Seaver's One-Hour Cleaning to get his suit cleaned and pressed, rid it of the goddamn jail smell, took another long hot soapy shower and a little nap, blew $8 on a T-bone and a few drinks at Manny's Steakhouse, did not though tempted try to pick up a broad in the Bar & Grill, got a good night's sleep instead with no bedbugs, sleeping until noon, got into his clean pressed suit, toted up his assets, $26.70, found Bremer Realty in the phonebook at the Y, had his shoes shined and went with no appointment and saw Margie Bremer, lucky to find her at her desk and, Hoss now surmises, in a good mood with a $15,400 house sale she made herself just wrapped up, ready to close.

And now by god he's in real estate! With a business card, a hundred cost him $4, "Harold E. Hossman, Sales Associate, Bremer Realty." He's still at the Y but has transportation, a clunky '49 Olds that eats oil priced at $795 on T.J. Hanrahan Auto Sales & Service Used Lot, Margie advancing the $100 down payment. He tells prospects, "This a loaner, my Caddy is in for a tune-up."

Margie, in fact, Hoss thinks, has been pretty damn good to

him. How long this will last, he doesn't know. But he's into her now for $250 with his draw and the down payment on the clunker and the more he owes her, he surmises, the more reluctant she'll be to dump him. And any day now, Hoss is sure, he'll close a deal, the Skooner place or another place. He has several prospects looking at various properties. There is one little fly in this ointment: Margie won't screw him. That's Bremer Realty policy, she says: Not with the help. But there seems to be quite a lot of loose quiff in Winatchee Falls. Hoss has checked that out while nursing a drink, making it last, at Manny's Bar & Grill, and one of these days, he closes a deal, has a little dough, he'll gets out of the goddamn Y and into an apartment.

Margie interrupts these pleasant thoughts. "Harold, come here a minute." Hoss obediently goes into Margie office. "The lawyer handled that trouble you had with the school bus and is handling your divorce, isn't he with Schott and Schott?" Yes, Hoss says. "Go see him tomorrow. Talk about your divorce and try and find out what Birdshot Schott plans to do with his dad's house. My guess, Birdshot will put it on the market and it's a hell of a property. It's an old mausoleum but prolly been kept up and that's a hell of a location, up on West College there. I'd list it at tweny-eight, maybe thirty. Birdshot will prolly want a MLS but that's all right, I list it. It's too soon, though, I call Birdshot myself. They're only burying Old August today. But you find out, much as you can."

"Will do," Hoss says, and goes back to his desk and phones Web Allen. But Schott & Schott is closed. "On account of the funeral," the female who answers the phone says. "I'm the owny one here." He'll call again in the morning, Hoss says, so informs Margie and does a little doodling on Wilma's desk blotter, betting on the come. Forty percent of five percent of thirty grand. $600! Enough, clean up his advances and put him right back on his feet.

* * *

In Hayfield, middle of the afternoon, alone in the new Village Court upstairs over Bonnie's Cafe, the new Village Court judge, Her Honor Jane Klamatty, seated at the desk she brought from her basement, is going through the Justice Court files in ragged manila folders piled on her desk, three folding chairs, the floor and in cardboard boxes and on the metal file cabinets also removed from her basement, from which these files came. They add to the mess and clutter already existing in the new courtroom: sawhorses, a step-ladder, stacked lumber, broken plasterboard, thirty new metal folding chairs piled in one corner, two folding tables, folded, etc.

The Village Council in its wisdom hired Ev Geisler's Uncle Herman to remodel the space over Bonnie's Café: install a half-bath, build a proper bench and a witness box and a partition dividing this space, not equally, the larger part overlooking Main Street the courtroom, the smaller part overlooking the alley Her Honor's chambers. But Herman somehow got this division backward and persons with business before the court coming up the stairs from Bonnie's would have had to pass through Her Honor's chambers. Herman subsequently removed the partition and is supposed to be putting it up again where it should be. But Herman views this as a lot of extra work he won't be paid for and he's not rushing it. He was in for a while in the forenoon, muttering and measuring, but said he had "another job" he has to finish and left. He may be back tomorrow or he may not. The Village Council is just about ready to sue Herman, failure to fulfill a contract. The half-bath has been eliminated, Herman's "estimate" for that considered too high. Her Honor and members of the legal profession use Bonnie's bathroom. Other persons with business before the court have to go up the street to the Muny Liquor or the Standard station.

Klamatty sighs. She hates clutter and somebody is thumping up the stairs. It's Web Allen in a dark suit and sober tie, looking fir and tanned. He circles a sawhorse.

"Web!" Klamatty says. "You old goat! What a nice surprise! Where have you been anyway? How was Montana?"

"Nice." Web says. "I saw a grizzly bear. With binoculars. He didn't see me. I don't think. He didn't have binoculars. Otherwise, other points west, taking depositions. Objecting to numerous motions the MSP&P lawyers are filing. We now have two clients who, encouraged I suspect by their local physicians, claim to have suffered severe whiplash injuries when the train hit the truck. Guess you know, there's nothing like a whiplash, muddy the legal waters."

"True," Klamatty says. "And elsewhere on the legal front? I've been so busy getting organized here I'm out of touch."

Web Allen lifts a metal folding chair from the pile in the corner, sets it up, sits in it and brings Klamatty up to date. "Well, Celestial Vanderhoeven and several Custer Women are holding off on their action to recover for personal injuries suffered when run down by a raging boar and much subsequent pain and suffering and anguish. Because, thanks to a recent remarkable decision handed down in a court that no longer exists, a decision worthy of King Solomon I believe read somewhere, they do not know which of two parties to sue. Or we may sue both of them, opening that can of worms all over again."

"How about Chief Wyncoop? And the MSP&P and Whip Rahilly?"

"Wyncoop dropped his suit. He was on duty at the time and the Volunteer Fire Department's insurance paid for his new dentures. TheMSP&P's suit and Rahilly's countersuit are somewhere in District Court. Their respective insurance companies got into it so don't hold your breath, those are settled."

"Web," Klamatty says. "I know you told me you weren't and you were the first to congratulate me on my appointment. I thank you for the phone call. But were you upset, even a little, when I found your client Mister Hossman guilty on that school bus thing? And socked it to him?"

"No," Web says. "I was surprised. Not at the time knowing all the circumstances. But I was not upset. I thought all along

Mister Hossman was guilty as charged. Anyway, it worked out for you, Jane. That's the main thing. I'm curious though. Did you ever hear anything from Diptill? Or Louella? After you socked it to Mister Hossman?"

"No, except his letter appointing me." Web wants to see that. Klammatty digs it out her desk. "I'm going to get it framed. Like a diploma. Hang it in my chambers."

"Penned by an aide, no doubt," Web says. "One with an advanced degree in bureaucracy. But some things, I suppose, are best left unsaid. Do you think, Jane, you got the appointment because you were so mean to my client Mister Hossman?"

Klamatty shrugs. "Probably. Who knows? Who cares? I got the appointment. I am the Village Court judge. As we often said, that was the main thing. And any day now I'll start campaigning, get elected in November."

"There was a mysterious phone call that morning," Web Allen says. "Old Dobermann called August and August wrote himself a note but forgot all about it. Mabel Murphy found it. All it said was, Tell Allen let justice be done. Were you upset when Judge Kelly, my favorite judge, reduced Hossman's sentence?"

"No. Don't be silly. How is Mister Hossman anyway?"

"Well, his wife, Louella, is in the process of divorcing him on numerous grounds including adultery. I'm handling his end and he's not going to contest it. He's in real estate now. Selling for Bremer Realty. He latched onto that, day or so after he got out of jail. Do you know Margie Bremer?"

"No. Well, I've heard things. But nothing you could charge her with, I guess."

"You mentioned campaigning? You foresee any opposition?"

"Elmer Hooter, endorsed by the Star & Shopper. But I was elected JP ten times and Celestial Vanderhoeven is my campaign manager. Celestial browbeats voters. Elmer doesn't scare me. In fact, his father, Win, I was in the drugstore, told me in confidence he will not vote for Elmer."

"How are things going otherwise? New court and all?"

"Same as before, far as I can see," Klamatty says. "I've only had about a dozen cases. Piddly little cases. I miss Trooper Redhardt. You know he was transferred?" Web Allen nods. "He came and saw me when he found out. He was heartbroken. He hates the North Woods and so does his wife. And he wondered why he was transferred. I don't understand that either. It was Trooper Redhardt apprehended Mister Hossman in the first place and the way it looked to me at trial, it was Trooper Redhardt pretty much prepared Doodle's case."

"My guess," Web Allen says. "Is that early on when Governor Diptill and my client's wife Louella had it in mind to save my client's neck on the school bus thing, Diptill requested or suggested a transfer for Trooper Redhart. Put it in the bureaucratic hopper. Hossman told me was going to ask Marky and, I quote, 'Get that asshole trooper transferred the hell-and-gone up the boonies.' End quote. That was before the plan to save my client's neck was dropped. Or amended. His fault or your friend Little Nell's fault. Whatever, I expect Governor Diptill's request or suggestion was in the pipeline, never rescinded by him, and when it came out the other end of the pipeline, the governor's name on it, bingo! Trooper Redhardt was headed for the boonies."

"Makes sense to me," Klamatty says. "Incidentally, Little Nell McNeeley, on whom I now look with great fondness, did not spend much time at Bonnie's. She's a cocktail waitress at Manny's in Winatchee Falls now. How'd old August's funeral go? I thought about going but."

"Oh Lord!" Web Allen says. "But you asked so I'll tell you. Funeral went off well enough. Bit of a wait since Wednesday. But Birdshot had a big Labor Day weekend up at his lake place planned. He didn't think August would mind the delay. Said lots of August's friends would be up at their lakes too, Labor Day weekend. Guess they came back. Church was full anyway. Eulogy ran a little long. Reverend Mensch traced August's life from birth to grave, finding no fault therein, good husband, wonderful father, generous employer, a shining example to one and all and so on and so on.

"But the burial now! Old August has not been buried yet, Jane. There was some kind of a mix-up at Everlasting Rest Gardens. There was no grave for August. Well, there was a grave or gravesite. But it was filled in and somebody else was in it. Man named Bremer, the young fellow who seemed to be in charge said. Werner Bremer. Snuggled up next Elaine, so to speak. Mister Dobermann's orders, the young fellow said. Mister Clyde Dobermann, Everlasting Rest Gardens president.

"Birdshot was livid. Can't say I blame him. Then Mabel Murphy started howling. Keening, the Irish call it. Scared a dozen crows out of the cornfield across the highway. Couple girls from the office finally got her settled her down and took her away. One girl told me Mabel was bitterly disappointed. She said Mabel was going to throw herself into old August's grave. But he wasn't in it and it was covered up, so that didn't work out. It was Mabel, you know, who found old August. She thought he was asleep in his chair. He often was. But he was dead. Massive stroke or massive coronary. Mabel by the way is retiring, end of the week.

"Birdshot wanted the Bremer person disinterred then and there so we could bury August. But the young fellow, he seemed to be conversant with cemetery law, said not without a court order or Mister Dobermann said so. Clyde Dobermann. But Clyde wasn't there. Nobody knew where he was. They finally put August in Ranfranz's hearse and took him back to the funeral home. Far as I know he's resting comfortably in Ranfranz's cold room, waiting for a grave. Birdshot will be in District Court first thing tomorrow, Judge Kelly, seeking a disinterment order. The mourners drifted off then and so did I. Thought it was time I came and saw you. Before Birdshot asked me to locate Mister Bremer's next of kin. I'll do that but not today. I'm going to start with the real estate woman. And I should tell you. Birdshot's offered me a partnership. I think I'll take it."

"Congratulations," Klamatty says. "Leave it to Clyde Dobermann, screw things up. I'm sorry now I wasn't there. But I wanted to finish with these files. Mine and those of my several predecessors. They date to 1870. I want to store most of them. Might give the Historical Society a few. I tell you, Web." Klamatty slaps the files piled on her desk. "The stuff in here, you saw it, it would shatter your faith in humanity. And the Good Life in the Heartland of America. I have here eighty-plus year of man's inhumanity to man. And women. And children and animals. My predecessors saw a lot of cruelty to animals before farmers got tractors. Specifically, I made a list. You want to hear it?"

"Why not?"

Klamatty reads from her list: "Adultery, one case only, defendant convicted and fined twenty dollars. Aiding a Suicide. Arson, malicious and for the purpose of gain. Assaults, domestic and on non-family persons, with and without the use of dangerous weapons. An Abduction for the purpose of a marriage, which failed. Bestiality, which also covers fowl, an interesting case involving a turkey. Bribery and several attempts to bribe public officials. Burglaries galore, in the night and in broad daylight. Corrupting Public Officials in attempts to influence their votes. Damage to Real and/or Personal Property, malicious or otherwise, and to public library materials. Defamation of Character, Slander and Libel, old Colin Trudd doing business as the Star and Shopper a frequent defendant. Disorderly Conduct, a broad range that includes fighting, the use of loud offensive obscene or profane language, and peeing in public. Escapes from Custody and Attempts to. Failures to Provide Child Support. Failures to Appear for a Judicial Process. Failures to Confine Dangerous Animals, mainly dogs and bulls. Failures to Provide a Flagman in Advance of an Automotive Vehicle. Failures to Register for Selective Service, two cases in the early Forties, both mine, federal crimes initiated before me. One was a Jehovah Witness, a bona fide conchie. The other one said he just forgot and agreed to register, thus escaping prosecution, but he was killed somewhere in Italy. Fleeing Peace Officers performing their duties. Flights to Avoid Prosecution. Flights to Avoid the Establishment of alleged Paternity. The Filing of False Statements and False Insurance Claims. Frauds, various scams, some successful, some not. Frauds by Check, a lot of those, with insufficient funds, on closed accounts, no accounts, never had an account. Forgeries for the Purpose of Gain. Fornication, a misdemeanor, rarely charged. For which, perhaps, we should be thankful. Incest. Lots of that. Brothers, fathers, favorite uncles, granddads. Before the automobile came along people and got out of the house. Off the farm. Then the automobile spawned Careless Driving, Reckless Driving, Operating a Motor Vehicle in a Grossly Negligent Manner, Speeding in excess of the posted limit, Driving with a Suspended License, Revoked License, no license, never had a license, DWIs and Auto Theft. Gambling in any form other than a church Bingo game and/or Possession of a Gambling Device or devices, meaning pinball machines, if banned by local ordinance. Illegal Possession of burglary tools and/or explosives. Illegal sales of Intoxicating Liquors, meaning bootlegging, a raft of those in the Twenties. The Possession and/or Consumption of those said Liquors and/or Malt Beverage by Persons Not Yet of Legal Age, meaning twenty-one. Illegal Sales of Tobacco or Tobacco-related Products to persons not yet eighteen years of age. Molesting a Child. Murder Ones, two in the 1890s, preliminary hearings only in Justice Court, defendants bound over for trial. Likewise some Murder Twos and a few Manslaughters, prelims only. Malicious Mischief. Neglecting and/or Endangering a Child. Obstructing a Legal Process. Perjury. Possession of a sawed-off shotgun. Prostitution, the solicitation thereof and/or the profiting therefrom. Not much of that but a Jay J. Doodle pled guilty to Operating a Disorderly House in Hayfield in 1902. Public Nuisances, the maintaining thereof, mainly barking dogs. Receiving Stolen Property. Recklessly Discharging a Firearm. Rustling, the taking by theft of live cattle, sheep or swine or their carcasses. I should have nailed Len Steckle with that. Robberies, in the night and otherwise, by force, with the use of dangerous weapons or threats of bodily harm. Tampering With a Witness. Theft, Grand and

Petty, legally the taking of personal property belonging to another and/or gas or electric services, documents, household pets, whatever. Trespassing, on or within the property of another, with or without criminal intent, but an act likely to disturb, distress or frighten the owner of said property. Soliciting a Juvenile for the Purpose of Commiting a Crime. Sodomy. The Making of Terroristic Threats. The Taking of Indecent Liberties. Remember the Ding Dong man? Which frequently led to Carnal Knowledge, the taking of liberties more indecent still. Vagrancy, meaning able-bodied person eighteen years of age and older with no permanent place of abode and no plans to seek employment who subsist by begging or fortune-telling or similar pursuits, or hopped off an MSP&P freight and soon were thought be a Public Nuisance. Vandalism in many forms. Vehicular Homicides. Wrongfully Obtaining Public Assistance, or trying to. That's the one Republicans equate with High Treason. And numerous conspiracies to commit all of the above."

"Enough!" Web Allen says.

"But I'll say this for our community," Klamatty says. "I have not found a single case of Treason, not counting the Welfare frauds, Inciting to Riot or Interfering with a Military or Naval operation. I still have two boxes to go through though."

"Leave them for another time," Web Allen says. "What with all I just heard and Old August's botched burial, I need a drink. The Muny Liquor? That's if the Village Court judge drinks in public. I know judges who do. Then if you're free we'll have dinner at the Fish House."

"Sounds good to me," Klamatty says. "Muny's fine. Shoot, I'll do a little campaigning, anybody there looks like a voter."

"I do have one question," Web Allen says. "Did you ever find out or figure out whose boar that was? Hennessey's or Strudel's?"

"No. I asked Steckle, did it have a black spot like a football on its right shoulder? That was Hennessey's principal claim. Steckle said he didn't notice."

* * *

The sign outside the old stone Holy Redeemer Catholic Church on Second Avenue West in Winatchee Falls says "Confessions, 4-5 p.m. Daily." Mabel Murphy, still in her good black funeral dress, goes up the stone steps into the church, dim and dark, a dozen faithful scattered among its dark oak pews. An old woman with a cane shuffles out of the confessional and Mabel goes into it and kneels, bowing her head to conceal her identity. The priest seen dimly through the screen in the confessional looks like the Holy Redeemer pastor, the Rev. Bernard (Penance) Griffin. He smothers a yawn.

Mabel makes a sketchy Sign of the Cross and mumbles the words drummed into her by the nuns at Holy Redeemer School and never forgotten. "I confess to you, Father, and to Almighty God, that I have sinned. Since my last confession thirty-two years ago."

That gets the Rev. Griffin's attention. He shoves his nose against the screen but all he'll see of this penitent is the top of Mabel's black straw hat. And, Mabel thinks, the saying goes, he ain't heard nothin' yet. "I failed to make my Easter Duty thirty-one times. I committed adultery. Quite a few times. I fornicated with a married man. And other men. I engaged in uh sodomy. Quite a few times."

What sounds like a low whistle escapes the Rev. Griffin. I bet, Mabel thinks, he's sorry (the Rev. Griffin comes honestly by his nickname) the True Church dropped the sackcloth-and-ashes and wonders: what will her penance be (thirty-one thousand Rosaries?) and do priests ever talk about the things they hear in Confession? Not specifically, of course, no names, but she can imagine the Rev. Griffin, slicing the pork roast at dinner, priests eat high on the hog, telling his assistant pastor, Fr Manfred, "I had one today would curled your hair! First Confession in thirty-one years, she said. But that was just for openers."

* * *

District 33B State Rep. Wolfe Strudel brakes his new '56 Ford pickup to a stop beside the mailbox at the end of his long driveway and tells Imogene, "Get out and get the mail. See you can do that right!"

Imogene climbs out of the pickup. She missed the homebound school bus. The Consolidated School called and Strudel had to go get her. She was waiting in Dr. Kammerfuss the principal's office. Her story was, "I had a go the bathroom and that Wade drives the bus, he jist drive off and left me."

Ordinarily, this would have set Strudel's hackles to rising, and he did give Kammerfuss an earful in regards to the big mistake the Consolidated School was, the high cost of its school bus operation and the hope that the driver Wade would get a good flogging. Three dozen lashes. But Strudel otherwise had had a pretty good day and went easy on Imogene. His talk to the 4H leaders went off well, applauded twice, once in the middle when he said "I want to make just one more point" and again at the end, because, perhaps, it was the end. And in the afternoon the claims adjuster from the insurance company came and, quick to assess damage suffered by a member of the Legislature, offered $300 for corn damaged by the hail. More than Strudel expected.

Imogene opens the mailbox. But she's staring at something in the muddy ditch beside the driveway. She goes down into the ditch and into the mud and picks this something up.

"Imogene!" Strudel says. "What are you doing? Get out of the mud!"

Imogene gets out of the mud and up out of the ditch, triumphant. "My flute!" she says. "I found my flute! And the case!"

And so she has. Strudel examines them. The flute is somewhat rusted, full of mud, and the case, likewise full of mud, is half rotted. But so what.

"I be dammed!" Strudel says. "They must fell in the culbert

when you drop them, that guy almost kilt you. Rain last night run through the culbert and wash them out! Okay, get the mail."

Imogene gets the mail, it's mostly junk mail, and climbs into the pickup. "What a we gonna do with my flute, Pa?"

"What we are gonna do with your gotdamn flute," Strudel says. "Is you are gonna clean it up, Imogene. And the case. Then you take them the gotdamn school and tell the band teacher tell that fella from that gotdamn music company, he comes around. I guess it be a new fella now, not the one almost kilt you. He can have them back. Soon's the gotdamn music company send me a check, eighty-nine-ninety-five. Or else by got I by got sue that gotdamn music company! I by got Replevy them that check I give them!"

TO BE CONTINUED

NORMANDALE COMMUNITY COLLEGE
LIBRARY
9700 FRANCE AVENUE SOUTH
BLOOMINGTON, MN 55431-4399

NORMANDALE COMMUNITY COLLEGE
LIBRARY
9700 FRANCE AVENUE SOUTH
BLOOMINGTON, MN 55431-4399